**Oh, he knew what he did. He knew what
pleasure he could bring her.**

Julian knelt between Elspeth's legs like a Greek supplicant before a goddess, his head thrown back, his neck
corded with tense muscle. His face was one of agony, his
mouth open and shining, his eyes squeezed shut. It was an
expression that made her want to hold him, to console him
in his extremity.

For a second, his head dropped, slumping between his
shoulders, but then he looked up, and his expression was
so vulnerable that her heart gave a pang. He looked boyish, his eyes wide, his mouth soft and uncertain, and he
jolted to his feet as if he would run.

"No," she said softly, gently, as if instead of the arrogant, cynical Mr. Greycourt, he were a roebuck, poised to
run from a clearing. "Stay. Stay with me. Please?"

PRAISE FOR
ELIZABETH HOYT

Not the Duke's Darling

"Hoyt...marries her irresistibly witty writing style with an intrigue-steeped plot that is generously spiced with lively banter and lush sensuality."
—*Booklist*

THE MAIDEN LANE SERIES
Duke of Desire

"Passages of intrigue are charged with palpable suspense and danger, while the steamier bits crackle and singe."
—*Entertainment Weekly*

"4½ stars! Top Pick! Readers will be transfixed by this poignant tale of revenge and redemption."
—*RT Book Reviews*

Duke of Pleasure

"Hoyt once again successfully deploys her irresistible literary triumvirate of marvelously engaging characters, boldly sensual love scenes, and elegant writing brightened with just the right dash of dry wit."
—*Booklist*

"4½ stars! Top Pick! Always unique, wonderfully romantic and highly sensual, Hoyt's stories take readers' breath away."
—*RT Book Reviews*

Duke of Sin

"A complete triumph."
—*Booklist* (**Starred Review**)

"4½ stars! Top Pick! Hoyt delivers a unique read on many levels: a love story, a tale of redemption, and a plot teeming with emotional depth that takes readers' breaths away. Kudos to a master storyteller!"
—*RT Book Reviews*

Sweetest Scoundrel

"4½ stars! Just as enchanting as fans could desire.... It is a story that takes your breath away and leaves you uplifted. Hoyt does it again!"
—*RT Book Reviews*

Dearest Rogue

"[This] superbly executed historical romance is proof positive that this RITA Award–nominated author continues to write with undiminished force and flair."
—*Booklist* (**Starred Review**)

"Scintillating romance."
—*Publishers Weekly*

Darling Beast

"Hoyt's exquisitely nuanced characters, vividly detailed setting, and seemingly effortless and elegant writing

provide the splendid material from which she fashions yet another ravishingly romantic love story."
—*Booklist* (**Starred Review**)

"4½ stars! Top Pick! Wondrous, magical, and joyous—a read to remember."
—*RT Book Reviews*

Duke of Midnight

"Richly drawn characters fill the pages of this emotionally charged mix of mystery and romance."
—*Publishers Weekly*

"4½ stars! Top Pick! There is enchantment in the Maiden Lane series, not just the fairy tales Hoyt infuses into the memorable romances, but the wonder of love combined with passion, unique plotlines, and unforgettable characters."
—*RT Book Reviews*

Lord of Darkness

"Hoyt's writing is imbued with great depth of emotion.... Heartbreaking.... An edgy tension-filled plot."
—*Publishers Weekly*

"Illuminates Hoyt's boundless imagination.... Readers will adore this story."
—*RT Book Reviews*

Thief of Shadows

"This one did not disappoint."
        —*USA Today*

"An expert blend of scintillating romance and mystery.... The top of its genre."
        —*Publishers Weekly* (**Starred Review**)

"All of Hoyt's signature literary ingredients—wickedly clever dialogue, superbly nuanced characters, danger, and scorching sexual chemistry—click neatly into place to create a breathtakingly romantic love story."
        —*Booklist*

"When [they] finally come together, desire and long-denied sensuality explode upon the page."
        —*Library Journal*

Scandalous Desires

"Historical romance at its best."
        —*Publishers Weekly* (**Starred Review**)

"With its lush sensuality, lusciously wrought prose, and luxuriously dark plot, *Scandalous Desires*, the latest exquisitely crafted addition to Hoyt's Georgian-set Maiden Lane series, is a romance to treasure."
        —*Booklist* (**Starred Review**)

Notorious Pleasures

"Emotionally stunning.... The sinfully sensual chemistry Hoyt creates between her shrewd, acid-tongued heroine and her scandalous, sexy hero is pure romance."
                    —*Booklist* **(Starred Review)**

Wicked Intentions

"4½ stars! Top Pick! A magnificently rendered story that not only enchants but enthralls."
                    —*RT Book Reviews*

NO ORDINARY DUCHESS

OTHER TITLES BY ELIZABETH HOYT

ELIZABETH HOYT

NO ORDINARY DUCHESS

A GREYCOURT NOVEL

FOREVER

New York   Boston

Forever
Hachette Book Group
1290 Avenue of the Americas, New York, NY 10104
read-forever.com
@readforeverpub

First Edition: December 2024

Forever is an imprint of Grand Central Publishing. The Forever name and logo are registered trademarks of Hachette Book Group, Inc.

The publisher is not responsible for websites (or their content) that are not owned by the publisher.

The Hachette Speakers Bureau provides a wide range of authors for speaking events. To find out more, go to hachettespeakersbureau.com or email HachetteSpeakers@hbgusa.com.

Forever books may be purchased in bulk for business, educational, or promotional use. For information, please contact your local bookseller or the Hachette Book Group Special Markets Department at special.markets@hbgusa.com.

ISBN: 9781538763582 (mass market), 9781538763599 (ebook)

Printed in the United States of America

BVGM

10 9 8 7 6 5 4 3 2 1

This is for everyone who has been told that they must change to be loved. Please remember: right now, this minute, you are perfect.

ACKNOWLEDGMENTS

Thank you to Amy Pierpont, my editor since 2007, when she radically changed the cover of *To Taste Temptation* and set me on the path to becoming a *New York Times* bestselling author. It's been a wonderful seventeen years. I'll miss you.

Thank you to Alex Logan, who gracefully stepped in as my editor midrevisions without missing a beat. I hope we'll have many years together.

And finally, thank you to Cecilia Tan, who found me a sensitivity reader, and to Cameron Quintain for being that expert reader. You both rock!

NO ORDINARY DUCHESS

CHAPTER ONE

Once upon a time a baby girl was born in a palace.
The baby had golden-brown eyes and downy black
hair and a nose that was far, far too big for her face.
When her father, a courtier to the king, saw her,
he beamed with pride. Her mother,
however, was silent....

—From *Lady Long-Nose*

OCTOBER 1760
LONDON

Private libraries were extraordinary, Lady Elspeth de
Moray mused. To have an entire room filled with books—
in one own's *house*—seemed quite fantastical. If *she* had
a library, she would never leave. She'd eat, sleep, and day-
dream surrounded by *stories* and be completely happy.

Footsteps sounded outside the door, rapidly coming
closer.

And—more practically—a library held a multitude of
excuses right at hand, should a lady be discovered skulk-
ing in one.

Elspeth reached for a large book and opened it, perch-
ing on the library ladder as she did so.

Just in time, as it happened, for a tall, severely handsome gentleman to slide into the Duke of Windemere's

library. His eyes narrowed as he spotted her. "What are you doing here?"

His tone was not friendly. Actually, if one were to be frank, his voice was rather icy. Which was a pity since he was otherwise intriguing. His black hair was braided into a long queue, and he wore a gray pearl earring dangling by the sharp angle of his jaw.

Elspeth met his gaze. His clear gray eyes were the same color as his pearl earring—beautiful and almost otherworldly. Unfortunately, he looked at her as if she were a bit of manure he'd just discovered adhering to his shoe.

Humph. "I am reading," she replied loftily to his question, and then glanced down at the book.

She blinked in surprise. A rude engraving covered the page.

The gentleman walked to her, his movements graceful. Sinuous. He reminded her of a viper gliding toward a particularly plump sparrow—the sparrow in this case being she.

He stopped in front of her, so close Elspeth could see the small wrinkles at the corners of his eyes when he narrowed them again.

"Are you?" His gaze flicked down to the illustration of...a couple? Possibly two couples? There were a confusing number of limbs. One ebony eyebrow rose censoriously as he looked back at her. "Reading, that is?"

Quite unfair that *she* was unable to raise her eyebrow in return. She felt heat invade her cheeks. "Yes."

His mouth twitched irritably, and she couldn't refrain from staring at his lips. They were thin but perfectly formed, the cupid's bow wide and defined, the bottom lip just a fraction plumper.

She was still staring when those lips parted and he asked, "Who are you, and how did you get into this library?"

Her gaze abruptly jerked up to meet his stony one.

Elspeth lifted her chin. "I don't see how that is any of your concern."

If she hadn't been watching, she would've missed the tiny curl of his upper lip.

He seemed to dismiss her, glancing about the library as if he were looking for something—or perhaps *some-one*? The room was rather gloomy. Bookshelves rose up to a second story, accessible only by means of the ladder she sat on. The walls were gilt and bloodred, shadowed and menacing. It was an atmospheric room.

Perhaps that was why she felt a frisson of alarm trip up her back when his attention snapped back to her. "Why are you here?"

"Why does anyone frequent a library?" Elspeth shrugged. "For the books, of course." She smiled. "Why do you ask? Do you perhaps have another reason for being here?"

His face frosted over, all expression gone, as he stared at her. "You haven't answered my question."

The gentleman was persistent.

And a bit formidable.

Elspeth swallowed. "Nor have you."

He said with a cutting edge, "I hardly think—"

Whatever horrible words he meant to throw at her were interrupted. Outside the door, the sound of voices was approaching fast.

Before Elspeth had time to think, the gentleman seized her, turning her bodily around to face the ladder. The scandalous book dropped from her fingers to the floor.

He placed his palm on her bottom and gave a hard shove. "Move!" he hissed, herding her up the steps.

Despite his rude push, Elspeth scrambled into the upper story of the library. It would do her no good to be found here. A narrow walkway ran around the room, with an iron railing to keep one from accidentally falling.

Once he'd ascended the ladder himself, the gentleman led her into a dark corner where there was a window covered in grime. Both the corner and the window were obscured to those below unless one stood quite at the opposite side of the library.

Abruptly, he sat and pulled Elspeth down, and she belatedly realized they were hiding—that *he* must have some reason to hide as well. How very interesting. They squeezed together, the gentleman with his back against the window and Elspeth between his legs.

The door opened.

Candlelight suddenly brightened the room below as someone—two someones—walked into the library.

The gentleman tightened his hold about her middle. Her bottom was firmly wedged against the V of his thighs, his heat enfolding her. Elspeth had to pull her mind away from the sensation of his breath against the nape of her neck to listen to the men below.

"...the matter," the Duke of Windemere was saying.

Oh Goddess. Of course the library was the duke's, but she'd rather hoped that he'd not return home before she left.

"Yes, Yer Grace." The other man spoke with a guttural London accent.

Elspeth was distracted by an intriguing scent. Something...spicy. Perhaps mace? Or cloves—she always had trouble telling the two apart. She turned her head and drew in a long breath.

"What are you doing?" the gentleman hissed, so close to her ear it tickled.

"I'm sniffing you," she replied as softly as she could.

"*Don't.*" His whisper had the hint of a growl.

Well, that would mean not inhaling, and as she needed to breathe, that was a silly command.

He seemed prone to ire over the least little thing.

As was the duke. His Grace was speaking sharply to the man with the London accent now. "...and you must be discreet."

Drat. She'd missed something again.

But it was hard concentrating on what sounded very much like a lecture while being held in a gentleman's arms. He might be chilly and abrupt, but his arms were warm and very solid. Quite muscular, in fact.

Elspeth placed an experimental hand on his thigh. Yes, his legs were muscular as well. And encased in velvet. It made one want to run one's hands down the soft yet hard length of his thigh.

The gentleman stiffened before pulling her hand from his leg and placing it in her lap.

She looked down. He hadn't let go, and it was fascinating how big his hand was next to hers—his fingers encased her wrist quite easily. He wore a dully gleaming gold ring on his forefinger. The ring seemed to have some sort of carving. Elspeth tried to bring both their hands closer to her eyes to examine the ring, but of course he wouldn't let her.

Strict man.

She bent over their hands instead. The light wasn't

good, but she could just make out...a snake? Something serpentine in any case, curling around the flat head of the ring. How extraordinary. The de Morays' emblem was the merlin, and she remembered inspecting her father's gold ring—very similar to this one, though of course with a bird instead of a snake. It was almost as if—

"...what in the hell?" the duke said suddenly. "Who took this book from the shelf?"

Elspeth's head jerked up. Windemere's voice was calm, nearly bored in fact, but what if he decided to search the library? She couldn't afford to be found here. Her search had only just begun, and if she was discovered—

The gentleman's arms tightened around her as if he meant to protect her.

A soft thump—the sound of a book being shelved.

"Where was I?" Windemere muttered. "Ah, yes. You'll have the rest of the money once the deed is done and not before." There was a scraping from below as if someone was standing from a chair. "Be discreet when you leave my house—the less you're seen, the better— and make sure your men know as well. I expect a report within the week, do you understand?"

"Aye, Yer Grace."

The door opened and then closed, taking the candle-light with it.

Elspeth moved to stand, but the gentleman restrained her. "Stay. Don't move."

She rolled her eyes. It wasn't as if she had a choice. Elspeth began to wonder. Why was he so wary of being discovered in the library? She knew her own reasons for hiding, but what were his?

Elspeth realized that her breath matched his. In. Out.

In. Out. It was so comfortable simply sitting like this, his warm body against her own, waiting.

She yawned.

"For God's sake," he muttered into her ear, and then he broke her peace by rising and pulling her to her feet.

Elspeth shook out her skirts before she looked up to see that the gentleman was already climbing down the ladder. He jumped onto the main library floor and then motioned to her impatiently.

She descended the ladder more slowly. Halfway down, she felt his hands grip her hips and lift as if she were as light as a newborn chick—which she most certainly was not.

He was quick to let her go once she stood on two feet.

She turned.

He was staring down at her in almost an accusatory way.

"Well," she said brightly, "wasn't that exciting?"

"You should leave," he clipped out. "If—"

"I wonder why," she interrupted, "you were so insistent we hide?"

The gentleman's aristocratic nostrils flared. "I *beg* your pardon."

The words might be polite, but his frosty tone made it more than clear that it was Elspeth who should be begging.

Silly man. As if she'd ever beg.

She smiled instead. "It's just that if you had leave to explore Windemere's library, I doubt you'd need to hide from him. Are you a thief?"

His face iced over. "Listen to me, girl," he said with excruciating precision. "You do not want to come to the

Duke of Windemere's attention. Trust no one in this house. Leave as fast as you can. Do not linger. I do not want to see you in the duke's library or anywhere in his house ever again. Do you comprehend?"

Elspeth nodded slowly. The gentleman's instructions were quite understandable, not to mention ominous.

"Leave," he said, taking her arm and marching her to the library door.

She shivered as she walked away. She could feel his gaze fixed upon her back like icy fingers. No doubt he was making sure she obeyed him and took the correct hallway to the front door.

Not that she would, of course.

She shook her head. Whatever his reasons for lurking about the duke's library, the gentleman was a fascinating man—so rigid, so severe, so *contained*. She couldn't help but wonder what it would take for his ice to melt.

But she hadn't time for her curiosity. She was in London for a very important reason: to save the Wise Women and return to her home in Scotland.

And to do that she needed to find and steal a book hidden in one of the Greycourt libraries.

* * *

Julian Greycourt watched the sway of the young woman's skirts disappear around the corner of the hall. He *wanted* her.

He closed his eyes.

These...urges were loathsome, and yet they plagued him near constantly. He'd been in London over a month now with no remedy. Perhaps that was why he'd found himself drawn to the girl.

She was pretty and bright and innocent, and she had

smelled of wild roses. She would not welcome his touch. No sane woman welcomed his touch—not at least without being paid.

Julian shook his head and started down the hall, pushing the girl and his perverted needs out of his mind. He had other, more important things to think about.

Such as the person he'd expected to meet in the library—Peg McDonald. Peg had sent him a note telling him the day, time, and place.

And yet she wasn't there.

Maybe she'd lost her nerve. Peg was a housemaid— one of the few who had been in service to the Greycourts since Julian was a little boy. More importantly, Peg had served his mother until her death. It had taken Julian months to coax her into meeting him.

The woman had been terrified.

Julian turned a corner in the hall and came face-to-face with the reason for Peg's fear. Augustus Greycourt, the Duke of Windemere—and Julian's uncle. The duke was a short, rotund man a bit over sixty. He wore a simple white wig with a minimum of curls. His cheeks were rosy, his eyes the Greycourt gray—the same as Julian's own.

By rights Augustus should be a jolly man.

Appearances in this case not only deceived but gave no forewarning of the madness within.

"Nephew," Augustus greeted him with a smile.

"Uncle." Julian kept his tone even.

"Do you mean to attend the duchess's gathering?"

"I do," Julian replied, watching him warily. The duchess had invited him to her afternoon tea, a ready-made excuse for him to be in Windemere House.

His uncle feigned surprise, his eyebrows arching up,

his hands spread wide. "And yet this is not the way from the front door to my wife's salon. Have you become lost?"

Augustus knew damn well he wasn't lost. Julian had lived in this hellish house for four years before he'd escaped at the age of one and twenty. "I stopped in the library to look for a book."

"A book?" The old man's expression metamorphosed from one of pretended kindly concern to one of sly amusement. "Perhaps one of...licentious drawings? Is that the book you were interested in?"

"Yes," he replied without inflection. He could not give away the girl's presence in the library, even if it meant humiliation in front of his uncle.

The duke cocked his head like a curious robin—or a feral dog about to attack. "You should be careful of such base desires. I've known them to wreck a man."

Julian felt a chill down his spine. He'd made sure to indulge his sexual requirements only in the country and in secret. If his uncle ever realized what Julian craved, the duke would destroy him with the information.

The duke continued, "You must've been bored waiting in the library." The old man's smile widened until he grinned maliciously. "I expect it was disappointing when *my maid* Peg McDonald didn't come."

Julian stilled. Peg was dead. He knew it as certainly as if he'd witnessed her death. Julian felt hot rage boil within his chest—at his uncle, at *himself* for imperiling the woman. But he contained his anger, tamping the feeling down, locking it behind iron walls of indifference.

He would not give his uncle the pleasure of his heartache. Augustus fed upon others' grief, their terror and rage. Julian had learned long ago to never show emotion.

"Your maid?" Julian asked in a deadened tone. "Perhaps your mind is softening with age, Your Grace. I do not *meet* with servants."

His uncle's face twisted with fury before he spat, "Just as well since she seems to have disappeared."

"Pity." Julian calmly held Augustus's gaze. "If you'll excuse me? I'm late already to Her Grace's party."

"Of course." Augustus moved aside. "Enjoy the tea and my wife's clever conversation."

Julian brushed against the savage old man as he passed. He was two strides away when the duke spoke behind him. "Oh, and Julian?"

He froze before slowly turning to look back at his uncle.

Augustus smiled. "I think it's about time Lucretia married, don't you?"

Julian breathed slowly, watching the old man.

His uncle chuckled softly. "And I've found the most marvelous bridegroom. I think you'll be most surprised."

The duke was too delighted with himself. Julian knew that the nameless man was someone entirely wrong for Lucretia.

He felt the impact of the duke's words. Inside he was growling, fighting down the urge to wrap his hands around the old man's throat and *squeeze* until Augustus choked on his own bile. Outwardly he turned without comment and continued down the hall.

He must've walked automatically, for he stopped at the doors to the pink salon without remembering how he'd arrived.

Julian blinked. The duchess's tea had been an excuse, a reason, should he need it, for being in Windemere House. But now he felt a desperate urge to see his sisters in person. To make sure they were alive and well.

He pushed the tall painted doors open.

The pink salon was a huge room. The walls were a deep, shrieking pink, embellished with light-gray plaster bas-reliefs of flower baskets. If one had the misfortune to look up, a ceiling entirely painted with Roman figures at a banquet assaulted the eyes.

The Romans were pink, white, sky blue, and gold, a rococo excess.

At the far end of the salon, a group of ladies were gathered, their silk gowns almost as colorful as the ceiling. Julian could see his sisters sitting together, their shining black hair in contrast to the rest of the party.

He breathed, feeling his chest loosen, and walked toward them.

As Julian approached, a ridiculous Italian greyhound ran at him and attempted to shred his stockings by jumping at his legs.

Julian deftly caught the animal and continued his progress, stopping before his sister Messalina. "Yours, I presume?"

Messalina glanced up, the gloss of her ebony hair reflecting the light. "Oh, Daisy!"

The puppy wriggled happily.

Daisy had taken an idiotic liking to Julian—despite his best effort to dissuade the animal. For a moment he curled his fingers into his velvet-soft fur, wishing...

Then Julian dropped the puppy onto his sister's lap.

He turned to his hostess, making a leg. "Your Grace, I beg your forgiveness for my tardiness."

Ann Greycourt, the Duchess of Windemere—and Augustus's third wife—was only three and twenty, a full decade younger than Julian. She was a pale, rather retiring girl who looked too delicate to survive his uncle's Machiavellian machinations.

Ann gazed at Julian with a rather nervous smile. "Not at all. Not at all. I'm so glad you came."

He nodded at his sisters. "Messalina. Lucretia. Good day."

Messalina, the elder, smiled as she fed a tidbit to Daisy.

Lucretia glanced at him, and Julian rejoiced at the bored expression in her pretty gray eyes. She didn't know. She had no fear.

"I didn't think you were invited," she drawled.

Lucretia's skirts twitched as if Messalina had kicked her in the shin. No matter. He cared not that his sisters thought him cold and uninterested. It was better, in fact, that he maintain the facade.

He was their shield, standing between them and Augustus.

"Indeed I was invited," he replied dryly.

Messalina cleared her throat. "Have you met everyone here, Brother?"

At his no, she began the usual introductions, which were rightfully the duchess's duty.

He glanced at Ann and found her slowly angling her hand in a sunbeam, perhaps to make the ring on her finger sparkle. Poor girl. Marriage to the duke could not be enjoyable. Augustus wanted a child badly. As it stood, Julian himself was the duke's heir—a fact he enjoyed rubbing in his uncle's face.

Julian returned to the introductions to bow and bow again. The names and faces were a blur of words and feminine giggles until Messalina came to the last woman.

The room seemed to quiet.

"Have you met Lady Elspeth de Moray?" Messalina asked with a warning stare at Julian as a familiar face looked up at him.

De Moray.

The girl from the library was a de Moray. The sister of *Ranulf* de Moray.

His enemy.

He returned Messalina's glower with a small arch of his eyebrow. Did his sister think he'd become violent at the name?

Julian turned deliberately to examine the de Moray girl. She was plumper than was fashionable. Her generously round hips overflowed the seat of her chair, and her pillowed breasts pushed against her stays as if they wanted freeing. She had full cheeks, pink against her white skin, and her hair was a glorious blond red like the dawn of a new day.

A smile played about her lush lips.

He felt his own mouth tighten. "We haven't been introduced."

Messalina nodded. "Lady Elspeth, my brother, Julian Greycourt."

Lady Elspeth's blue eyes held the hint of a merry twinkle, which Julian didn't like at all. What *had* she been doing in his uncle's library? He realized she'd never given him an answer. How very suspicious.

He bowed and took her hand, soft and white, in his. "An honor, my lady."

His lips brushed the air over her knuckles, and for a fleeting second, he wanted to put his mouth to her hand and discover the taste of her skin.

Madness.

He straightened.

"I trust your delay in arriving wasn't caused by something dire?" the minx asked with an innocent air.

The only empty chair was next to hers. He sat, his gaze never leaving hers. "Not at all. My horse wasn't saddled when I asked for it."

"Oh, you have a horse," she replied nonsensically, her eyes softening. "What sort?"

What was she about? "A bay mare."

She smiled, and the room seemed to grow a little brighter. "And her name?"

He cleared his throat. "Octavia."

Lady Elspeth tilted her head, gravely considering. "The Greycourt family *does* seem rather fond of ancient Roman names. Save for Daisy, of course."

"Obviously." He turned pointedly to watch their hostess pour the tea. But the scent of wild roses seemed to tap at his shoulder, keeping him aware of the woman beside him.

Across the gathering, Lucretia sighed. "I can't think why our ancestors considered it a good idea to use Roman names. There are only so many, after all, and quite a few made famous by tragedy. I mean *Lucretia*, of all people."

"My namesake isn't much better," Messalina murmured. "But it's tradition, dear."

Lucretia snorted, and they were off, debating names and ancient figures. He felt a swelling of not-unfamiliar affection for the two.

"Sugar?" Ann asked, holding a tiny, delicate teacup.

"No. Thank you, Your Grace." Julian took the dish of tea.

Beside him, Lady Elspeth shifted. He imagined her body heat warmed his side. "I don't understand how you can drink tea alone without sugar or milk. It's far too bitter."

"Perhaps I enjoy bitterness," he replied. Of course, he wouldn't taste the tea in Windemere House. Even if Ann looked innocent enough, he knew better than to trust anyone under Augustus's power.

He could feel Lady Elspeth glance at him, but he kept his gaze steadfastly on Lucretia.

Lady Elspeth took a breath. "That seems rather self-defeating."

"Do you think so?" He finally turned to her and found those wide blue eyes far too close. He steeled himself and straightened away. "But then you know nothing about me, my lady."

She nodded. "I think that's why I have the desire to peel you apart like an orange. Surely your insides must be sweet?"

He clenched his fists, fighting down any physical reaction. "I doubt anyone has ever described me as sweet."

"No? But that only makes me more curious about what you hide at your center." She cocked her head, and for a moment, he had the awful sensation that she could see inside him. "Of course, I know a *few* things about you." She looked as if she was fighting a smile. Was she mocking him? "I know you can move very fast up a ladder."

"Hush," he breathed. Was she mad? It was her reputation that would be ruined if it came out that they'd been alone together in the library.

She raised her eyebrows, murmuring lower, "Are you so humorless, Mr. Greycourt?"

He stiffened. "I don't have time for humor."

"Don't you?" She sounded almost pitying now, and he shot a sharp glance at her. She shrugged. "I think humor is the spice to our days, Mr. Greycourt. It makes everything that much livelier. That much more delightful."

This time he didn't bother answering her, giving her his shoulder.

Across the table, the ladies were chattering about hats or some other frippery. Lucretia picked up another dainty cake from one of the plates before them—her third since he'd entered the room. His lips softened. His youngest sister had been fond of sweet things ever since she'd been a child.

As was he.

But Julian knew better—any sort of indulgence was a weakness waiting to be exploited.

Lady Elspeth leaned forward to make her own selection from the tray of treats—a confection of pink sugar roses atop a tiny cake. He watched, appalled, as Lady Elspeth ignored her fork and brought the cake to her lips with her fingers. Julian swallowed. What would the icing taste like licked from her fingers, sweet sugar and her? The thought was too sensual. Too tempting in every way.

He was so intent on his thoughts, he almost missed her next words. "I suppose you haven't time for pleasure, either." Her voice was low for a woman's, almost husky. "I'm afraid it rather begs the question what you *do* have time for. Perhaps your horse. Or a dog. Do you have a dog?"

"No," he bit out. *Not since I was seventeen.*

He had to get hold of his mind.

Focus on what his uncle had revealed of his plan for Lucretia. Augustus was head of the family and he had the power to force Lucretia into marriage. Just as he had done only two months ago when he'd made Messalina marry Gideon Hawthorne—a disastrous misalliance.

Hawthorne had been Augustus's bullyboy, a violent, immoral man who had emerged from the manure pile of one of the seediest areas of London: St Giles.

"No dog," mused Lady Elspeth beside him, persistent as a kitten begging for attention, her needle-sharp claws pricking and scratching his skin. "Of course not. Too frivolous, I suppose." Did she wish to draw blood? "I have noticed some London gentlemen—and ladies—quite interested in tobacco. Do you smoke or snort or otherwise take tobacco?"

As it had turned out, Hawthorne had not been *quite* as awful as expected. Messalina appeared to be smitten with the man—proving that Julian would never understand the inner workings of women, let alone his sisters.

"Perhaps cards?" Lady Elspeth murmured, her voice lowering to an unbearable purr. "Or books? I did, after all, meet you in a library."

But the fact remained: Julian had been out of town when Augustus had forced the union. Julian had arrived far too late to help Messalina.

He'd been useless. Too far away, too distracted by—

"The sensual arts?"

His head whipped about at her whisper.

Her eyes widened at his sudden movement. "*Oh*."

"That is not a subject for unmarried ladies," he said sternly.

She looked both surprised and innocent, but perhaps she was an actress. "Isn't it?"

What was she playing at? "Of course not."

Everyone must be looking at him. He felt heated by the combined stares. He slid his gaze about the circle of women, but no one seemed to have noticed their little exchange.

When his eyes returned to Lady Elspeth, he found himself the object of her too-intent inspection. "How very interesting," she said, her sky-blue eyes trailing from his neck to his chest to somewhere about his belly. "One would never think from your cool exterior that you might be a liber—"

"Hush."

Sparks had trailed behind her gaze, flying perilously close to dry tinder. He felt as if he might go up in a blaze at any minute.

"Your words and thoughts are intemperate, my lady," he replied coldly, and for a fleeting moment, he saw the flare of hurt in her face.

He made himself ignore her dismay. Julian stood and bowed to the duchess. "Your Grace, you must forgive me, for I have a pressing matter to attend to."

He barely waited for Ann's confused nod before striding from the room and heading for the front door.

Outside, Octavia waited patiently for him under the supervision of a groom. Behind her was a large carriage with no emblem. Two shifty-eyed men lounged on the box while an enormous brute picked his teeth by the side.

Gideon Hawthorne's men.

Julian would never like his sister's husband, but he had to admit Hawthorne made sure Messalina—and by extension Lucretia—was well guarded.

Julian nodded to the big man by the carriage and turned to mount Octavia. For the moment, Lucretia was safe.

He just had to make sure she stayed that way.

CHAPTER TWO

Two weeks later, the entire court gathered for the
baby's christening. As the child's blanket was drawn
back, everyone leaned forward to see her.
Whereupon there was a collective gasp that turned
into whispering that led to a murmuration so loud
the pigeons perched on the roof took wing.
What everyone was saying was:
Lady Long-Nose....
—From Lady Long-Nose

Almost an hour later, Elspeth was the last to enter the Hawthorne carriage. She sat opposite Messalina and Lucretia and twitched her skirts into order thoughtfully. "Does Mr. Greycourt often come to tea parties? He doesn't seem the sort to be interested in little cakes and gossip."

Lucretia snorted. "No, he's not."

"Julian is worried about us." Messalina said as she stroked Daisy, drowsing on her lap. "Or at least I believe that's why he accepted the duchess's invitation."

Lucretia rolled her eyes. "Julian's actions are entirely opaque."

"Are they, though?" Messalina looked thoughtful.

"What do you mean?" Elspeth asked curiously.

Messalina bit her lip. "I think Julian holds himself to blame for Aurelia's death."

Elspeth shivered. Ah. That night fifteen years ago when Aurelia Greycourt, the eldest Greycourt daughter, had been killed. And Elspeth's own brother, Ranulf de Moray, now the Duke of Ayr, was whispered to be her murderer.

Elspeth hesitated and then blurted, "*Should* Mr. Greycourt be blamed for Aurelia's death?"

"I don't think so." Messalina sighed. "Of course I was asleep when it happened, so I can't say with absolute certainty, but in any case, because of Aurelia's death, I believe Julian is doubly worried about Lucretia and me." She looked at Elspeth. "He doesn't want to lose another sister."

Elspeth's eyebrows shot up. "Are you in danger, then?"

Messalina winced. "There is our uncle. The duke is..."

"A beast," Lucretia said bluntly. "He's an evil old man who delights in making people unhappy."

"Hence Julian's urge to guard us."

"Like some sort of mastiff growling over a bit of beef." Lucretia wrinkled her nose. "I swear I can feel him staring at me whenever we're in the same room together. It's not at all nice."

"Darling," Messalina murmured in a chiding tone, "he cares for us."

"Does he?" Lucretia challenged. "He hardly speaks to us, aside from the usual courtesies. I think we're a duty to him, not sisters he loves."

Messalina looked unhappy, but she didn't refute Lucretia's claim, Elspeth noticed.

The carriage dipped and bumped over the uneven cobblestones.

Mr. Greycourt was very...intense, Elspeth mused, glancing out the carriage window. She remembered his pale-gray eyes drilling into her as he warned her away from the duke, the library, and indeed all of Windemere House. His eyes had been so hard, so cold.

And yet...

There was something about him that made her want to crack him. Make him take off that icy mask and acknowledge that he saw her.

She must stop dwelling on the man.

The carriage shuddered to a halt, and Elspeth straightened and looked out the window. "Oh, we're at Harlowe House."

Harlowe House was the London home of the Dukes of Harlowe, the latest of whom was Elspeth's brother-in-law, Christopher, better known as Kester to the family. Freya had married him only a month ago in a small ceremony.

"Convey my love to Freya," Messalina said. "And tell her we're looking forward to her ball next week."

Elspeth nodded as she stepped from the carriage. "I will."

Both ladies waved as the driver started the horses.

Elspeth turned to inspect Harlowe House.

It was a grand townhouse on par with Windemere. But Harlowe House had been built much more recently and thus boasted lovely Palladian columns, rising loftily along the facade.

Palladian. Elspeth wrapped her arms around herself and wriggled happily. It was so wonderful to see architecture that she'd only read about in books before.

She mounted the front steps and narrowed her eyes at the waiting butler. The man called himself Fletcher and was tall and thin, with ridiculously bushy eyebrows. Elspeth didn't trust him in the least. Butlers were *very* suspicious. They lived in all the great houses, and who knew what they really did? She kept an eye on Fletcher as he ushered her to Freya's sitting room.

Freya was lounging by the fire, but she rose at Elspeth's entrance, holding out her hands in greeting. "I expected you hours ago. Her Grace's tea must've been quite long."

Elspeth crossed to her sister and let her cheek be bussed as she took Freya's hands. "You wouldn't believe how long. But there were little iced cakes to console me."

Freya looked amused. "Thank goodness."

They both listened as the door to the sitting room closed behind Fletcher.

Immediately, Freya pulled Elspeth to sit with her on a settee near the fire—away from the door and any listening ears. "Well?"

"I was interrupted," Elspeth said, remembering Mr. Greycourt striding into the library, proud and distant. "I didn't have time to find Maighread's diary."

Freya's brows knit in concern. "You were discovered?"

"Not by the duke."

"Thank Goddess!"

Elspeth winced. "But Julian Greycourt saw me in the library."

"I'm not entirely certain that's any better," Freya said grimly. "He was there the night Aurelia was killed and Ranulf was beaten so badly. He never came to our brother's defense."

"But you've made up with Messalina and Lucretia since?" Elspeth asked curiously.

Freya twisted her lips. "*They* had nothing to do with whatever happened at the Greycourt manor. Besides, Kester was there as well, remember? My husband has told me that it was Julian who wouldn't let him help Ranulf as he was beaten by the duke's men."

"Oh." Elspeth swallowed, feeling a bit ill. Ranulf had lost his right hand as a result of that beating. Mr. Greycourt must loathe the de Morays. "He was at the tea afterwards, I'm afraid. *And* he sat next to me."

Freya asked fiercely, "Did he threaten you?"

"No, not at all," Elspeth said slowly. "Mr. Greycourt was quite abrupt and rather disapproving, but he only warned me to stay away from the duke."

In fact, shouldn't Mr. Greycourt have been more hostile when he realized she was a de Moray? After all, he believed her brother had killed his sister.

"Well, he was quite right about that." Freya hesitated and then seemed to make up her mind about something. "I'm sorry, dearest. I know you think that finding Maighread's diary will somehow gather the Wise Women back together, but is it really worth the danger?"

"Yes." Elspeth knew she was thrusting out her chin defiantly. All three of the de Moray sisters—Freya, Caitriona, and herself—were rather known for their stubbornness. As the youngest, Elspeth had had to learn early to defend her ideas against her older and more articulate sisters. "Maighread reformed the Wise Women nearly a thousand years ago, writing our laws and reminding us that we served *all* women. It is only because of her that the Wise Women still exist. The Hags must listen to her writings."

"Must they, though?" Freya pursed her lips. "What if the Hags aren't interested in Maighread's teachings? They are, after all, the leaders of the Wise Women. Most follow the Hags' decrees like baaing sheep."

Elspeth inhaled and took a moment to order her thoughts.

The Wise Women were an ancient, secret organization

pledged to help all women in Britain. Their compound was in the north of Scotland, and Elspeth and her sisters had grown up there after Papa had died. Elspeth had been only six when they'd lost Papa.

Freya had left their home years ago when she had been made Macha—the Wise Women's spy. But Elspeth and their middle sister, Caitriona, had stayed in that isolated world.

Within the Wise Women's compound was an ancient library full of knowledge from all over the world. The keeper of this library was called the Bibliothacar. When Elspeth turned thirteen, the Hags had decided she should become the Bibliothacar's apprentice.

Fortunately, Elspeth had found she enjoyed the work. The Bibliothacar who mentored her had been a very old woman called Rikvi. She had been stern but kind, and Elspeth had loved both her and the library. When Rikvi died, Elspeth should have inherited the title.

But there had been changes in the Hags as some died and were replaced. The new Hags had become fearful. The Wise Women had always been secretive, but now the Hags decided that the risk of discovery and destruction was too great. They abandoned the women outside their walls, closed the gates, and pushed out the Wise Women who disagreed—including the de Moray sisters.

Freya had been in London when she'd received orders to either comply with the new rules or quit the Wise Women. She'd chosen the latter. Caitriona and Elspeth had been forced to leave the compound, Caitriona traveling to see their brother, Lachlan, in Scotland, and Elspeth making the journey to London and Freya. She'd arrived only weeks ago and had immediately started laying plans to search the Duke of Windemere's library.

The Wise Women were simply too precious to let shrivel and die because the Hags were afraid.

Elspeth opened her eyes. "You're right. When I bring Maighread's diary to the Hags, they might dismiss it, but I believe that there are enough people in the Wise Women who still honor Maighread's teachings. Rikvi thought the diary was important."

"I'm sure she did," Freya replied, sounding soothing— so irritating! "But she'd never seen the diary, had she?"

"No living Wise Woman has," Elspeth said with some excitement. Wouldn't it be wonderful when she found the near-mythical book?

"Then how do we know it's still extant? Perhaps it was burned decades ago."

Elspeth's eyes widened. "Why would anyone destroy such a precious artifact?"

"Oh, darling, you've been out in the world only a month," Freya said gently. "Maybe someone read it. After all, it was written by a woman whom most outsiders would see as, at best, a rebel against society, or worse, simply mad."

Sometimes Elspeth found it very hard to understand outside society. But... "I can't give up my search because of what *might* have happened."

"And if it never existed?" Freya asked. "Perhaps Maighread's diary is simply legend."

"No, it's not." Elspeth knew she was correct in this. "Rikvi was certain the diary was in a Greycourt family house. The information has been passed down from Bibliothacar to Bibliothacar."

"Well." Freya sat back against the settee. "I suppose I can't convince you to change your mind, but you must be careful, darling." She met Elspeth's gaze. "Mr. Greycourt is dangerous, the duke more so, and there are Dunkelders in London."

The Dunkelders were humorless people—mostly men, naturally. The rest of Britain might have given up on witch burning, but the Dunkelders still hunted Wise Women.

Elspeth shuddered at the thought. "I will be careful, but I must find that diary."

Even if that meant crossing paths with Mr. Greycourt again.

* * *

Julian rode along the street that evening. The wet paving stones, the looming houses, and the air itself felt murky and macabre in the dimming light. Footsteps sounded from the dark, some near, some far, but Julian was alone on the street. Not even the moon, hidden behind clouds, kept him company.

Maudlin thought.

A cat suddenly darted across the cobbles, causing Octavia to shy, and Julian realized to his chagrin that he'd not been paying attention to what was happening around him. The mare's hooves struck the cobblestones with a clear *clop-clop*, the sound echoing off the shuttered buildings. The dark had fallen fully now. Ahead, two shadows lingered within an alleyway.

Unmoving.

Keeping silent.

Suspicion was an ingrained habit now after years of threats, feints, and outright attacks from Augustus.

The duke didn't want him to inherit the title.

Julian wheeled Octavia around at the thought, kneeing her into a canter back down the street. A shout and a *bang* came from behind him, and he instinctively crouched over his saddle, heart racing in his chest. They turned into a more crowded street, and Julian reined Octavia back to a trot. She shook her head, nervous after their abrupt retreat.

Julian patted her neck as he guided her onto a different route.

Only a few minutes later, the White Horse Inn came into sight, and Julian breathed a relieved sigh. He and his younger brother, Quintus, had taken rooms here.

Had Father lived, there would have been a London townhouse. But Augustus had held the purse strings of the family ever since his brother, Julian's father, had died. When Julian had turned one-and-twenty, the duke had handed over his inheritance—a pittance.

Julian knew—*knew*—that there had been more money, but what could he do against the Duke of Windemere?

Hence the inn.

The White Horse was a large posting inn. A carriage stood in the middle of the courtyard, hostlers unhitching the horses and leading the tired animals to the stable, while the coachmen threw down the luggage, and what looked like the last straggling passengers entered the inn.

When Julian at last deposited Octavia's reins into the hands of a stable boy and went inside, he found the common room packed. Smoke, the smell of roasting beef, and the loud voices of dining travelers assaulted his senses.

"You there," Julian called, stopping a hurrying tavern maid. "Some of that roast beef I can smell for our rooms as well as a bottle of wine."

"Aye, sir." The girl curtsied and ran toward the bustling kitchen.

Julian had little hope of seeing their meal anytime soon.

He turned to the left, begged pardon of an elderly country squire, and climbed sturdy wooden stairs to the floor above. There were only a few tallow candles on the wall and no windows, making the corridor dim. Julian stopped at the third door on the right and knocked.

There was a thump from within and then a scrape before the door was unbarred and opened.

Quinn peered out, his black hair a wild tangle around his head. His bulky shoulders filled the doorway.

"Jules!" Quinn seized Julian's arm and pulled him into the room, slamming the door behind them. "I saw her. I saw Aurelia again today!"

"Did you?" Julian gently shook off his brother's grasp and walked to the table and chairs before the small fireplace. He took off his gloves and hat, throwing them on the table.

"You sound doubtful."

Julian turned.

Quinn was scowling at him, obviously ready for a fight.

Julian closed his eyes. He didn't want this. To argue with his brother. To try to tear down Quinn's hope—his belief—that Aurelia, Quinn's twin, might still be alive. Until a fortnight ago, his brother had been almost daily in his cups.

But then Quinn had seen a woman with gold hair and a certain way of holding her head. Only a glimpse, mind, in the crowd at Covent Garden market, but he was convinced it had been Aurelia. Never mind that Aurelia had died fifteen years before. Never mind that Aurelia had been sixteen when she died. Never mind that she'd be one and thirty had she lived, and who knew what she might look like? Quinn was convinced that he'd seen his twin.

At least this new hope—however tenuous it might be—had Quinn curtailing his drinking.

Julian took a breath. "Can we argue this later?"

"Aye." Quinn grunted and threw himself into a chair, making it creak. "How about Peg? Did she give you any information about Augustus?"

"Peg wasn't there." Julian met his brother's gaze grimly. "What's more, Augustus stopped me in the hall after I left the library. He told me that Peg was gone."

"Fuck," Quinn muttered. "He must've discovered she was going to speak to you. How?"

Julian shrugged. "The old man has filled Windemere with spies loyal to him. She must've let something slip. I can think of no other explanation. Augustus wouldn't have let her live once he recognized the possible danger to himself. It was a miracle that Peg McDonald had remained alive and in his employ all these years."

"Have you any idea what she meant to tell you?" Quinn asked.

"No." Julian dropped into the chair opposite his brother. "Perhaps she knew nothing. Perhaps I was merely chasing a fleeting hope—and she died for it."

"She must have known something against the old man," Quinn growled. "Why else would he have killed her?"

"Sheer malevolence?"

"Don't jest." Quinn glared at him.

"What makes you think I am?" Julian raised his hands in surrender. "I think someone shot at me on the way home."

His brother swore savagely. "When will you take your own safety seriously? You know not to travel at night."

"Or in crowds, in places I frequent, in places I'm not familiar with…" Julian smiled bitterly. "The problem is that I'd be under a bed night and day if I worried about my own safety so much. I cannot. I cannot hide and keep my family safe, too. I *will* not."

"This is your life," Quinn said fiercely. "Jules."

"It's what I must do," Julian said quietly. "I take what precautions I can." Frivolous words. The duke had already made one failed attempt. It was only a matter of time before he made another. And this time the old man might very well succeed. "I'll not leave you his heir."

Not and paint a target on Quinn's back instead.

Quinn scoffed. "You had better not."

"Besides," Julian continued more lightly, "maybe the old man will finally get an heir on Ann. Then all our worries will be over."

Quinn looked at him from under the untamed locks of hair falling in his eyes. "I think we will have worries until our uncle is in the grave. You know my opinion on the matter."

"I do know," Julian said calmly. Quinn had several times suggested that hastening their uncle's death would be beneficial to the entire Greycourt family. "And I also know that one or both of us hanging for the murder of a peer would destroy this family."

"There won't be much of a family if we lose another member." Quinn restlessly rose from his chair.

And really wasn't that the heart of the matter? Aurelia's death fifteen years ago had split apart the family—literally. Mother had died not that long afterward, the girls were sent to a distant elderly uncle, and Quinn and Julian were condemned to endure Augustus's household.

The quiet was broken by the slam of Quinn's fist into the wall.

Pieces of plaster fell to the floor.

"They'll charge us for that," Julian murmured dispassionately.

Quinn paced to the opposite wall. "Perhaps Augustus killed Peg because she knew Aurelia was alive."

Julian looked at his brother and hardened his heart. "Aurelia is dead."

Quinn stared at him. "I saw her, Jules, I saw her on Bond Street today, and I saw her a fortnight ago. She was tall and slim. She had hair the color of a guinea, curls that blew in the wind, the same as Mother's in that portrait that hangs in Greycourt. It was Aurelia."

Julian held up his hands. "Before you hie off to search for a sister who may only be a will-o'-the-wisp, let us save the flesh-and-blood sister we have with us. Lucretia needs our help."

Quinn scowled. "If this is some—"

"Augustus means to marry off Lucretia," Julian said grimly. "He says he already has a bridegroom."

"Jesus." Quinn looked stunned.

"Exactly," Julian said. "I haven't told her yet. I'd hoped to have a plan for her escape before I broke the news, but..." He grimaced. The ideas were still spinning in his head. "In any case, I'll have to tell her tomorrow."

"Aye." Quinn stood and paced. "What are your thoughts?"

Julian steepled his hands before him. "We must get her out of England—or at least London."

"The duke'll have spies watching her," Quinn growled. "Probably watching us as well."

"Yes." Julian placed the tips of his fingers under his chin, thinking hard.

Quinn ran his hands through his untamed hair. "Christ. We don't even know who the man is."

Julian frowned. "Right. You'll have to discover the man for us, and I—"

A rap came at the door.

"Enter," Quinn said.

The door was opened wide by Vanderberg, Julian's valet. Behind him was a maid bearing a huge tray of food.

Vanderberg bowed as the girl placed the tray on the table before Julian. "Forgive me for my tardiness."

Julian thanked the maid and watched her depart before turning to his valet. Vanderberg was a short, slight man who should be earning much more than Julian could afford. "No matter. Have the kitchens prepare two baths."

Vanderberg looked doubtful. "It may be some time before a bath will be ready."

Julian waved him toward the door. "Nevertheless."

The valet bowed and left.

Quinn sat and tore apart his bread. "Will you be able to pay him for much longer?"

"I hope so," Julian replied. "Vanderberg is loyal."

"That he is." Quinn nodded. "What were you about to say before our supper arrived?"

"We have to find someone to help us with Lucretia." Julian glanced up at his brother. "Someone we can trust."

* * *

The next morning, Lucretia Greycourt wandered into the Whispers library as Elspeth was working. Whispers was

Gideon Hawthorne's house and, apparently, had been near empty when Messalina married him.

"Oh my goodness, whatever are you doing up at this hour?" Lucretia demanded, patting back a yawn.

Elspeth glanced at the clock. "It's nearly nine of the clock."

"Ghastly," Lucretia muttered, sinking into a settee and draping her arm over her eyes.

There was a companionable sort of silence.

The library was a vast room lined with shelves waiting to be filled with books—empty save for the clock placed there so that Elspeth wouldn't miss supper when she worked here.

Messalina had acquired at auction a huge collection of books from the estate of some deceased peer. Unfortunately, the collection had not been catalogued—or, for that matter, in any way sorted.

Naturally, Elspeth had offered to catalogue and shelve the library when she'd seen the crates of books. Messalina had accepted the offer with what had looked like relief and had even said Elspeth might sleep at Whispers during her work.

Now the floor was littered with stacks of books from one end of the room to the other, rather as if children had pretended the floor was a sea and the books islands and decided that they could traverse the space only by jumping from one pile to the next.

Elspeth had her own sorting method for a library, based loosely on the method Rikvi had taught her. Each stack represented books with a common theme. Perhaps Poetry or History or Tedious. Not of course that there weren't some books that presented problems. The *Aeneid*, by Virgil, for instance, which could be placed in either of the first two categories and might, one could argue, be catalogued in the third as well.

Elspeth could muse over such fascinating conundrums for hours on end if given the opportunity.

However, she was organizing this delightful library for Messalina, not for herself, so she attempted to keep to her task.

Mostly.

As she sat on the floor sorting books, Elspeth mulled over the problem of returning to the Windemere library to continue her interrupted search. It had been pure luck that the Greycourt sisters had been invited to their aunt's tea so soon after Elspeth had arrived in London. She couldn't rely upon happenstance again.

Could she somehow insinuate herself into the duke's household? The difficulty was that she'd already been introduced to London society as Lady Elspeth de Moray. She couldn't pretend to be a maid or a cook or a widowed lady willing to be seduced by the duke.

Elspeth wrinkled her nose. Especially not the last.

What then did that leave her?

She could sneak into Windemere under cover of darkness and burgle the library! It would be difficult and a tad dangerous, but most probably it could be done without discovery.

Elspeth bit her lip. Freya would be most disapproving of such a scheme.

She sighed.

Obviously, she should think of a more conventional idea.

"Lady Elspeth."

She started at the deep voice so close to her. She looked up to see Mr. Greycourt staring down at her, his gaze so intent she was surprised she hadn't felt it immediately. He was frowning and seemed tense.

"Mr. Greycourt," she replied sedately. Even though Freya had warned her against him, Elspeth couldn't help a shiver of anticipation at the sight of him. "Good morning. Are you looking for your sisters?"

Behind her, Lucretia snuffled and settled into a gentle snore.

Mr. Greycourt pursed his lips—possibly in disapproval, though whether of her, Lucretia, or the entire world was hard to tell. "Yes." He glanced at his sister asleep on the settee, and for a moment his face gentled. Then he looked back at Elspeth, and he was icy again. "What are you doing sitting on the floor?"

"Cataloguing books for Messalina," she said, gesturing to the assortment of volumes lying all around her. "Do you know I've discovered four copies of Izaak Walton's *The Compleat Angler*, and I still have those boxes to unpack." She pointed at half a dozen crates stacked at the far end of the room. "Why would anyone purchase four copies of the same book?"

"I have no idea." He glanced at the piles of books and then back at her, his eyes narrowed. "You seem to have an affection for libraries."

He sounded suspicious.

She raised her brows. Was he always this wary? It must be terribly exhausting. "Well, yes. I do love libraries and books and reading, but then doesn't everyone?"

"Not in my observation."

Her cheery mood faltered a bit. "Perhaps, but *you* must, surely. After all, I met you in a library."

"Which you had no right to be in." He stared at her coldly.

Well, of course she hadn't, but..."Does that mean," she asked, concerned, "that you *don't* enjoy books?"

His gray eyes flickered, and then his lips pressed together. "I haven't the leisure to read for pleasure."

She felt a sharp pain in her soul. "How can you possibly survive without literature?"

"Quite easily." He sounded mocking.

"No," she replied quietly. "I don't believe you're such a clod."

His eyebrows winged up at that. "What?"

Elspeth spread her arms. "One can *live* without books. Birds live. Cats live. Even the best of dogs live. But only humans can *soar* on the words from a book. Stories fling us high into the clouds with imagination. Poems make hearts weep with emotion. Science stuns the mind with wonder." She let her hands fall to her lap. "Without the stimulation of literature, you can live, yes. But your soul will be earthbound. A clod without imagination."

"I..." He blinked as if taken aback for just an instant before assuming his usual haughty expression. "I assure you, my lady, I live perfectly well without books."

"No." She shook her head, pitying him, this severe man who thought he wanted for nothing. "No. You breathe and you move, but inside, in your mind, there is only gray. You don't know what it is to soar."

She locked eyes with him. The atmosphere was thick with tension as his nostrils flared, his thin lips parted, and his gray eyes turned stormy, and for a moment—only a moment—she thought that his expression was very similar to what his passion would look like.

Then, behind her, Lucretia groaned. "Are you arguing with my brother? Don't bother. He always wins."

Mr. Greycourt turned, and the moment was gone. "Good morning, Lucretia."

Lucretia yawned extravagantly. "Good morning to you as well, Brother. I haven't any idea where Messalina is, though I did see her at breakfast, so she must be somewhere about."

He raised his brows. "What makes you think I've come to see only Messalina?"

Lucretia looked confused. "Haven't you?"

Mr. Greycourt merely looked at her, a faint trace of what might be amusement about his eyes. "Actually, I have something I need to discuss—"

"We plan to leave soon," Lucretia blurted.

"Do you?" Mr. Greycourt's mouth thinned as he tapped his walking stick on the floor. "That works perfectly with my plans. I'll accompany you to Bond Street."

Lucretia bridled. "Bond Street? I never said we were going to Bond Street. And why would you accompany us in any case?"

That was rather rude. Elspeth held her breath, half expecting that Mr. Greycourt would scold her friend.

Instead he merely looked implacably at his younger sister.

Elspeth shivered as the library seemed to become stifling.

Then Lucretia made a moue and glanced away from her brother. "Oh, very well. We'll make an outing to Bond Street."

"Thank you," Mr. Greycourt said softly.

"But Elspeth shall come with us," Lucretia demanded. She turned to Elspeth. "That is, if you'd like to visit Bond Street?"

Of course she would! Elspeth had heard of it, but she'd yet to visit the famed shopping center. She smiled at Lucretia. "Oh, yes."

"Then it's settled," Lucretia pronounced with a defiant glare at her brother.

Mr. Greycourt, for his part, was staring at Elspeth with what looked like ambivalence. "Very well," he said slowly, then glanced at the clock. "Let us leave at eleven of the clock. Lucretia, please find Messalina and tell her."

Lucretia muttered to herself but marched from the room obediently.

Elspeth looked down at her dusty hands. "I'd best go freshen up."

A hand appeared before her face.

Startled, she looked up and found Mr. Greycourt standing before her.

He arched an ebony brow. "My lady?"

Elspeth blinked and put her hand in his.

He drew her to her feet with no effort but then pulled her closer so that they were nearly embracing. She could feel his breath on her lips when he spoke. "I hope, for your sake, that I can trust you."

Elspeth pulled her hand free from his. "You can."

She turned and left the room without further words, but she couldn't help but wonder: what was Mr. Greycourt planning?

CHAPTER THREE

The father raged and roared, and even complained to
the king, but still the awful name stuck.
Her mother dosed Lady Long-Nose with potions and
smeared her with poultices to stop her nose growing.
But nothing reduced the size of the baby's nose....
*   —From* Lady Long-Nose

"Did I tell you what I found in your library this morning?" Lady Elspeth asked Messalina eagerly.

Julian watched Lady Elspeth as the carriage bumped toward Bond Street. Her cheeks were flushed prettily, a dimple appearing by her mouth as she smiled.

She looked the very picture of innocence.

He glanced away to stare out the carriage window. He'd have to tell his sisters soon about the marriage threat to Lucretia, but not yet.

From beside him, Messalina said, "No, what did you find?"

"A very old piece of a folio. I think it's part of Bede's *Ecclesiastical History of the English People.*"

"*No,*" Messalina exclaimed in a whisper.

Julian hadn't thought of Ran's youngest sister in over fifteen years. Yet now she seemed to have installed herself in Lucretia's and Messalina's lives quite easily. Was Lady Elspeth spying for her brother?

Ran certainly had reason.

"What exactly is that?" Lucretia asked with what sounded like reluctant interest.

Lady Elspeth looked startled.

"Darling." Messalina sighed. "Bede. The father of English history?"

"Oh, that Bede," Lucretia replied airily. "I thought you might mean the Sicilian Bede or even that one in France."

Julian closed his eyes. They might be his sisters, but he felt alien when Lucretia and Messalina were frivolous like this. He'd spent four years in Augustus's house—a place where no one could be trusted. Where servants and guests alike spied on him, eager to report any slight thing. If he smiled at a maid, she disappeared the next day. If he picked up a book, Augustus would make Julian watch as he burned it. If he frowned at a footman, he was forced to apologize.

"You made that up." Lady Elspeth sounded fascinated.

While at the same time, Messalina said, "There are no other Bedes! It's just the one."

Lucretia mumbled, "Killjoy."

His every expression, every little move was studied, picked apart, and used against him until Julian had learned to hold himself still, to express neither joy nor sorrow nor anger. He'd buried all his thoughts and feelings so deeply inside himself that sometimes he thought he'd lost them altogether.

Messalina snorted in an unladylike manner. "Even if *some* people are sadly ignorant of Bede, I'm terribly grateful that you found the manuscript, Elspeth."

"I'm enjoying the work tremendously," Lady Elspeth said, and in Julian's mind's eye, he saw that dimple again. "It's as if I'm exploring an unmapped country. I never

know what I might find—illuminated psalters or philosophical texts in Greek or—"

"The collected poems of Aphra Behn, woman poet,"
Lucretia piped up. "Do you know she's buried in Westminster Abbey?"

"Truly?" Messalina sounded surprised. "I'd have
thought she was far too scandalous for such a prominent
cathedral."

The carriage jolted over something in the street, and
Julian opened his eyes. Lady Elspeth was looking right at
him, her mouth still in a soft smile. Why? Why would the
girl constantly smile at him when he'd been nothing but
dismissive of her? Those curving pink lips should make
him suspicious. Should raise his hackles and make him
reach for a weapon.

"We ought to visit Westminster Abbey and look for
her," Lucretia said, bouncing on the carriage seat.

Messalina stared at her sister. "*You* want to visit an
abbey?"

"An abbey where scandalous people are buried,"
Lucretia retorted. "It's quite different from some village
church."

"I would like to tour the cathedral," Lady Elspeth put
in. "I've heard that there's an absolutely ghastly effigy of
Queen Elizabeth in it."

He was older than she, a cynical husk of a man trying
and mostly failing to shield what remained of his family. Why in the world should she look at him so gently?
Did she lack the instinctive wariness of any small, soft
creature?

And yet he found himself relaxing under her stare, a
feeling of warmth and comfort coming over him.

Dear God, Elspeth de Moray was dangerous, but not for the reasons he'd first assumed.

"Lovely," Lucretia said. "Then we shall all go together."

"Wonderful," Messalina said sardonically. "I've always wanted to see a ghastly effigy."

Julian glanced out the window. They were nearing Bond Street. He had to speak to them now.

He cleared his throat. "I have something to tell you both. The duke has made plans to wed Lucretia to an unknown man."

Beside him, Messalina gasped. "Dear God."

Lucretia was frozen, looking at him with wide, frightened eyes.

Messalina clutched his sleeve. "She needs to leave London. Go to Scotland or—or France. Somewhere she can hide."

He put his hand over his sister's fingers. "Yes. And we will get her out. Quinn and I are thinking of plans."

"But can't Lucretia simply say no?" Lady Elspeth asked.

Was she bamming him? Julian stared at the girl, but her expression was entirely open, her blue eyes watching them with confusion.

How could anyone be so naive?

"No," Lucretia said quietly. "Uncle Augustus can force the wedding. Just as he did Messalina's marriage."

"What?"

"Blackmail," Messalina said. "The duke had me kidnapped and then held Lucretia's safety over my head."

"She had no choice," Julian growled, remembering his anger and shock, the desperate ride to London to try to save Messalina. The realization that he'd arrived too late.

"Fortunately, I came to love my husband," Messalina said crisply. "I've forgiven Gideon long since."

"*I* haven't," Lucretia muttered.

The carriage rolled to a stop.

Julian glanced out the window. The carriage was off Bond Street, but the street was still crowded. Good.

He turned to nod at Lucretia. "You needn't fear, Hawthorne's men are here and so am I. No one can snatch you from the street."

She raised her head proudly. "I know."

Messalina nodded at Julian. He glanced at Lady Elspeth to find her watching him as if trying to solve a puzzle.

The carriage door opened and the step was set. Julian jumped down first. He helped Lucretia and Messalina down before wordlessly holding his hand out to Lady Elspeth. She placed her little gloved fingers in his grasp as she stepped down. She shot him a glance from under lowered eyelashes, and for a moment, warmth lit his chest. Then she let go, and the cold returned. She lifted the hood of her dark-blue cloak over her head.

"Shall we?" Lucretia pointedly linked her arm with Messalina's and set out down Bond Street.

"My lady?" Julian proffered his arm for Lady Elspeth, and for a second, she merely stared at the limb as if nonplussed.

Was he so loathsome?

Then she nodded and took his arm.

He inhaled the scent of wild roses and couldn't stop his body from tightening in reaction. The temptation to lower his face to her neck, to find the source of that perfume and...

Julian cleared his throat and made himself move forward.

Their progress was slow, the way jammed with both the fashionable and the working class. An exquisitely bewigged pair of gentlemen bowed to a trio of giggling ladies. A floridly rotund country squire escorted his family: a matronly lady and three excited girls. A scarlet-coated soldier winked at a milliner, who tilted her chin in the air, clutching her bandbox as she hurried by.

"I don't blame you, you know," Lady Elspeth said suddenly.

For a split second, he wondered if she could somehow sense his longing.

Then he came to his senses. He lowered his head to hear her. "Blame me for what?"

"Ranulf."

His heart froze. "You know nothing about that time."

"I know that my brother lost his right hand."

He wanted to close his eyes, step away from this conversation, and sear the memory from his brain.

Ran had been an artist.

"And you think that's my fault." *It was. It was.*

"No, that's what I'm trying to tell you," she said, almost scolding. "I don't know whose fault it was, if it was anyone's, but I don't blame you."

She should. "That's very kind of you."

"Now you're being sarcastic." She sighed. "Ranulf refuses to answer any of my questions."

He looked at her. She wore a white cap underneath her hood, the lace framing her face like the petals of a flower. "You've seen Ran?"

She wrinkled her nose, which was ridiculously adorable. "I haven't *seen* him, no. I don't think any of our family has in years, except for Lachlan, who has to consult

Ranulf about the ducal lands. But I do write both of my brothers."

Julian blinked. Rumor had it that Ran was a recluse, hiding away in some townhouse in Edinburgh. "What..." He took a breath. "What does he say?"

She laughed, too loud, too boisterous, and utterly charming. Everything he did not deserve. "He tells me about anatomy."

"What?"

She smiled up at him. "He's taken a great interest in it and consults with learned men all over the continent." Her smile fell. "Via letters, of course."

"Of course." Julian had thought that Ran had given up. Had retired from the world, never to return. But if he was pursuing his interests, was in contact with others...

That was good. Very good.

His guilt should lessen at the news. Except Julian would have to fool himself first.

He knew what he'd done to Ran.

Lady Elspeth said, "There is really no need for us to be enemies. After all, your sisters are friends to me."

"My sisters," he said through stiff lips, "forget that your brother killed Aurelia." He glanced at her, making his expression harden. "You and I can never be friends."

She looked up at him with solemn eyes. "Can't we?"

Why was she even trying? Didn't she know he'd been the architect of Ran's fall? Didn't she know how base his desires were?

No one should be friends with him.

There was a shout behind them, and Julian turned just in time to see a skinny lordling chase after a tattered urchin, shoving aside a man in a bottle-green waistcoat in the process.

Julian faced forward again.

Lady Elspeth pulled at his arm, and he realized that his sisters had stopped by a shop window, their heads together as they peered inside. It wasn't until Julian and Lady Elspeth caught up to them that he saw that the shop sold books.

"Shall we go in?" Messalina asked Lucretia.

Lucretia rolled her eyes. "Don't you have enough books?"

Messalina answered, "No."

While at the same time, Lady Elspeth said excitedly, "I don't think one could ever have enough books."

Julian's lips twitched. "Of course you don't."

"Oh, come in," she said in mock affront, and they followed his sisters into the shop.

Inside, closely set bookshelves created a warren, the scent of ink, mildew, and, faintly, decay in the air. The shop held both new editions and older volumes. There were two customers already peering at the shelves, but otherwise the store was empty.

Messalina and Lucretia immediately wandered to inspect some large volumes lying in a glass case.

Lady Elspeth looked around, her face lit with something close to rapture. "Let's check down here," she said, leading him into an aisle.

The scent of old paper was stronger here, reminding Julian of his father's library at Greycourt. The hours he'd spent reading poetry in a window seat, dust motes floating in the sunlight. That time was like a paradise forever lost. He'd been a daydreaming boy, unprepared for Augustus and his evil.

"Oh, look," Lady Elspeth called, tearing Julian out of his thoughts. "What a lovely set of Mr. Johnson's *A*

Dictionary of the English Language. Aren't they beautiful?"

Lady Elspeth was gesturing to a tall, dusty glass case, inside which were four folio volumes. The case was naturally locked.

"And expensive," Julian said dryly.

Lady Elspeth pouted. "But they're still beautiful. Even if unaffordable to most."

He fought back an urge to lean closer, perhaps to feel her warmth on his skin. "Point."

She nodded as if having proved something to herself and walked deeper into the store.

Julian shook his head, strolling after Lady Elspeth. He caught up with her as she stood on tiptoe trying to reach a thin folio on an upper shelf. She clutched two other books in her other arm.

Julian reached over her head and easily took down the book, presenting it to her.

"Oh, thank you." She took the book and opened it, smiling faintly. "It's *Hero and Leander* by Christopher Marlowe. I've always wanted to read it."

"Have you?" He contemplated her. "It's a bit risqué for an unmarried lady."

"I think you know I don't worry much about the opinions of others." She had a smudge of dust on the tip of her nose, and he wanted—very badly—to thumb it away.

Instead he murmured, "No, you seem to live by your own rules."

Elspeth either ignored him or didn't hear his words. "Oh," she said, frowning ferociously at a *Daemonologie* by King James VI. "What a hateful book."

He glanced at the book in question—a tattered copy

facing out—and snorted. "You don't believe in witches, do you?"

She looked at him strangely. "Do you?"

"No, not really." He shrugged. "But at the border where I grew up, the superstition was still alive. And of course there were strange women who wanted to be thought witches. They called themselves Wise Women and dealt in herbs and the like. Simply nonsense."

Her face had closed for some reason, and he couldn't read her eyes.

"Elspeth," Messalina called from behind him, "are you ready? Lucretia wants to visit the glove maker."

"I'm coming," Lady Elspeth replied. "I just have to buy these."

They went to the tiny counter where the proprietor sat dozing. He didn't seem entirely happy to be disturbed for business but was quick to settle the transaction with Lady Elspeth and tie the small stack of books together.

"Thank you," Lady Elspeth said politely, and she reached for her parcel.

Julian picked up the books before she could. "Allow me."

"That's very kind of you," she said stiffly.

He couldn't help arching a brow. "Very few ladies have had cause to call me kind."

Beside them, Lucretia snorted.

Oddly, Lady Elspeth frowned at his sister.

Outside, Hawthorne's men were waiting patiently.

Julian nodded to them as he followed the ladies. As he did so, he noticed a flash of green behind them.

The man in the bottle-green waistcoat was lingering by the shop before the bookstore, seemingly interested in a display of lace-trimmed tricornes on the table in front.

The shop boy was staring at the green-waistcoated man with suspicion, and well he should be. The man didn't seem the sort to be able to afford a lace-trimmed tricorne, let alone to wear one.

Julian casually turned back to trail after the ladies. Perhaps the man in the bottle-green waistcoat wasn't following them. Perhaps he was too suspicious.

But there was another possibility. Perhaps Augustus had set a watcher on them, either to kill Julian...

Or to make sure Lucretia didn't flee before the marriage.

*   *   *

"Well," Elspeth said the next day, "this is certainly depressing."

"Isn't it?" Lucretia agreed faintly.

"What?" asked Ann Greycourt, the Duchess of Windemere, sounding confused.

All three ladies stood with Messalina, looking down at the gravestone of Aphra Behn, woman poet, in the cloisters of Westminster Abbey. It was black and set flush with the stone floor and read:

MRS APHRA BEHN
DYED APRIL 16
A.D. 1689.
HERE LIES A PROOF THAT WIT CAN NEVER BE
DEFENCE ENOUGH AGAINST MORTALITY.

Elspeth tilted her head, studying the inscription. "Do you think that is what she wanted her gravestone to read?"

"Noooo," Lucretia moaned. She seemed to be taking the inscription very hard.

The duchess merely blinked and gazed around a bit absently. Elspeth wasn't entirely sure how she'd come to be with them at the cathedral. Something about Messalina inviting her after the duchess appeared at Whispers that morning. The sisters and Elspeth had agreed to act as normal as possible until a way for Lucretia to flee had been decided on.

"It does seem unlikely that Mrs. Behn wanted this on her gravestone," Messalina said. "Unless she became quite religious toward the end of her life. Like John Donne."

"John Donne was religious?" Lucretia asked, diverted.

"He became a priest," Messalina said, and one could tell she very much wanted to roll her eyes.

Elspeth bit back a smile.

It was a cold, dreary day. Rain was dropping aimlessly on the cloister garth outside as if unable to commit to a storm.

Elspeth shivered. She wasn't entirely sure what a garth was. It looked like a square garden to her.

Lucretia was still frowning at the stone. "I don't think Aphra wrote this."

"Aphra?" Messalina looked incredulously at her sister. "You're on intimate terms with her now?"

"Yes," Lucretia said, her chin set quite firmly.

"A man wrote it," Elspeth said with certainty, even though she knew very little of Aphra Behn. "Her husband or perhaps a brother, someone who was quite jealous of her talent and wanted to have the last word."

"You have a low opinion of the male sex," a very male voice said from behind Elspeth.

She jumped and turned to see Julian Greycourt standing there. "You startled me apurpose."

He tilted his head slowly to the side, staring at her as

if she were almost, but not entirely, interesting. "Perhaps you simply don't pay attention to your surroundings."

Elspeth narrowed her eyes. "You were behind me. I haven't eyes in the back of my head like a…a…"

"Owl?" he inserted.

"Owls don't have eyes in the back of their heads." Elspeth frowned. "They merely turn—"

"Quite." Why did the man feel the need to interrupt her? "Perhaps Janus," he continued musingly. "The two-headed god. Though the analogy is somewhat clumsy."

Elspeth fought to keep from propping her hands on her hips like a baker arguing with a customer. "I didn't say Janus. *You* did."

She could see his lips parting and was aware once again of how beautiful his mouth was. It was stern and hard, the vertical indentation between upper lip and nose so sharp it might've been carved in marble. And yet…his lips held the possibility of softer moods.

Sensuous moods.

What would he look like if he were to taste a sweet custard, licking the cream from his upper lip—or even her fingers—his eyes half-closed…

She was brought abruptly back to the present by Messalina's voice. "What are you doing here, Julian?"

Mr. Greycourt's attention turned to his sister, and Elspeth felt a momentary pang of disappointment at the loss.

He said to Messalina, "I've come to see Westminster Abbey with my sisters and Lady Elspeth." He bowed to the duchess. "And, of course, my aunt."

"I didn't think you would remember our discussion from yesterday?" Lucretia looked a bit startled.

Mr. Greycourt raised his eyebrows. "Naturally, I remember what my sisters talk about."

It was a gentle rebuke, but still a rebuke. Elspeth watched Mr. Greycourt's face, but he gave no indication he might be hurt by Lucretia's lack of faith in him.

Lucretia, on the other hand, looked thoughtful. Perhaps she was realizing that her brother cared more for her than she had thought?

"Naturally, you're welcome to walk with us, Julian," Messalina said in an even tone.

Mr. Greycourt inclined his head to his sister before he held out his arm to his aunt. "May I escort you?"

"Oh, thank you." The duchess flushed a pretty pink. "But I think I'll walk with my nieces."

Her Grace took Lucretia's arm and began strolling to the abbey's entrance with Messalina bookending her on her other side.

Mr. Greycourt stood staring after them.

"Ahem." Elspeth cleared her throat.

He ignored her.

Elspeth tried a little louder. "Ahem."

Mr. Greycourt turned his frosty gray eyes on her. "Have you a cold, my lady?"

"Not at all." Elspeth looked pointedly at his elbow.

He raised an eyebrow but held out his arm. "Shall we?"

Elspeth tucked her hand into his elbow. "Yes, we shall."

He led her back along the chilly cloister corridor.

At first she'd been incredulous when Freya had explained that it was considered proper and polite for a gentleman to offer his arm to a lady. Elspeth thought the idea that a woman was so weak that she had to lean on a man just to walk was ridiculous.

Nevertheless, the position was quite warm, if nothing else. Mr. Greycourt radiated a great deal of heat. Elspeth cozied up to him and smiled when he shot her a puzzled look.

They climbed the few steps into the abbey proper, and Elspeth stopped dead. "It's amazing, isn't it?" She looked in wonder at the ceiling high, high above them. She'd never been in a building so big. "It makes one feel rather like an ant."

"Does it?" He tilted his head back. "I'm not sure what an ant feels like."

She stared at him, eyebrows raised. He'd made a joke?

He turned then and looked her in the eye, and there was a faint curve at the corner of his mouth.

"Perhaps..." Elspeth licked her lips and couldn't help but notice when his gaze dropped to her mouth. "Perhaps very small."

He arched an eyebrow.

"The ant, I mean." Elspeth took a breath to steady herself. "It would feel very small and insignificant."

"Is that what you feel?"

"No." She smiled as she realized. "No, I don't. I feel rather exuberant."

"Because of the ceiling," he murmured.

She tilted her head, trying to read him. "That's certainly part of it." Something flared behind his eyes. Something private and vulnerable.

Before she could completely process what she'd seen, his expression froze over, becoming impossible to discern.

"Come," he said. "We're lagging behind."

"You care for your sisters," Elspeth said.

"Of course I do." His arm stiffened under her fingers. "I'm their brother. Is that so odd?"

"It is, actually," she replied, thinking. "Lucretia at least seems to be a bit estranged from you."

There was a flash of something almost like hurt in his cold, cold eyes before he turned away from her. He faced forward, not answering.

"I beg your pardon," Elspeth said softly. "I was perhaps mistaken in the matter."

"No," he replied stonily. "You're quite right."

Ahead, Lucretia, Messalina, and the duchess were standing before a tomb. When Mr. Greycourt and she came abreast, Elspeth could see that the other ladies were gazing doubtfully at a gentleman in a doublet and ruff who was reclining lazily on his side atop his coffin.

"I...don't understand," Her Grace murmured. "It seems strange for him to not be lying flat."

Lucretia tilted her head. "He seems rather jolly, don't you think?"

"He's certainly colorful," Elspeth said, eyeing the bright yellow hose.

They started strolling again, and Mr. Greycourt leaned down to murmur, "We were all destroyed that summer. The summer Aurelia died. My mother passed away within a week, leaving my uncle in control. He sent my sisters to an elderly cousin and took Quintus and me to London. It was...difficult. I didn't see Messalina and Lucretia again for four years. That's probably why she thinks me distant."

His last words were whispered, and she felt a pang of sympathy. It seemed that all the children of both the de Moray and the Greycourt families had been scattered from their homes. She tried to remember Ayr Castle, but all she could conjure in her imagination was the smell of the stables and the nook under the servants' stairs where she used to hide from her nurse.

She asked impulsively, "Have you been back to Greycourt

since that summer?" Greycourt Hall was the country seat of
the Dukes of Windemere. Their lands adjoined those of the
Dukes of Ayr, with Greycourt on the English side of the border and Ayr Castle on the Scottish side.

He shook his head.

She nodded. Had any of them returned? Well, Lachlan
must have, simply to see to the care of Ayr Castle. But
besides him? Perhaps no one. Greycourt and Ayr Castle
were almost like fairy-tale palaces, locked away behind
walls of thorns, forgotten by all until some prince or princess might wake them again.

It was a forlorn thought.

Elspeth looked up as they climbed a series of stairs
into the chapel beyond the transept. "Oh," she breathed.
Above them was a magnificent ceiling, all carved fans
and pendants, each worked into intricate designs like
lace. She turned in place, head tilted back, examining the
ceiling. When she glanced down, she met Mr. Greycourt's
gray eyes watching her. "Isn't it beautiful?"

"I suppose it is," he said slowly, never looking away.
"Quite unique and beautiful."

She caught her breath at the intensity in his gaze. It
was strange, for he hadn't seemed to even glance at the
ceiling. But she was aware suddenly of how serious he
was, as if the ceiling was the most important thing he'd
ever contemplated.

Lucretia called to them, and Mr. Greycourt blinked
and looked away from Elspeth.

She breathed a sigh. His close regard was almost too
intense, as if he'd cracked open a door to his soul and
she'd been blinded by the light within. But that couldn't
be. Mr. Greycourt was a cold, unmoving, unfeeling man.

Wasn't he?

All this time he'd been leading her to Lucretia, Messalina, and the duchess. The sisters had paused with Her Grace before an enormous family monument.

"Why," Lucretia asked in an appalled tone, "is the father dressed as a Roman soldier? Surely he hadn't those muscular arms when he died at eighty?"

Elspeth examined the carved marble. "There always seem to be naked babies," she mused, peering closer at the winged ones about the Roman father's head. "Do you think—"

The father's nose suddenly chipped off, almost as if—

A *crack* echoed around the abbey.

CHAPTER FOUR

*Lady Long-Nose grew into a young woman.
She learned to dance and to paint. To play the
harpsichord, the lute, and the violin. She spoke
nine languages, two of them quite extinct. She rode
as if she were a centaur, sang like a lark, read—
and moreover understood—the most labyrinthian
philosophies, and wrote sublime poetry.
Yet all anyone talked about was her long nose....*
—From *Lady Long-Nose*

Julian shouted, "Get down." And at the same time, he pushed Lady Elspeth to the floor.

Lucretia dropped, pulling Messalina and Ann down with her, the three of them sprawled in yards of lavender, yellow, and pale-pink skirts.

Julian rolled over onto Lady Elspeth, shielding her with his body. The shot had been very close. It must've flown inches from her head. He found he was shaking. This was his fault. The bullet had no doubt been meant for him. He'd put them all in danger by simply being present. Damn it. He'd thought it safe to accompany them inside a cathedral.

Whoever was shooting was very bold.

"Are you all right?" Lady Elspeth's whisper came from

beneath him. He could feel the brush of her breath against his cheek, the warmth of her arms clasped in his hands. The scent of wild roses enveloped him.

He ignored her, scrutinizing the Lady Chapel. No one else was in it, but they were trapped at the far end, the only way out the steps back into the nave.

"You're trembling," Lady Elspeth said.

He glanced down at her. "It'll stop soon."

Her sky-blue eyes were wide in a face gone pale. "It was very close to you."

The shot had been much closer to her than to him. Almost as if it had been meant for her. No, that couldn't be right.

"Julian," Messalina called.

"Hush." His gaze flicked to his sisters. "Stay still. Just a minute more."

He could hear Hawthorne's bullyboys in the abbey, shouting to one another.

"But—" Messalina protested.

"Do as I say!" Julian didn't know where the assassin was, or if he still had a clear shot, or even who, exactly, he was aiming for in their party.

Footsteps were approaching at a run, and he tensed, crouched over Lady Elspeth, ready to attack or push her to safety if it was the assassin. A round little man appeared, huffing as he climbed the stairs to the chapel. "I say, you mustn't bring guns into the abbey. Have you lost your wits?"

Julian met the man's gaze. He was dressed simply, as if he was a sexton, and seemed more irritated over what the shot might've done to the abbey than to the people in it. Still. "Do you have the shooter?"

"What?" The little man paused, his face red as he panted. "I beg your pardon, but the shot came from within the Lady Chapel."

"No, it didn't." Julian finally rose, helping Lady Elspeth to stand as he did. "It came from without."

"I don't understand." The man looked behind him and faced Julian again. "But there was no one else in the abbey."

"I assure you I wasn't the one with the gun," Julian said without heat.

"Missus!" The biggest of Hawthorne's men had arrived, his eyes wild. Thankfully, he also held a pistol. "Are you 'urt?"

"No, we're all quite fine." Messalina tugged Lucretia closer.

"Oh, thank Gawd for that," the big man said, bracing his empty hand on his knee to breathe heavily. "The guv would've 'ad me balls otherwise, sure enough."

"My hand," Ann said quietly. "I think a chip from the monument hit me."

"Oh, Your Grace," Messalina exclaimed. She took the other woman's hand, pressing a handkerchief to the small bit of blood.

"Have you found the shooter?" Julian interrupted impatiently, directing his question to Hawthorne's man.

The big man straightened. "Not yet, though me boys are searching the abbey. Do you know where the shot came from?"

Julian shook his head, angry with himself for his inattention.

"We were all examining this monument." Lady Elspeth gestured to the marble sculptures. "Perhaps there was someone—"

But the sexton gave a cry as his gaze went to the memorial. "His Grace's nose!" He rushed past them to examine the broken statue, muttering to himself.

"We need to get the ladies to safety," Julian said, taking Lady Elspeth's arm.

"Righto!" The big man turned and placed two fingers between his lips, giving a shrill whistle. "Oi! Red, get 'ere quick-like." He turned back to Julian. "Red'll 'elp you get the missus and the other ladies to the carriage. I'll stay with the rest of the boys and keep looking."

A scrawny red-haired man skidded to a stop at the bottom of the steps, nodding as the big man gave him orders.

"Thank you, Reggie," Messalina said quietly, and the big man flashed her a gap-toothed smile before jogging back to the nave.

Julian paused as he saw a scrap of white on the top step.

"What is that?" Lady Elspeth asked as he bent to pick up the bit of paper.

Julian straightened, examining it, and then sniffed. Gunpowder. Faint but lingering.

"Well?" Lady Elspeth asked in an impatient tone.

He glanced up. All four ladies were waiting with expectant faces.

Julian shook his head, pocketing the scrap. "Nothing. Merely a bit of paper."

Lucretia scowled at him suspiciously, but Messalina led her sister and Ann around Julian and Lady Elspeth, murmuring as she did, "Perhaps it was an accident."

Lucretia snorted. "Are you saying someone brought a primed pistol into the abbey and *accidentally* fired it?"

Messalina humphed. "Are you saying that someone

brought in a pistol, loaded it, and then deliberately shot off the duke's marble nose?"

"Were we shot at?" Ann asked, curiously impassive.

"No, dear, I don't think so," Messalina said. "It seems more likely to me that…"

His sisters walked ahead, Red stalking in front of them, alertly guarding.

Lady Elspeth took Julian's elbow as they followed. "What was that paper really?"

"Wadding." He shut his mouth. Why the hell had he told her?

But it was too late. Her clever mind was already spinning.

"You mean for a pistol." Her brows were furrowed in thought. "Wadding to pack a pistol when loading it. That means…" She halted, pulling him to a stop, and glanced back to the Lady Chapel steps. "The shooter stood there. He would've seen us in the chapel." Her gaze met his, her blue eyes solemn. "This was no accident."

He sighed, nudging her into motion. The last thing he needed was Lady Elspeth becoming curious. "No. It wasn't."

She was silent as they passed Saint Paul's Chapel and John the Baptist's, and Julian almost sighed in relief, hoping she had moved on from thinking about the shot.

"Who wants to murder you?" Lady Elspeth asked suddenly, proving him wrong.

He made sure not to look at her and said curtly, "I can't think of anyone."

"Can't you?" She hummed to herself. "That seems very unlikely. You must have enemies. Your uncle, for instance."

"If I do, it's none of your concern," he replied. She couldn't intrude into his feud with Augustus. If she drew his uncle's attention...

The mere thought made his blood crystallize with fear. And her next words gave him no comfort.

"Just because it's not my concern doesn't mean I won't find out." Lady Elspeth smiled up at him angelically.

He blinked at that look, the shining certainty in her face. He had to make her stop.

He felt a pain burst from behind his left eye as he tried to repress his worry for her. His lust for her. He had to control himself.

"No," he clipped out coldly as he lengthened his stride. "You will not. I don't need some..." He raked his eyes over her plump little body, so sweet and unattainable. "Some featherbrained girl barely out of the schoolroom"—her eyes had widened in what looked like shock, shock and hurt, but he could not reverse course now. "Stop following me about like a puppy. You are ridiculous."

They had made the north entrance. Finally.

Lady Elspeth pulled away from him.

His head throbbed in pain.

She took a step outside into the dripping rain and then turned and looked at him.

He'd expected tears, recriminations, something, and he'd braced, telling himself that his cruel words were only for her safety.

But she only looked at him. Drops clumped her eyelashes and ran down her cheeks, but they were from the rain, not her tears. "I'm not featherbrained, and I haven't seen a schoolroom for quite some time. Don't think you can drive me away with cruel words. I'm not a girl."

She turned to walk unhurriedly to the waiting carriage. The other three women were already climbing inside.

Lady Elspeth entered the carriage, and then closed the door. Leaving him standing in the rain, alone.

Which was exactly what he'd wanted.

* * *

Julian walked into Otto's coffeehouse late that afternoon, having left Lucretia, Messalina, and Lady Elspeth safely at Hawthorne's house.

He glanced about. Even this near to evening, the room was crowded. Men sat at tables and booths, smoking long clay pipes while bent in discussion. Some wore periwigs, some were in curled and powdered wigs, and some—a few—wore their own hair. Otto's was known as an egalitarian coffeehouse where the customers were interested in trading in stock.

It wasn't Julian's regular coffeehouse.

He procured his tankard of coffee at the counter and made his way through the tables. The man he wanted sat alone at a table near the smoky fireplace.

Julian nodded as he took a chair opposite him.

The other man looked up. "Greycourt."

"Archway."

Francis Archway was a man of middling years, his face deeply lined, his brown-and-gray hair falling to his shoulders. The table before him was littered with news-sheets and a half-filled tankard. "May I be of service?"

"I hope you might," Julian said carefully.

"Money?" Archway was quite wealthy, despite his ordinary attire. It was rumored that he'd begun life as the son of a fisherman somewhere in Cornwall, but if he had, he hadn't retained his Cornish accent.

Still, Julian could believe that Archway had traded and bargained his way into riches. The man was quiet but perceptive.

"Thank you, but no." Julian took a sip of his bitter coffee. "It's more in the way of a favor."

Archway merely looked at him.

Julian examined the room, making sure no one had drifted close to the table, before saying, "My uncle."

The other man said flatly, "Your uncle is a very powerful man."

"Yes. Few men are stalwart enough to cross him."

Archway narrowed his eyes. "You make such a man sound like a knight rather than a fool."

"Perhaps." Julian took another mouthful of coffee. "Perhaps I'm in search of a foolish knight."

"Why?"

Julian looked up into the other man's eyes. "Because Lucretia, my younger sister, needs help."

Archway frowned, the lines above his nose deepening until he looked a caricature of himself. "I thought she was in the schoolroom."

"No." Julian shook his head. "She's three and twenty, and she's in danger."

"From your uncle."

"Yes."

Archway spread his hands. "I do not see how I can help you. Windemere is an aristocrat. I work in much less lofty spheres."

"And that is why you may help me." Julian leaned forward. "I need her gone from London. To the Continent or further. It's vital."

"Then why do you not take her yourself?"

"Because I have reason to believe that he's put a price on my head."

"He's mad," Archway murmured. "Quite mad."

"Yes. Mad enough to search me out wherever I might go." Julian watched Archway as he said quietly, "I'm a danger to my family already. Lucretia has a much better chance of disappearing without me. I need someone Windemere would never suspect to take her."

"I sympathize with your plight, Greycourt," Archway said, and he even sounded as if he might mean it. "I have two daughters nearly the age of your sister. I would shudder to think of them in Windemere's power."

"Then you'll help me?" Julian asked with little hope.

"No." Archway shook his head. "If you need funds, I can lend you money, but I have a family of my own. I cannot risk coming to the attention of the Duke of Windemere."

Julian nodded. These were the same reasons that two other men had given for turning him down. Archway had been the last on his small list of men who were bold and discreet and could be trusted with his sister.

There wasn't anyone else in London whom he knew.

Their only hope now lay with Hawthorne. Julian had informed his brother-in-law of the problem after he'd returned with the ladies from Bond Street yesterday. He didn't particularly like Hawthorne, but the man had connections Julian did not.

Hopefully, Hawthorne's inquiries would prove more fruitful.

Julian drank the last of his coffee and stood. "You'll not tell anyone of this discussion."

"Of course not," Archway assured him. "You have my word."

Julian nodded and donned his tricorne.

Outside Otto's, the sky was darkening as the daylight people hurried home—shop owners, hawkers who sold out of wheelbarrows and dogcarts, clerks, butcher's boys, and many more. They were replaced as in the changing of a guard by linkboys, young bucks in search of entertainment, footpads, watchmen, prostitutes, and those who huddled around bonfires to keep warm.

Julian passed shuttered shops as he walked toward the White Horse Inn, his thoughts on how to help Lucretia. It wasn't until he'd been strolling ten minutes or so that he noticed the man trailing behind him. How long had the follower been there? He was far enough behind that Julian hadn't seen him until the street was near empty.

Well, why not?

Julian stopped and turned, drawing his pistol from his coat pocket. The follower—the man in the bottle-green waistcoat from Bond Street—took another couple of strides before he realized that his quarry had halted.

"Stop or I shoot," Julian said just loudly enough to reach the man.

For a second the man stood still.

Then he charged.

Julian exhaled and aimed the pistol with a steady hand even as the man bore down on him. He had only one chance.

His shot echoed around the buildings.

Bottle-Green Waistcoat collapsed.

Julian was on him before the smoke had dissipated. He'd aimed well, a shot to the shoulder, probably breaking the bone. The man was whining horribly between gritted teeth, the whites of his eyes reflecting what light there was in the shadowed alley as he clutched the wound.

"What do you want?" Julian asked. "Who sent you? Was it the Duke of Windemere?"

The man pressed his lips together. Julian ground the butt of his gun into the wound. The man's eyes rolled to the back of his head before closing, his hand going limp. Julian waited a moment and then checked the man's breath.

Bottle-Green Waistcoat had fainted.

Julian scoffed and stood. He didn't really need the assassin's answer.

He already knew who wanted him dead.

* * *

When Elspeth slipped out the Whispers House kitchen door that night to burgle the Windemere Library, it had nothing at all to do with Mr. Greycourt and his unkind words to her at the abbey yesterday. Her mission in London was to find Maighread's diary. In order to dismiss Windemere House's library as a hiding place, she needed to finish her search of it.

Mr. Greycourt didn't come into her decision at all.

Well, maybe he did a little.

It was well past one o'clock in the morning, and the shadows were deep in the back of Whispers House. Thankfully so because Mr. Hawthorne's men stood guard over the house, which was rather a bother. She crept quietly to an overgrown boxwood, crouching next to it as she surveyed the back garden.

The thing was, Mr. Hawthorne's men were guarding

to keep nefarious persons *out* of the house. She was gambling on their being less inclined to keep one woman *in*.

She waited, barely breathing, until she heard drunken singing, which signaled her paid distraction. He was a one-armed soldier she'd found not far from Whispers, begging by the street earlier that evening. The man had been quite happy to aid her once she'd shown him her purse.

And from the shouting, it sounded as if her accomplice had successfully drawn the attention of the guards.

She needed only a moment.

Elspeth raced through the garden and to the door that led into the mews. There appeared to be only one guard in the mews, fortunately looking toward the shouting. She pulled her shawl over her head and walked the other way.

It wasn't until she'd reached the end of the mews that she let out her breath. Windemere House was to the east. Not a short walk, but quite easy for a woman raised in the Scottish hills.

Elspeth set out with determination.

She'd never taken orders well—as a girl or as a woman. Perhaps to others she might seem docile because she often did exactly what was asked of her—why not, if it caused her no problem?—but Elspeth also had a mind of her own with very definite opinions. Just because someone *told* her to do something didn't mean she *would*.

Up ahead, male voices were raised in a terribly off-key song. As she looked, three soldiers staggered around the corner, led by a small linkboy with a lantern.

Elspeth ducked into a narrow alley just to be careful. As the men neared, she backed away from the entrance to the alley and, in doing so, nearly tripped on something soft under her foot.

She turned, startled, and found a dog lying behind her. It was too dark to see what the dog looked like, but she saw when the animal raised its head.

"Shh," she whispered to the dog. "Just a moment more, and I'll leave." She remembered suddenly the sweet biscuits she'd hidden in her pocket to savor later. Elspeth fished one out and offered it to the dog.

The animal very gently took the treat from her hand.

"What a good boy," she whispered, although the dog might well be a good girl.

She peered out of the alley and saw that the soldiers were nowhere in sight. Hastily she continued her journey. Elspeth turned at the next street and wondered if she should've brought a lantern. But it would've been hard to sneak out of the house with one.

She was passing near a house with a lamp hung by the door when she heard footsteps behind her. Well...not *footsteps*.

More like paws trotting behind her.

She halted and turned.

The dog—some sort of hound but with short, stubby legs—stopped and looked up at her. Its eyes were incredibly sad, and she could see now that he was male.

"Are you following me?" Elspeth asked him.

The dog sat down.

Elspeth glanced around, but she'd reached a part of the street that was quite deserted. No owner in sight. She shook her head and studied the dog for another moment before setting off again. No doubt the dog would tire of, well, *dogging* her steps and find his own way home.

The dog got up and trotted alongside her, quite seriously, as if he'd decided she needed a companion to steal into Windemere House.

Elspeth ignored him—as best she could—and concentrated on remembering the way.

A man stepped out of the shadows right in front of her. "Where you goin' in such a hurry?"

Elspeth sighed and fished in her pocket. The dog growled as she drew her pistol. "That's none of your concern."

By the time she'd ended the sentence, the man had disappeared again. She nodded, pleased with herself, before pocketing the pistol again.

Then Elspeth peered at the dog. "That was rather nice of you."

His tail wagged once.

She hardened her heart. Now was not the time to become enamored of a stray dog.

It was another half hour or so before she came within sight of Windemere House. The street was wider here, the houses large and well kept, and there were lanterns hanging by every door.

Well, every *front* door.

Elspeth made her way around the back and into the mews. It was quiet here, the horses and stablemen asleep. Only a cat raced across her path, disappearing into the shadows again.

She glanced down at the dog.

The dog looked back at her.

"Aren't you meant to chase cats?" she whispered.

He cocked his head but gave no other reply.

Elspeth ventured on until she found the Windemere gate, where she had a short moment of worry before discovering it was unlocked. Cautiously she opened it, creeping into the garden.

The dog followed.

Elspeth stole to the back of the house and looked up. Windemere House was very large, with window after window in back. She frowned and counted.

Then counted again.

A mistake would be catastrophic.

When she was certain she had the right window, Elspeth finally looked at the house itself. The brickwork was smooth, but there were two iron trellises, one almost directly under the window she wanted.

Elspeth put her foot on the bottom horizontal bar on the trellis, testing it. The iron held firm.

She glanced back at the dog and whispered, "No barking."

The dog sat down and opened his mouth to let his tongue loll out.

Elspeth supposed that was the best answer she'd get. Climbing up the trellis was slow because she had to carefully test each rung, but it wasn't particularly hard. Breaking the window, however, made her heart race. She froze for a second after the glass tinkled into the room, waiting for someone to call an alarm.

The house was silent.

She pocketed her pistol again—she'd used the butt to hit the glass—and carefully laid her shawl over the sill.

Then she climbed in.

Elspeth couldn't help but grin. She'd successfully broken into the Duke of Windemere's house! Really, she was quite proud of herself.

Searching for Maighread's diary was another matter altogether. The library was dark, almost black, the only light coming from the broken window.

Luckily, she'd searched the main level of the library last time, before she'd been caught by Mr. Greycourt. But that still left the upper balcony, which meant several hundred books—maybe a thousand? She'd never been good at maths.

Elspeth found a candelabra that she'd noticed before sitting on a table. She lit it with a flint and steel from her pocket. Then she carefully climbed up the ladder with the candelabra and began methodically searching. Each book she removed from its shelf and quickly paged through. Some books didn't even need that—the atlas was quite obviously an atlas and besides, far too large for a diary.

She worked for hours, until the room began to lighten with the sunrise. Her face and hands were grimy with dust, and she'd found nothing. But she couldn't linger longer. The servants would wake and eventually arrive at this part of the house to light the fire. She had to leave.

Elspeth climbed back out the window and down the trellis and found to her surprise that the dog was still at the bottom, in the same spot she'd left him in. He yawned and stretched as she stepped onto the gravel path.

Voices came from the basement kitchens, and she caught her breath. It was later than she'd thought—the servants were up already.

She didn't let herself panic. Elspeth walked swiftly to the back gate. But she was only halfway there when she heard a shout behind her. "You! Why are you lurking there?"

Elspeth grabbed her skirts and ran as fast as she could. There were raised voices behind her, but she didn't dare look. She scrambled through the gate and kept running down the mews and into another street. Finally she had to stop to catch her breath.

Beside her the dog was panting happily.

She eyed him as she caught her breath. "I think you enjoyed that."

Elspeth threw her shawl over her head and turned to begin the long walk back to Whispers House.

But a heavy hand descended on her shoulder, halting her. She looked up into Mr. Greycourt's stormy gray eyes as he growled, "What in hell are you doing?"

CHAPTER FIVE

*Now, Lady Long-Nose had a distant cousin. He
was tall and broad-shouldered, his eyes the blue of
cornflowers and his hair golden. When he smiled,
two dimples appeared on his face, and any ladies—
or lords—who were nearby found themselves
becoming overheated.
His name was Sabinus, and Lady Long-Nose fell
quite helplessly in love with him. . . .*
—From *Lady Long-Nose*

Lady Elspeth didn't look like a lady at all.

Julian frowned down at her, taking in the smudges on
her cheek and chin, the rough shawl over her head, and
her plain brown skirts. Add to that her overly innocent
expression, and he would've been suspicious even if he
hadn't seen her fleeing Windemere House.

It was only by happenstance that he had seen her. Sleep
had eluded him due to his concern for Lucretia and the
knowledge that he must see her safe before Augustus's
assassin succeeded in killing him. He'd risen before the
sun and headed to his uncle's house in the hope that he
might see a footman or chambermaid or even a stable boy
he could bribe to give him some information on Augustus's plans.

And whom should he see dashing from the Windemere House mews but Lady Elspeth.

Of course.

He felt like shaking her. Like marching her off to her room and locking her in. He'd warned her. Had she no idea how much danger she placed herself in whenever she was near his uncle? Augustus could hurt her, could kidnap her, and Julian would never know if she was alive or—

"You need to listen to me," he ground out, both hands on her shoulders now, his fingers flexing in suppressed irritation. "No matter how curious you may be about libraries, my uncle is deadly. If you—"

He was interrupted by a growl from somewhere about their feet.

Julian glanced down and met the eyes of an oddly short mongrel, its lips pulled back from sharp teeth. "Whose dog is this?"

"Mine." Lady Elspeth looked down at the dog with a small frown. "Although I'm still thinking of a name. How do you feel about Thomas?"

Julian stared. "What?"

"No, I agree," Lady Elspeth continued, still examining the dog. "He doesn't seem like a Thomas." She snapped her fingers. "Bobby! Stop growling."

If anything, the dog's rumbling was louder now.

Lady Elspeth sighed. "I don't think he fancies Bobby, either."

He shook her. "Listen to me!"

She looked him in the eye and said very gently, "No."

And his fear and frustration and longing, and all that he'd kept so carefully tamped down deep inside himself, simply exploded.

He pulled her roughly into his arms and bent his head

to devour her lips. She was sweet and soft, and her taste was like balm for his wounded soul. He opened her mouth with his tongue, thrusting inside almost desperately, as if her depths held all the secrets he needed to sustain life. She moaned low in her throat, so softly he felt more than heard it, a tremor against his lips, and he moved his hand to her jaw so that he might press his thumb against the pulse of her throat and understand the emotions that swept through her.

He would've stood there, this small, lush creature in his arms, consuming her lips and her essence forever, feeding on her innocent warmth and happiness endlessly, except that a dogcart rattled by, the boy leading the cart whistling rudely at them.

Julian straightened, appalled. When had he become so lost to propriety, so destroyed by his own terrible desires, that he would kiss a lady in the street? "I beg your pardon," he said, and even to his own ears the words were covered in frost.

Good. Quite. It was a relief to pull his adamantine mantle about his shoulders again. To bury deep any hint of softness—of *weakness* that could be used against him.

Lady Elspeth stared up at him, softly touching her lips. "Oh." She tilted her head like an inquiring titmouse. "Why are you asking for my pardon? I rather liked that."

He felt the visceral jolt that gave him, a loosening of his restraints, a weakening of his chain mail resolve, and he pulled back sharply, tightening his control until his chest felt banded by iron. "Come."

Julian took Lady Elspeth's arm—he didn't trust her not to scamper off—and strode toward Whispers.

"What are you doing?" she asked breathlessly.

"Taking you home."

"But what if I don't want to go home?" she asked in a tone that sounded like pure curiosity. "What if I and my dog wish to continue our walk?"

Julian glanced quickly down to see that the dog was indeed trotting along with them. He scowled. "That dog should've bitten me when I assaulted you."

She scoffed. "Constantine is much more civilized than that, and besides, you didn't *assault* me. *We* engaged in a kiss."

He stopped, aggrieved out of all proportion. "What are you babbling about? I embraced you without any regard for your feelings or wants. My actions were those of a roué. You would do well to remember that you cannot physically stop a man from doing whatever he will with you. You need to be more careful."

"Actually, I could've stopped you had I wished." She took a tiny but lethal-looking pistol from somewhere on her person and brandished it before his eyes. "But I *didn't* wish to prevent you from kissing me."

Julian blinked and felt the foundations of his walls shake. She could have shot him. Could have intentionally wounded him or even killed him, and he would not have been able to prevent her.

He had thought he was in control of their embrace, but in reality, it was *she* who had held the control all along.

He closed his eyes—for a second, only that—and felt the thrill of the thought thrum through his body and harden his prick.

Her control.

Then he wrestled back his desires, shuttered his barriers tight, and started walking again. They had to be close to Whispers House now. "You took that pistol to Windemere House."

The pistol had disappeared again, and Lady Elspeth's voice was a bit shifty. "Well, yes."

"You have no business at Windemere House," he said coldly. "I don't know if you're spying or—"

"Whyever would you think me a spy?" she asked, sounding honestly perplexed.

He gritted his teeth. "Perhaps because every time I see you, you're lurking suspiciously about, usually in one of my family's libraries."

"You've seen me *twice* in a library," she said, her voice ridiculously outraged. "And the second time, your sister had hired me!"

He halted so suddenly he had to jerk her back to him. "And this morning? Where did you go in Windemere House?"

Her absurdly charming pout was all the answer he needed.

"Quite." Julian nodded and linked her elbow very firmly with his as he set out again. "Either you're spying, or you are unnaturally attracted to libraries."

There was no answer to that.

He looked at her, only to find that there was a contemplative wrinkle between her brows.

"To be fair," she said musingly, "I am very attached to books and libraries."

He raised a dubious brow. "Enough to go breaking into houses?"

She opened her mouth, and for a minute he thought that she was going to continue and claim to be an insane bibliophile.

Lady Elspeth snapped her mouth closed and shook her head.

"That's what I thought," he said, but the victory brought

him no happiness because it meant that Lady Elspeth was indeed up to something.

Which meant his warnings about the Duke of Windemere were falling on deaf ears.

The beginnings of a headache twinged behind one eye. First Lucretia and now Lady Elspeth, and of course Messalina and Quinn. He had to keep them all safe from his uncle. He was juggling too many lives, and if he let one fall, the crash would be devastating to all.

Julian was drawn from his bleak thoughts by the sight of Whispers House. The sun was fully up now, and there was nothing for it but to hustle Lady Elspeth up the steps—followed naturally by the mongrel—and knock at the front door. He hoped he wasn't late.

It was opened by a butler looking neat and alert, even though it couldn't yet be seven of the clock. "Sir?" He glanced at Lady Elspeth. "Good morning, my lady."

Lady Elspeth smiled gorgeously, so bright she put the sun itself to shame. How the butler didn't stagger back was a mystery. "Good morning, Crusher. What do you think? I had the most marvelous luck and ran into Mr. Greycourt on my morning stroll." Crusher's gaze had lowered to fix on the dog. "Oh, and I acquired a dog as well, as yet unnamed."

The butler blinked once and nodded. "Of course, my lady." He opened the door wider, letting them all in.

Lady Elspeth immediately trotted to the stairs without another word and disappeared to the upper regions of the house, trailed by the dog. She didn't even look back at him.

Julian snorted and turned to the butler. "I'd like to see Mr. Hawthorne."

"Certainly, sir. If you will wait here, I shall find if he is available."

Julian was shown into a small receiving room just off the hall. It was painted a bright yellow, and a set of delicate chairs were arranged next to a fireplace.

Quintus rose as he entered the room, his eyebrows lowered. "What took you so long? I was beginning to think I'd have to meet with Hawthorne all on my own."

Before Julian could answer, Hawthorne strode through the door. "Greycourt. Quintus."

"Hawthorne." Julian nodded, while Quintus merely grunted his greeting. It was something of a miracle that his brother was awake at this hour.

Gideon Hawthorne was a sleek, muscled man, a little shorter than Julian himself. His speech still held the tinge of St Giles, where he'd been born and raised.

The door opened again, and a maid came in, bringing the scent of coffee.

Hawthorne nodded to her and waited until the door closed again before pouring three cups. "Well?"

Julian shook his head. "Archway refused." He looked at his brother. "Quinn?"

That man took a gulp of coffee before speaking. "I haven't found the man who wants to marry Lucretia yet. I do, however, have a few suspects. Augustus met with Earl Evening and Lord William Speckling at the city coffeehouse, so either of them might be the man—or he might not."

Julian nodded and looked at Hawthorne. "Have you had any luck?"

Hawthorne leaned forward. "I've made inquiries about people who could smuggle Lucretia out of London. I might have someone. They're a bit rough."

"Do you trust this person?" Julian asked.

Hawthorne grimaced. "That's part of the problem."

Quinn sighed and tilted his head against the back

of his chair. "This is maddening. What if I take her to Dover?"

"You'll be followed," Hawthorne grunted. "Both by Windemere and possibly the bridegroom, whoever he is."

Julian took a sip of his coffee. "Your men are still guarding Lucretia?"

Hawthorne nodded. "As you know."

"Thank you," Julian said. He remembered Lady Elspeth roaming the streets. "You might want to remind them that they are to guard against not only people coming into your house at night but those leaving as well."

Hawthorne raised his eyebrows. "Very well."

"You heard of yesterday's shooting at the abbey?"

Quinn muttered angrily to himself because, of course, Julian had already told him the night before.

Hawthorne's expression became colder, but he merely nodded.

"If anything..." Julian shook his head. There was no point in tiptoeing around it. "If I die." He met Hawthorne's black gaze. "You'll do your best to see them safe? Both Messalina and Lucretia?" He coughed. "And Lady Elspeth as well?"

Quinn's brows knit.

Hawthorne gave Julian an odd look but didn't comment on the belated addition. "Yes," he said gruffly. "You needn't worry about that."

"Good." Julian inhaled and continued briskly, "I hope to have Lucretia out of London soon. Until then..."

"I'll double the guard around Lucretia and Messalina. But Greycourt"—Hawthorne's gaze was serious—"the Duke of Windemere has far more money and power than I. For Lucretia's sake, you both need to move quickly."

"Yes." Julian's fingers clenched. "I know."

He rose and bowed as Quinn drained the last of his coffee. He walked with his brother to the door and left the house.

Quinn waited until they had descended the front step. "Lady Elspeth?"

Julian cursed under his breath. "Lady Elspeth *de Moray*. The youngest de Moray sister. She's staying at Whispers."

"Ah," Quinn said, his voice giving nothing away.

Julian dodged around a child in leading strings and shot a suspicious glance at his brother.

His lips were pressed together as if he were trying to keep from smiling.

"Damn you," Julian snapped.

At which point Quinn burst into laughter, startling a passing maid. "Now, now, no need for foul language."

God, his brother could be irritating.

"She's Ran's sister," Julian growled. "There's nothing there."

"No?" He could practically feel Quinn's eyes on him. "You named her, Jules, right along with our sisters. That means something, I think. Even if you don't want to admit it."

Julian merely shook his head. If he said anything more, he'd merely be feeding Quinn's speculations, ridiculous as they might be.

Lady Elspeth wasn't for him, no matter how much she challenged him.

Julian frowned. He should've made it plain to Hawthorne that his guards had let Lady Elspeth slip out of the house. It would've been the safe thing to do. The right thing to do. But he couldn't betray her in such a way.

Fool that he was.

*   *   *

"Elspeth?" Messalina's voice came from the door to the library that afternoon.

Elspeth looked up, hoping her weariness didn't show too badly. She'd been able to catch only a couple of hours of sleep before she'd had to rise at her regular time. No point in provoking suspicion.

Well. Besides Mr. Greycourt's suspicion. Or was it hatred? His kiss had been so very angry.

His mouth so very hot.

She sighed, attempting to put both the kiss and the man from her mind. "I'm sorry, I've been woolgathering. What is it you need?"

Messalina smiled, walking nearer. "Nothing really. Only there's a strange dog in the kitchens, and Sam seems to think it belongs to you."

Sam was a boy of about eight or possibly ten—Elspeth had never been good at judging the ages of children— who looked after Daisy.

The mongrel dog Elspeth had found that morning had followed her to the library after luncheon.

She glanced about the room now. Stacks and stacks of books lay in haphazard piles on the floor, with more books in the wooden boxes at the back of the room. The dog was nowhere to be seen. "Oh, bother. I hope he hasn't been making a nuisance of himself?"

"Not at all." Messalina sat in a chair near Elspeth, who was herself sitting on the floor, her skirts spread about her. "He growled at Daisy, but I think he was just putting Daisy in his place."

Elspeth winced. "I'm so sorry. He seems to have attached himself to me."

Messalina cocked her head. "When? I've never noticed him before."

"That's because I only found him this morning," Elspeth replied, trying to keep to at least the semblance of the truth. "On my morning walk."

"Of course you did." Her friend smiled with amusement. "You do seem the type to attract strays in need of a home and comfort."

"Thank you." Elspeth smiled. "I shall take that as a great compliment."

"As you should. What have you found today?" Messalina gestured to the piles of books. "Unpacking the library is like a treasure hunt, and I'm afraid that I'm quite enamored of its jewels."

"My most recent finds are rather more like rocks than diamonds or gold." Elspeth winced. "I believe you may have three different editions of *The Rape of the Lock*, one of them in German?"

Elspeth pointed to one of the smaller stacks of books.

Messalina looked confused. "But there are five books there."

Elspeth sighed. "Yes. Two editions have two copies."

"Ah." Messalina wrinkled her nose. "I'm not really that fond of Pope."

"Good," Elspeth said with satisfaction. She rather loathed Pope. "Then perhaps we can sell a few of these?"

"All of them." Messalina nodded.

The door opened, and a maid entered with tea and some lovely little cakes on a tray. Daisy came romping in, trailed behind by Elspeth's mongrel and Sam.

"There you are," Elspeth said happily.

In the full light of day, his short coat had a background of white with large splotches of reddish brown and black.

His ears were overlarge and hung limply on the sides of his head. But his eyes were a liquid, soulful brown, the prettiest eyes she'd ever seen on a dog.

And right now, those eyes were fixed on the cakes.

Elspeth frowned. "Didn't you feed him, Sam?"

"I did, ma'am," he piped up. "An' he et two plates o' scraps."

"Well then," Elspeth said to the dog, "you really don't need anything else."

The dog sighed as if in disappointment and lay down at her feet.

The maid cleared her throat. "Where shall I place the tea, ma'am?"

"On the center table, please." Messalina rose. "Come. Let's take tea properly."

"Very well." Elspeth got to her feet in what was probably a very ungainly manner. "I'm surprised Lucretia isn't here."

"No doubt she's napping," Messalina murmured. "I do love my sister, but I vow she's the laziest creature in London."

Daisy gamboled over to his mistress, only to be cowed when Elspeth's dog rumbled under his breath.

"Is your dog going to 'urt Daisy, m'lady?" Sam asked, sounding worried.

"I don't think so," Elspeth replied as she took a seat across from Messalina. "He's simply showing Daisy that he's older and therefore Daisy needs to be respectful to him. I do apologize for his growling, though." She glanced sternly down at the dog, now sitting alertly.

"What do you call 'im, then?" Sam asked.

The maids finished setting out the tea things and quietly left.

Daisy had recovered at the sight of the cakes and watched closely as Messalina poured the tea.

"I haven't found the right name yet," Elspeth said thoughtfully. "It's rather an important event, naming things, don't you think?"

"Quite," Messalina said gravely.

Sam's brows wrinkled. "'Ow's 'e 'spose to come then if 'e doesn't know 'is name?"

"That's a very good point," Messalina murmured.

"Yes, it is." Elspeth met the dog's liquid eyes. "Perhaps you might help me, Sam. Messalina has told me that you were the one to name Daisy. What do you think of Spotty?"

"Erm... seems a bit common-like," Sam said diplomatically.

"Of course," Elspeth said, holding back a smile. "What do you think, Messalina?"

"He's rather severe," Messalina commented. "Perhaps Abraham?"

Elspeth shook her head. "Too old."

"Sweetie?"

Elspeth laughed. "Too young."

Messalina's lips twitched. "You ought to name him after Julian—he's severe as well."

Elspeth thought of that kiss, the way Mr. Greycourt had almost compulsively drawn her into his arms. He hadn't been at all severe then. She felt her ears heat and hastily said, "That might cause confusion." She turned to Sam. "Have you any other ideas?"

The boy stared earnestly at the mongrel. "Plum."

Messalina blinked. "I beg your pardon?"

"Plum." Sam looked shy. "The fruit."

Elspeth cocked her head. "Hm. I think I like that name, but what made you think of it?"

"I like plum pudding the best," Sam declared with a small grin.

"A very good reason for a name." Messalina nodded sagely.

"Then Plum it shall be." Elspeth looked at the dog at her feet. "What do you think, Plum?"

The dog wagged his tail.

Messalina laughed "I think he approves."

"Good boy, Plum." Elspeth broke off a piece of her cake and gave it to him.

Daisy—who might've been jealous—tried to scramble into Messalina's lap, making it only halfway before falling back to the floor with a squeak.

Messalina bent to the puppy, but Daisy scampered to Sam, wriggling about his feet.

Messalina shook her head. "Perhaps it's time for Daisy's run in the back garden."

"Yes, ma'am." Sam picked up Daisy carefully and left the room.

"I think Daisy might like Sam more than me." Despite her words, Messalina was smiling. "It must be the running around the garden."

"Dogs do like to run about." Elspeth peered down at Plum. "At least most dogs do."

"Doesn't Plum like to run?"

"Yes." Elspeth concentrated as she finished the last of her cake.

"You've hardly had Plum a day," Messalina replied, pouring a second cup of tea. She glanced doubtfully down at the dog. "He doesn't seem built for speed."

Elspeth remembered Plum galloping out of the Windemere House garden. "I think he would surprise you."

The door to the library was flung dramatically open,

revealing a rather disheveled Lucretia. "Have you eaten all the cakes?"

"Not all of them," Messalina replied, sounding perfectly tranquil. "Come have a seat, dear."

"Oh, thank goodness," Lucretia said, and plopped into one of the chairs.

"The cakes are very good," Elspeth said helpfully. "They're filled with strawberry jam."

Messalina rang for more hot water, and for a few minutes, the ritual of serving tea took precedence.

When the maid left, Lucretia cleared her throat. "I wonder when Uncle is planning to marry me off."

Messalina sent her a worried look. "Julian and Quinn consulted Gideon this morning, and I have faith that they will find a way to remove you from London."

Lucretia sighed. "They can get me out, I suppose. But what if Uncle sends men to retrieve me? What then?" She poked at one of the cakes on her plate with her fork. "I wish I didn't have to rely on others. I want to be able to protect myself."

"If only the Wise Women could help," Elspeth said in frustration.

Messalina looked at her. "The Wise Women? I thought you and your sisters had to flee them?"

"Yes, we did," Elspeth said grimly. "But this situation is exactly the sort of thing that the Wise Women helped with. If Freya were still the Macha, she could send word to the messenger, who would in turn inform other Wise Women. There would be a chain of secret helpers smuggling Lucretia out of the country."

Messalina inhaled sharply. "So easily?"

"Lucretia would disappear so thoroughly, no man would be able to find her." Elspeth sighed. "But now, with the networks disabled? The Wise Women have hobbled themselves."

Messalina nodded. "I can see why both you and Freya mourned the collapse of the Wise Women."

Lucretia brought her hand down on the table in a loud slap. "I wish I could use a sword. I'd at least have a hope of defending myself." She turned to Elspeth. "Doesn't your sister know how to duel with a sword? Messalina said she dueled with Kester once and beat him."

Elspeth smiled with pride. "Freya is the best swordswoman I've ever seen. But really a knife would be more useful to you, I think."

Lucretia glowered. "Why?"

Elspeth mimed sliding a knife from her sleeve. "Easier to carry with you. Easier to hide."

"That makes sense." Lucretia nodded. "But does Freya know how to fight with a knife?"

Elspeth was about to reply in the affirmative. In fact, Elspeth and both her sisters had grown up learning to fight with different weapons.

But Messalina had another idea. "Darling, Gideon knows how to fight with a knife. He used to fight for prizes in St Giles, and he *won*."

Lucretia wrinkled her nose. "You want me to ask *Gideon* to teach me?"

Messalina looked a bit exasperated. "Why not? He is an expert, after all."

"I know," Lucretia said rather loudly, and then more quietly, "But will he agree? I haven't exactly been nice to him."

"No, but I think Gideon finds your attitude amusing more than anything else."

Lucretia's eyes widened in what looked like outrage.

"Which means he rather likes you," Messalina said hurriedly. "Ask him. I'm sure he'll want to help you."

Lucretia nodded and ate a piece of cake.

Messalina inhaled and quite obviously fixed a smile on her face before turning to Elspeth. "Are you sure you wouldn't like a table to work at instead of the floor? Truly, it would be no problem to bring one in."

"I like sitting on the floor," Elspeth said. "I feel closer to all the books, and I have almost the entire room for my stacks."

"Do you?" Messalina sounded dubious. "I really am quite grateful you're doing this, you know."

"It's my pleasure." Elspeth cleared her throat. "I'm surprised that you didn't have your own library when you wed."

"Well, of course I had *some* books," Messalina replied. "Would you like another cup?"

"Family books?" Elspeth asked, trying not to sound too interested. "And yes, please."

"Oh, no." Messalina took her teacup. "My uncle has all of the family books." She poured. "At least all of the books at Windemere House and Greycourt. Do you remember the Greycourt library at all?"

"Yes, I remember there was a magnifying glass with an ivory handle," Elspeth said. "I believe I was instructed not to touch it. I remember miles and miles of shelves. There must have been at least a thousand books."

"There were." Messalina pursed her lips. "But Uncle removed most of the books after my father's death. My grandfather had made a special disposition that Father might have the use of the manor while he lived, but he was the second son and, naturally, the estate reverted back to Augustus. The library was Papa's treasure. I remember that, before Mama died, she was quite distressed by my uncle's disregard of the library." She winced. "I'm afraid he burned many of the books."

Elspeth's heart fell, not only at the destruction of books but also because she'd already searched the Windemere library, and if there wasn't a library at Greycourt...

She cleared her throat. "There must be other libraries at smaller estates in the dukedom?"

"I'm not sure," Messalina said sadly. "There was one once at Heathers in Bath. I remember looking at the shelves for something to read. But Augustus..." She swallowed. "He really finds no use for books or libraries."

Elspeth stared at the teacup in her hands. If the duke had had the books in the Greycourt libraries burned, Maighread's diary might be already destroyed. Gone forever.

And with it her only chance to save the Wise Women.

CHAPTER SIX

Lady Long-Nose rode with Sabinus and fenced with him, too. She had long philosophical discussions with him and helped critique his poetry. They were very close. One day, Lady Long-Nose knew she could no longer keep her love silent. She determined to write him a letter filled with her hopes, her dreams, and her yearning....

—From *Lady Long-Nose*

Elspeth paused just inside Harlowe House's ballroom the next night and glanced suspiciously back at the butler.

Freya sighed. "Stop staring. Fletcher is not a thief or a murderer."

Elspeth transferred her glance to Freya. "How do you know?"

"Because," Freya said patiently, "Fletcher came with the best of references: a royal princess."

"The royal family is deeply suspicious," Elspeth said. "And besides, Fletcher might be biding his time."

"For what?" Freya demanded.

Elspeth narrowed her eyes, but had to confess, "I do not know."

Kester, the Duke of Harlowe and Freya's newly wedded husband, turned a chuckle into a cough.

"Don't encourage her," Freya murmured to Kester before turning to Lucretia.

Messalina, who was behind them in the receiving line with a bored-looking Mr. Hawthorne, said, "Why don't you take Elspeth to the punch, darling?"

"Of course." Lucretia nodded to her sister.

Freya smiled at another newly arrived guest.

"I don't like punch," Elspeth muttered a bit rebelliously as she strolled beside the other woman.

"No one likes punch," Lucretia returned.

"Then why do people drink it?"

"It's . . . festive?" Lucretia didn't seem at all sure.

Elspeth shook her head but was distracted by Freya's ballroom. She'd seen the room only once, when Freya had shown Elspeth around Harlowe House back when she'd first arrived in London.

Tonight the room sparkled.

The walls were a lovely pale greenish blue, decorated by white plaster bas-reliefs. The ceiling was quite high and entirely painted with a scene of . . . well, she wasn't certain, but there were quite a lot of naked bodies. Suspended over the guests were two enormous chandeliers, candlelight reflecting off the glass drops.

Hundreds more candles were lit around the room, the smell of beeswax and smoke heavy in the air. Massive bunches of white hothouse roses stood on pedestals and tables, their perfume mingling with the beeswax.

People crowded the room, silks and velvet in colors so bright it was like a spinning rainbow.

The ball was loud and odorous and hot and gloriously beautiful.

Elspeth had absently linked arms with Lucretia when

she spied Mr. Greycourt, looking bored as he lounged against a wall.

"Freya invited Julian?" Lucretia asked, following Elspeth's gaze. "I didn't think Kester was on speaking terms with Julian?"

"I don't think he is," Elspeth replied slowly, and then rather nonsensically, "Either Julian or Ranulf."

She had only fragmented memories of all three men being thick as thieves before the tragedy at Greycourt.

She glanced back at the receiving line. Both Kester and Freya looked unconcerned.

"Then why—?" Lucretia whispered.

Mr. Hawthorne's voice came from behind them. "I asked Harlowe to invite both Julian and Quintus."

Elspeth turned along with Lucretia to find Mr. Hawthorne standing with Messalina, her hand tucked in his elbow.

Messalina stared at her husband suspiciously. "What are you up to?"

Mr. Hawthorne's lips curled quite wickedly. "Must my actions be nefarious?"

"Yes," Messalina said with blunt certitude.

Elspeth's brows knit. "Aren't you glad your brothers are here?"

"The gossipmongers are the ones who will be glad," Messalina said in hushed tones. "Kester hasn't spoken to Julian since that summer, and it's well known that neither Julian nor the Duke of Ayr has spoken to him." Messalina shot an apologetic look at Elspeth. "I'm afraid everyone talks in London. It should only be our concern, but they all know."

Elspeth looked about the ballroom and understood

what Messalina meant. There were small groups of ladies and gentlemen chatting together, which was usual. What wasn't usual was that more than a few were darting glances between the Greycourt sisters and her and Mr. Greycourt.

"I had no idea that people still cared enough to gossip about it," Elspeth said slowly. "This must be so horrible for your brother."

Lucretia pursed her lips. "A few years ago, Julian was blackballed from every social club in London. He's probably used to gossip by now."

Elspeth glanced at Mr. Greycourt. He seemed supremely unaffected by the whispering, though he must hear it. He was such a private man, though. Could he really become immune to this public shunning?

Mr. Greycourt looked up as if he felt her gaze. His gray eyes seemed piercing, even across the crowded room, and for a moment, her heartbeat seemed to slow, and the noise disappeared, as if only they were in the ballroom. She suddenly remembered that she hadn't spoken to him since that one searing kiss the previous morn. Did he still think about their embrace as she did?

Or had he forgotten?

Elspeth inhaled and focused her attention on her friends.

"You look like you've bitten into an apple and found a worm," Lucretia said critically.

Elspeth sighed. "Not a worm, but rather your older brother." She looked again and saw that Mr. Greycourt now had his head pointedly turned away from her direction. That was fair, she supposed. If she could ignore him, then he was justified in ignoring her. The thought made her mood dip. She muttered, "And I saw Mr. Greycourt. I didn't bite him."

Mr. Hawthorne coughed into his fist.

Messalina blinked and seemed to dig her elbow into her husband's side as she asked Elspeth, "Have you had the punch yet?"

"No," Lucretia said, answering for them both. "We've been avoiding it."

"If you'll excuse me, ladies," Mr. Hawthorne murmured, "I see a gentleman I must speak to. Will you accompany me, my wife?"

Messalina beamed up at her husband. "Naturally."

They strolled away without further ado.

Lucretia sighed. "She's quite lost her head over him."

"Well," Elspeth said as they continued their perambulation of the room, "I suppose if one is going to lose one's head, a husband is just as well as any other man."

Lucretia snorted. "You have the oddest way of putting things."

"Do I?" Elspeth glanced at the other woman. "Then what do you think of the matter?"

"I think," Lucretia said, "that's it's a very good thing that Gideon worships my sister."

"Mm." Elspeth hummed a reply. "Have you started your knife lessons with Mr. Hawthorne?"

"Yes." Lucretia gave a shudder. "Much too early this morning. I can't tell you how sore my muscles are. I don't understand why learning to knife fight is so strenuous."

Elspeth fought not to smile. "Did you find the lessons useful?"

"That's the worst part," the other woman said in a put-out tone of voice. "They *are* useful. Terribly so. I feel I'm learning so much. I just regret the exercise involved."

"That is a pity," Elspeth said as levelly as she could.

But she must have given some sign of her amusement, for Lucretia squinted at her suspiciously.

Then the girl's eyes widened as she saw something behind Elspeth. "There's Arabella Holland," Lucretia exclaimed. "Shall we go greet her?"

Elspeth hesitated. She liked Arabella, but she had business to attend to. "I hope you don't mind if I decline and talk to your brother instead? I'm not sure I thanked him for saving me at Westminster Abbey."

"Oh." Lucretia glanced between her brother and Miss Holland as if undecided.

"You needn't accompany me," Elspeth said cheerily. "I think I can approach Mr. Greycourt by myself."

"Well, yes, but..." Lucretia bit her lip. "It might stir up the gossips more."

"They don't scare me." Elspeth withdrew her arm from Lucretia's. "I shall wave my handkerchief if I need help."

And with that she walked toward Mr. Greycourt. She couldn't stop anticipation tugging at her belly. Mr. Greycourt was severe and intimidating and oftentimes quite rude, but it was a facade, she knew now. Inside he cared to almost a fanatical degree. He was intelligent, sarcastic, and most definitely hiding something.

She wanted to rip open that false front and find what softness he hid inside.

"Lady Elspeth," he muttered as she drew closer.

"Mr. Greycourt." She dipped him a curtsy. "How wonderful to see you."

He raised an eyebrow. "You saw me just yesterday."

"I did." She nodded gravely. "But so much has happened since then."

"Such as?" he asked.

"Mmm…" She hummed while she thought. "I uncovered a *Don Quixote* in your sister's library, beautifully preserved and bound in red leather."

"Remarkable." His tone was bored, but she noticed that he hadn't looked away from her since she'd arrived by his side.

"Oh, it is," Elspeth assured him. "It's in Spanish and possibly one of the first editions published. Also, I named my new dog." She waited, but although he still watched her out of the corner of his eye, he didn't ask. "You should say, 'What is his name?' "

Mr. Greycourt exhaled slowly. As if tamping down exasperation.

"Plum!" She answered anyway. "I think it quite fits him."

"What do you want, Lady Elspeth?" he asked.

"The pleasure of your company," she replied gently.

For a moment, there was something in his expression. Surprise? Vulnerability? Longing?

Then his eyes iced over. "Not even my sisters enjoy my company, my lady. Cut line."

"I think they rather do," she said, but sighed when he gave no reply. "Books."

He blinked. "What?"

Elspeth cleared her throat. "I was discussing the Greycourt libraries yesterday with Messalina. She said that the Duke of Windemere wasn't interested in books, so he had many of the libraries dismantled." She paused and said carefully, "I wondered if you knew of any that survived? Perhaps he overlooked an obscure estate?"

He stared at her for a very long moment before speaking. "You're quite obsessed with libraries, aren't you?"

She cocked her head. "Isn't everyone?"

"No." He glanced away again. "Most people couldn't think of anything more boring."

"Then you have no library yourself?"

He looked at her, his eyes such a fathomless gray she couldn't tell what he was thinking. "I didn't say that."

Her hopes rose. "You must have a London townhouse."

"No." His mouth twisted for some reason. "My mother left me a hunting lodge from her family. Adders Hall."

"Ah," she said brightly. "Near to London?"

"No. It's almost to the Welsh border," he snapped.

Well, that put to rest any ideas of a day outing. Elspeth examined him, this man who kept such a tight rein on himself, and couldn't help saying, "I think you like libraries after all."

Something flared to life behind his eyes.

"Like libraries, my lady?" He stepped so close he loomed over her. "Let me tell you this: My father collected books. He loved them. Some of my earliest memories are of sitting on his lap while Father showed me his latest acquisition. He'd turn the pages and point to a griffin or a daffodil or a map of France. The library at Greycourt was my father's most prized possession." His icy, uninflected tenor was in sharp contrast to the passionate words he spoke. "Father had been buried only a day when Augustus began selling or destroying his books. There isn't anything left there. My mother was only able to save a single small crate of my father's books. She sent them to Adders. Everything else is gone." For a second—only a second!—his face twisted. "Yes. *Yes*, I like libraries."

"I'm so sorry," she whispered, her heart aching. "I can't fathom the loss if the library where I grew up were destroyed. All that knowledge. All those memories. A library is more than a space with books."

For the first time since she'd met him, Mr. Greycourt's expression seemed to soften. "Yes. My father's library was the best of him."

"And it's gone." She touched his arm with her fingers.

He glanced down at her hand, and his mouth tightened. "Now you've wrested my sad story from me, I think we are done."

She pressed her lips together in sudden irritation. "Are you this way with everyone you know? So abrupt and dismissive?"

"What do you care?" he sneered.

She exhaled forcefully, having lost all patience. "I care because I breathe and think and laugh and cry. I care because I'm alive. I suspect that you, Mr. Greycourt, have been dead for a very long time."

* * *

Dead? Julian stared after Lady Elspeth as she walked away. If he was dead, then why had she left him feeling so alive?

He ached to go after her, to catch her arm, make her stop, and tell her exactly what he thought of her and her opinions. But he could hear the whispers already. The gossips looking at him, at her, wondering what a de Moray might want with a Greycourt.

Julian turned to glare at the clump of young ladies to his right, making them scurry away from him. He might've scared the girls, but tomorrow, the spat he'd had with Lady Elspeth would be all over town.

She should know better.

She ought to be more discreet, more reserved, more ladylike.

Julian sighed.

Except Lady Elspeth wasn't and never would be either discreet or reserved. She spun around his family and around London as if she were some fae queen, without worry or fear. As if she'd been reared far from everything he understood. As if she'd come from another, wilder world.

Lady Elspeth burst into his awareness like the sun rising, bringing warmth and light, making his world iridescent with color.

And what was worse, he couldn't find it in himself to condemn her brilliance. He liked her. She argued with him, made him question his own opinions, made him *feel*. He was anything but dead in her presence.

Feelings, he reminded himself, could be a distraction. He was thinking about Lady Elspeth far too much. He was here to guard Lucretia. The thought made him jerk his head up, only to see Lucretia, still chatting animatedly with Arabella Holland and her mother.

Julian felt his shoulders loosen only fractionally at the sight of his sister. Right now, she was safe from Windemere's machinations—but for how long? Perhaps he should chance it. Take her to the Americas or the East Indies himself, even if that would put Augustus on his trail immediately.

If only...

A broad hand came down on his shoulder. "Enjoying the ball?"

Julian turned to glare at Quinn.

"Of course," his brother continued, "you seem to be spending it propping up the wall, which makes one wonder. But you've also talked to a certain pretty young lady."

"Quinn," Julian growled, knowing it was useless.

"I don't believe I remember her," his brother said softly. "But then she would've only been what? Five? Six?"

"Six." Julian could feel himself flushing.

Quinn nodded. "So one-and-twenty now. A bit—"

"Shut up."

"A *bit*," Quinn continued, "young, perhaps?"

"She's not in the schoolroom," Julian snapped, and then he winced.

Because Quinn grinned. "Oh no, of course not."

Julian closed his eyes. "It doesn't matter. She's not for me."

When he opened them again, Quinn had lost his smile. "Why not? I've never seen you taken so much by a woman. Except for—"

"No," Julian said. "Not here."

Quinn sighed. "As you like." His hand dropped from Julian's shoulder.

Leaving Julian cold again. "Have you any news for me?"

He could feel his brother looking at him before Quinn said, "No, Augustus's schedule has been the same, quite ordinary meetings with his solicitors and the like..."

His voice trailed off.

"What?" Julian asked.

"Nothing," Quinn said. "I just saw that Ann's here."

Julian turned around. "Where? Is Augustus with her?"

"No," Quinn muttered. "Some other gentleman."

Julian finally caught sight of the duchess, standing near a side entrance to the ballroom. Her hand rested on... "That's George Etherege, Earl Mulgrave."

"Mulgrave?" Quinn's nose wrinkled. "Isn't he a libertine?"

"Yes, there are rumors that he likes to hurt women,"

Julian said grimly, pushing through the crowd with Quinn behind. "What in hell is our uncle doing, letting Ann be escorted by Mulgrave of all people? Come."

It was nearing eleven of the clock, and the crush was at its thickest. People stood shoulder by shoulder, breathing each other's air, inhaling sweat and perfume. Julian was determined, though, and at last they stepped before the duchess.

"Your Grace," Julian said as he bent over her hand, "you look lovely." As he straightened, though, he realized he had lied. Ann's complexion was nearly gray, her eyes shadowed, and her fingers trembled in his. The change from only days ago made him ask, "Are you quite well?"

"Oh," she said, touching her temple, "it's nothing. His Grace has told me that I merely have a touch of melancholy. I'm here at his request. He feels I shall revive my spirits with company."

Julian wasn't entirely sure how "melancholy" could cause such pallor, but the bigger problem was the man with Ann. "I don't believe I've met your companion?"

Ann blinked. "Earl Mulgrave, these are my nephews, Mr. Julian Greycourt and Mr. Quintus Greycourt. And this is George Etherege, Earl Mulgrave."

Julian made a short bow, though Quinn didn't bother with the niceties.

"How do you know Her Grace?" Quinn asked aggressively.

Julian studied the man.

Lord Mulgrave had an aquiline face, handsome, with eyes that seemed to be habitually heavy lidded. He wore an ornate purple silk suit with gold-and-black embroidery at the wrists and pockets, and his white wig was curled and powdered exquisitely. He looked like any other aristocrat here, save that he also wore three black velvet patches on his face. Julian couldn't help but wonder if they covered syphilis pox scars.

"I am a friend of Windemere," Mulgrave replied with a dimpled smile. "Although I find myself rather insulted that I must explain to you of all people, Greycourt. After all, I'm not the one disgraced in society's eyes. Now if you will excuse us—"

"Not yet." Julian caught his arm, disregarding the earl's slur. After all it was true. "Your Grace, would you give me the privilege of escorting you?"

Ann's eyes widened. "What?"

"She doesn't need your escort." Mulgrave still held his smile, but something had gone wrong behind his eyes. They seemed as blank and unfeeling as a toad's. "I'm perfectly capable."

"You're a damned libertine," Quinn said, "and unfit to stand next to any woman."

"Come, Your Grace," Julian said, holding out his hand.

Ann visibly wavered before taking his hand.

Julian let Mulgrave go, tucking Ann's hand into his elbow.

The man exhaled a laugh. "You know this is all quite farcical," Mulgrave said while removing a snuff-box from his pocket. His words and face were calm, but his hands were trembling. "After all, I'll soon be your brother-in-law."

For a moment, all Julian could see was Mulgrave's dimpled smile growing wider. Mulgrave was the man Augustus meant to wed Lucretia to. He inhaled and said to Quinn, "Take Ann and find Lucretia."

Without a word, his brother led Ann away.

Mulgrave laughed. "Why bother hiding my bride?" he

asked as he carefully tapped out a line of snuff on the side of his thumb. "Augustus and I have already signed the marriage contract. We only need to set a wedding date." He inhaled the snuff and then sneezed into a handkerchief.

"You'll not be marrying my sister." Julian was fighting to keep his breathing even, to not let his rage past his defenses. "She doesn't want to marry you or anyone else at the moment."

"Indeed?" Mulgrave shrugged and put away his handkerchief. "But you must know that your sister's wishes matter not at all. Augustus is her guardian, and he has agreed to give her to me. I must say I'm looking forward to both her dowry and her . . . time."

The urge to take the man by the neck and shake him until Mulgrave's eyes bled was almost overwhelming. "Stay away from Lucretia," he rasped.

Mulgrave snickered. "I mean to collect your sister sometime tomorrow or the day after—we'll be marrying at my townhouse, I think. But I'm beginning to wonder if I should capture her tonight. I've enough footmen waiting outside the ballroom. What do you think?"

It had been only minutes since Quinn had left, and he was burdened with Ann. Even if he'd found Lucretia, he probably hadn't removed her from the house. Quinn needed more time.

Julian punched the earl in the jaw.

The man staggered back, nearly falling as several shrieks rose from the surrounding women.

"I say!" an older gentleman exclaimed.

"How dare you!" the earl screamed, his wig fallen to reveal a shaved head. "To me!"

The side door to the ballroom burst open and footmen—in Mulgrave's yellow livery—swarmed in. Julian just had time to hit Mulgrave one more time, and then he was pulled off by the footmen. He fought, of course, striking flesh, kicking legs, doing anything he could as more shrieks and yelling rose around them. But he was hit in the stomach, the face, and the back of the knee, the last making him fall to the ground, where he had little defense against the kicks coming from all sides.

"Enough!" the Duke of Harlowe—Kester—shouted. "Enough."

The footmen stopped, breathing heavily, as they backed away from Julian.

His ribs hurt. As did his face. He looked up and saw his childhood friend staring down at him. "What is going on, Jules?" the duke asked, thrusting his hand toward him.

Julian took Kester's hand and used it to get to his feet. "A disagreement."

"I'll have you arrested," Mulgrave growled at him.

"Stay away from my family," Julian snarled back, causing a couple of footmen to step closer.

Mulgrave waved his men away. "As I said, I'd have you arrested, but for the fact that it would drag my fiancée's name through the mud."

Julian surged forward, only to be caught by Kester. "Stop."

"Let me go," Julian growled to the duke.

"Jules," Quinn was panting beside him, "Kester is right. Mulgrave can have you before a magistrate."

Julian suddenly remembered what Quinn was supposed to be doing. "Lucretia—"

"Safe," Quinn whispered in his ear. "Hawthorne is with her. And I've seen Ann off. She looked quite ill."

"I think," Mulgrave interrupted, "you had better listen to whatever your brother is whispering to you."

"Fuck you," Quinn replied, tugging Julian backward.

Kester had disappeared, perhaps to find his own footmen to have Julian removed.

Mulgrave laughed. "I won't forget this." He gestured to the jaw that Julian had hit.

"We need to find Lucretia," Julian said, never taking his eyes from the earl as Quinn hurried him away. "Now."

* * *

Elspeth watched Mr. Greycourt and his brother approach the Duchess of Windemere and the gentleman escorting her. Odd. Both Greycourt brothers looked on edge, their shoulders squared.

She shook her head and returned to watching the dancers. They moved in a line in a very stately manner, a far cry from the wild dancing she'd seen in Scotland. Was that because—

Someone cleared their throat behind her.

She turned to find a maid. "Pardon me, my lady, but Her Grace would like to see you in her personal sitting room."

For a wild moment, Elspeth thought the Duchess of Windemere was summoning her before she remembered that Freya was also a duchess. "Thank you."

Elspeth began making her way to one of the ballroom's doors. It seemed rather odd that Freya would want to meet Elspeth during her ball. Was there some sort of emergency? But what sort?

She could see both Greycourt sisters and Mr. Hawthorne standing together on the other side of the room. And Kester was laughing with a couple of gentlemen.

Strange.

The hallway outside the ballroom was rather crowded with guests, but when Elspeth climbed the stairs to the upper floor, there was no one around.

She padded quietly down the hall to Freya's bedroom. Beside it was another door—her personal sitting room. Elspeth knocked and went in.

Inside, Freya sat with another woman on a settee. "Quick. Shut the door."

Elspeth closed the door before asking, "Who is this?"

The woman beside Freya was wearing a black cloak with a gray hood. She pushed it back, revealing a tangle of black hair loose around her shoulders and black eyes. "Don't you recognize me, little Elspeth?"

"I think I do?" Elspeth stared. The woman had one of those ageless faces—she could be anywhere from sixteen to five and thirty. "You're a Wise Woman, but I don't know your name."

"She's the Crow," Freya said very quietly, "and she's come to London at great risk to herself. Tell her."

"I went back when we were all recalled," the Crow said, "to see what the Hags were doing." She shook her head. "I don't know what you've said or done, little Elspeth, but they've sent a woman to kill you."

Elspeth felt her legs weaken, and she sat rather abruptly on a stuffed chair across from the settee.

She looked up. "They've set the Nemain on me?" The Nemain was a trained assassin—a woman who moved in the shadows, ready to kill any man the Hags ruled was deserving of death.

"No." Freya reached to place her hand on Elspeth's knee. "Listen."

"It's not the Nemain," the Crow replied. "I'm not sure where the Nemain is, frankly. No, this is a different woman. I glimpsed her only once, so she can't have grown up within the compound."

"Do you have a name?" Freya asked.

"I'm sorry, no." The Crow sounded regretful. "But she's unmistakable. Her upper lip is scarred, as if someone cut through it and the flesh was sewn back together badly. Other than that, she has brown hair and is tall and slim."

"Do you know where she is?" Elspeth asked.

"London," the Crow said grimly. "I followed her trail here, but then lost her several days ago."

"Several days ago?" Freya turned to Elspeth. "You said there was a shooting when you visited the cathedral."

"That was probably her work, then," the Crow said. "I've seen her carry a pistol."

Elspeth shuddered as she relived the shot fired at Westminster Abbey. At the time, she had thought that it was intended for Mr. Greycourt.

"Dear God," Freya murmured. "She'll know we're sisters. Perhaps you can hide with Messalina and her husband. Or"—she glanced at the Crow—"can we hire you as a protector for Elspeth?"

"I'm afraid not," the woman replied. "I start back to Scotland tonight. There's business I still have with the Wise Women at their compound."

The Crow didn't sound as if she considered herself a Wise Woman anymore, Elspeth thought with despair. What was she to do? Maighread's diary was needed now more than ever, but she was worried about being discovered by this killer sent especially to murder her. Would she even be able to return to the compound in Scotland if she did find it?

And then she registered the rest of the Crow's sentence.

"You're returning to Scotland?"

"Within the hour," the Crow said.

"Could you take someone with you?" Elspeth asked impulsively. "A woman being forced into marriage with an abominable man?"

The Crow didn't hesitate. "Of course, if she can be ready in time."

Elspeth turned to her sister. "Lucretia." She'd told Freya of Lucretia's peril only the night before.

Freya strode to the door and called for her maid.

"Your Grace?" The girl must've been waiting nearby.

Freya murmured some instructions and then shut the door again, looking at Elspeth. "She's wearing a ball gown."

"Then we must find her something else," Elspeth said. "Do you have anything?"

"Of course," Freya replied, opening the door that connected her sitting room to her bedroom. "But I'm shorter than Lucretia."

"And your dresses will be much too fine, I'm guessing," the Crow said. "What about that maid?"

Freya nodded, letting Messalina and Lucretia inside the bedroom along with Mr. Hawthorne. She turned back to the door and talked to the maid.

"What has happened?" Mr. Hawthorne demanded.

Elspeth squared her shoulders. "We've found someone to save Lucretia."

"Have you." His words were flat, and he was eyeing the Crow, who had donned her hood before everyone came in.

"Yes," Elspeth said. "And Lucretia needs to take off her dress, so I'm afraid you'll have to leave."

Mr. Hawthorne didn't exactly seem convinced, but he turned to look at Messalina.

She smiled at her husband and nodded.

That was all he needed, apparently, for without a word he left the room.

Freya came back inside. "Mary is fetching a gown."

"Let me help you out of that dress," Elspeth said to Lucretia.

"Who is she?" Lucretia asked, motioning to the Crow.

The Crow pushed back her hood. "I'm your savior."

Elspeth took down Lucretia's hair as Freya and Messalina dealt with her skirts and bodice. "She's a Wise Woman. We're sending you to Scotland."

"Just like that?" Lucretia asked, sounding alarmed. "But I haven't my clothes or—or anything of mine."

"I leave by half past eleven," the Crow said calmly.

Elspeth glanced at the clock on the mantel. It was already fifteen after.

"Either you come or you don't," the Crow continued. "Doesn't make a difference to me. But know this: if you come, I'll protect you with my life."

Lucretia swallowed and nodded.

Five minutes later, Lucretia stood in a plain dark-blue linsey-woolsey gown, her hair in simple braids pinned to her head under a large, floppy bonnet.

Both she and her sister were in tears.

Lucretia hugged Freya and Elspeth and lastly her sister.

"Goodbye, darling," Messalina said, holding Lucretia tight.

And then Lucretia and the Crow were gone.

Elspeth sank into the settee, feeling suddenly weary. Everything had happened so fast, and she still had to deal with the assassin who was after her.

Freya sighed. "I need to go back to the ball. People will comment on my absence."

Messalina nodded, blotting her face with a handkerchief. "You go. Give me a few minutes, and then both Elspeth and I will come."

Freya nodded, moving to the door, but it was suddenly slammed open.

Julian Greycourt stood there in front of Mr. Hawthorne and Quintus Greycourt, a bruise rising on one elegant cheekbone, and glared at Elspeth. "Where is my sister?"

Elspeth opened her mouth, but no words came.

"I'm sorry," Mr. Hawthorne said to his wife. "I tried to stop him."

Mr. Greycourt actually bared his teeth. "Stop me from what?"

"Jules," Quintus Greycourt murmured, "there's no need to shout."

"Then produce Lucretia," Mr. Greycourt demanded. He was still staring at Elspeth.

He was magnificent, she couldn't help thinking, entirely inappropriately, and then, even worse, what would it be like to have control over such a man? To order him to his knees.

She felt a flood of warmth.

Messalina said, "She's gone. We've sent her to Scotland."

"With whom?" Quintus Greycourt asked.

"With a friend," Elspeth said quietly.

"How dare you," Mr. Greycourt snarled. "She needs guards and a plan."

"No," Messalina said. "Lucretia needed a way to get out of London without anyone knowing. She's done that with Elspeth's help."

Mr. Greycourt turned on her. "And you simply trust Lady Elspeth with our sister's life?"

Elspeth inhaled, feeling the pain tighten her breast. He didn't trust her, it was clear. She might feel close to him, as if they were on the brink of a new realization, but he seemed still back in the Windemere Library at their first meeting. When he didn't know her at all.

"I do trust her," Messalina said. "With Lucretia's life."

For a moment, Mr. Greycourt stared, his eyes narrowed in what might be hurt. Then he strode from the room.

Quintus Greycourt gave one last glance at his sister and then followed Mr. Greycourt.

Mr. Hawthorne took Messalina into his arms. "I'm sorry. Quinn told me that they've discovered the man that was meant to marry Lucretia—Earl Mulgrave. And he was here tonight."

Elspeth's breath caught in her throat.

Messalina pulled back from her husband, her face gone white. "What?"

Mr. Hawthorne said grimly, "I don't know why Mulgrave decided to show, but Julian had an altercation with him outside. His mood is not your fault."

Messalina nodded absently and then turned to Elspeth. "Can Mulgrave follow them?"

"He could try," Elspeth returned, remembering why she'd sent Lucretia away with the Crow. "But he'd lose them."

"That's good," Messalina said.

Freya came back into the room. "Earl Mulgrave was at the ball. He must've sneaked in because I certainly didn't invite him."

"So we've heard from Mr. Hawthorne," Elspeth said.

Freya looked at the man. "Did you tell them that the earl and Mr. Greycourt came to fisticuffs?"

Mr. Hawthorne raised an eyebrow. "I didn't know."

Freya sat next to Elspeth and sighed. "Kester told me. I have no doubt that it will be the talk of the town tomorrow."

"I'm sorry." Elspeth frowned, thinking. "The earl may have left spies. And even if he didn't, everyone in the ballroom will be watching." She looked at Messalina. "You need to go back down. Act as if everything is normal."

"But shouldn't we leave?" Messalina asked.

"No," Freya replied. "Elspeth is right. If you leave early, it might create suspicion."

"Right." Mr. Hawthorne took his wife's arm, starting for the door.

"Wait," Messalina said, turning to Elspeth. "Aren't you coming?"

"In a minute." Elspeth glanced at her sister. "I need to discuss something with Freya."

Messalina looked between them but didn't ask any questions before leaving with her husband.

"What is it?" Freya asked.

Elspeth took a deep breath. "I need to search the library at Mr. Greycourt's Adders Hall."

Freya shook her head, sinking farther into a settee. "We haven't time for this tonight. We still—"

"Freya," Elspeth said.

Her sister stopped and looked at her.

Elspeth knelt and took Freya's hands. "I've a murderer after me. I need to leave London. I can escape after the ball—"

"You can't," Freya said. "Ladies do not travel alone."

"Then come with me," Elspeth pleaded. "It will be fun."

Freya closed her eyes as if weary to her soul. "Forgive

me if I don't wish to engender a scandal by stealing from Mr. Greycourt."

For a second, Elspeth felt awful for making her sister so tired.

But the point remained.

"I must leave London. Is it really stealing when the diary properly belongs to the Wise Women?" Elspeth asked earnestly.

"Elspeth." Freya sighed. "You know the tension that exists between Kester and Julian Greycourt. They won't even acknowledge each other in the same room. I won't be the catalyst that reignites their argument."

Elspeth nodded, considering. "Then I shall have to take the mail coach, I suppose." She wrinkled her nose. "I wonder what the nearest town to Adders Hall is?"

"Oh my Lord," Freya muttered, pinching the bridge of her nose. "I don't remember you being this—this *contrary* when we lived in the Wise Women's compound."

"That's because I was a child," Elspeth said gently. "Children take their opinions from their elders. Adult women make their own."

"You're right," Freya said. "Of course you're right. It just seemed easier to talk with you back then."

"Easier because I agreed always with you?"

"Perhaps." Freya gripped her hands together. "I'm afraid, darling. I'm afraid for you, I'm afraid for Lucretia, and I'm afraid for the Wise Women."

Elspeth nodded. "Is there a coach that travels near Mr. Greycourt's estate?"

Freya sighed heavily. "I'm not going to talk you out of this mad scheme, am I?"

"No." Elspeth waited for her sister to make up her mind.

"Then yes, I have no doubt that there is a mail coach," Freya said. "I can send one of Kester's men to check tomorrow morning."

Elspeth shook her head. "Now, please. I've stayed too long in London being distracted by balls and such. I want to find Maighread's diary and save the Wise Women."

Freya looked at her in alarm. "But you'll come back to London even if you find the diary, won't you? I'll want to see you first before you journey to Dornach, and besides, you'll need allies if you want to present the diary to the Hags." Freya stopped suddenly. "I can't believe you have me speaking as if the diary were a certain thing. You've made me lose my head to dreams."

Elspeth smiled. "The diary may be a dream, but if I find it, the Wise Women will change. The world will change."

CHAPTER SEVEN

One day Lady Long-Nose went riding with Sabinus.
They found a glade deep in the forest and
dismounted there for a picnic.
"I have a secret to tell you," Sabinus said. "I am in
love with the most wonderful woman in the world."
Lady Long-Nose's heart soared up high
into the sky with joy....
            —From *Lady Long-Nose*

The sky was turning that pinky-gray of predawn by the time Julian made his way back to the White Horse.

He felt as if he'd been awake for days, his very bones weary. He felt betrayed by his sisters, by Hawthorne, goddamn it, by Lady Elspeth. It was the last that stuck in his craw. He'd drawn closer to her without realizing it, and to find she'd gone behind his back...

He didn't notice the man standing in a shadowed doorway until Julian was almost on him.

The man stepped out, and Julian drew his pistol.

The stranger raised his hands immediately. "All right, all right. Ye needn't get nasty. I'd just like a word, m'lord."

Julian quickly glanced around. Was this some sort of trap? He didn't see anyone else in their vicinity, but he kept a close watch. "I'm not a lord."

"No?" The man had a Scottish accent. "Thought you'd be a lord, being the heir to a dukedom and all."

"Who are you?" Julian snapped, raising his gun.

"Peg McDonald's son." The stranger's voice was suddenly serious.

"Ah." Julian felt an ache beginning behind his left eye. "What can I do for you?"

"I'd like me ma back, but I reckon not even a high and mighty duke's heir like yerself can do such a thing." Peg's son looked bitter. "Told her she had to get out of the duke's service, but she was too afraid of what he'd do. Well, he had her killed anyway, didn't he?" His head turned in the barely lit street, his voice sharpening. "'Cause of you."

"I'm truly sorry," Julian said, lowering his pistol.

"Thanks much," the other man said dryly. "Bit late, ain't it?"

"I suppose it is," Julian answered wearily. "I had offered to bring her to my country estate."

"He could've had her killed there." The man sighed. "He could've had her killed anywhere. That's the thing about you lords and ladies—we're worms under your diamond-buckled shoes. If you crush us or don't, doesn't matter to you. Most of the time you don't even notice." Peg's son took a step closer, and his face came into the light. He was Julian's age, a big man, his hands square and heavy. "Did you even think of Ma as anything but a servant? Did you know she was a mother? A grandmother?"

"No, I did not. Again, I'm sorry." Julian took a breath. "What's your name?"

The other man shook his head. "Doesn't matter, m'lord. I'm here for one reason. Ma once told me that yer mother wrote in a small printed book as she lay dying, in the blank spaces at the sides. Yer mam would hide the book when a servant came into her rooms, but me ma knew what she did. That book was in the crate of books sent to yer manor—Adders, ain't it?"

Julian's heart nearly stopped. The information he'd wanted from Peg was here, laid before him almost as an afterthought. "Why are you telling me this?"

Peg's son grinned, his teeth glinting in the lantern light. "'Cause me ma said that if there was ever a way to bring the duke down, it was in that there book yer mother kept. I want you to end him, the Duke of Windemere. I want him to bleed like the rest of us worms."

That was highly unlikely. In theory, a duke could be brought before Parliament, but it was exceedingly rare.

But if Julian's mother had known something about Augustus, something secret, and if she'd written it in that book, well then, perhaps Julian could finally get the upper hand over the duke.

Peg's son turned as if to walk away.

"Wait," Julian said urgently. "You're in danger, too, if my uncle suspects your mother told you this."

"Aye," the other man said. "That's why I'm bound for the American Colonies. They say men are more equal there." He snorted. "Fairy tales, I have no doubt, but at least it's not England."

With that he walked away.

Julian stared after him before peering around again to make sure there was no one else about to step into his path.

· Then he dropped his pistol back in his pocket and strode to the White Horse.

He felt suddenly awake, his mind whirring as he made

plans. It was past time he returned to Adders Hall—but first he needed to provide a distraction.

The inn was bustling as Julian walked through the main room. Some travelers half dozed over tankards of small beer, while others hurried to the waiting coach. Ostlers shouted outside, and maids called orders to the kitchen as they ran to feed hungry patrons.

Julian took the stairs two at a time, impatiently darting around those slower than he. There was light beneath the door to the room he shared with Quinn when he made it.

A soft rap on the door, and Quinn peered out. "Well?"

Julian pushed past him and into the room, jerking his head at the door.

Quinn closed it obediently before returning to packing a satchel. Vanderberg was in the corner, rummaging among Julian's clothes, looking harried.

Julian nodded, sitting at the table to pour himself a glass of wine. "Hawthorne and I finalized the plan."

"And?"

"He'll be away with Messalina later this morning," Julian answered. "Bound for Newcastle. Apparently he has mines there." He shrugged. "If he can combine this with business, so much the better."

The plan was to confuse Augustus as to where Lucretia might've escaped to. With Newcastle's busy port, the route to the city was one of many that Lucretia might've taken if she'd fled abroad.

Julian took a sip of the wine and looked at Quinn. "Did you find a girl to play the part?"

Vanderberg dropped something with an exclamation.

"Yes," Quinn gestured to the floor. "A French lass in the inn below. She wants to return home. She's more than happy to share a carriage with me in return for free transport to Dover."

Julian nodded. "Good. I'll leave this afternoon bound for Bristol. One of Hawthorne's maids has family there and is glad to have a month's leave to visit them. I've procured a horse for the maid to ride. I'll take Octavia and then ride her to Adders to spend the fortnight afterwards."

"Shall I come with you, sir?" Vanderberg asked. He'd packed a soft bag for Julian to travel with.

"No," Julian replied. "I'm not sure I'll even need you at Adders." He looked at Quinn. "What about you?"

His brother grimaced. "I'll stay in Dover for a bit—maybe a week—before I return to London with the carriage. It'll cost a bit to stable the horses and put up the drivers while I'm in Dover."

Julian shook his head. "Can't be helped. Hawthorne and Messalina will be at least a month in Newcastle. Our times are staggered both leaving London and returning. Hopefully, it'll put Augustus off the scent long enough to let Lucretia escape."

"What about Mulgrave?" Quinn asked.

"What about him?" Julian returned sharply.

Quinn shrugged. "He doesn't strike me as a man to give up easily."

Julian nodded. "You think he'll pursue Lucretia himself."

"From all I've heard of him?" Quinn looked grim. "I think he'll be hot on her trail."

Julian knocked back the rest of his wine. "Then we'll have to hope our ruse will fool Mulgrave as well."

* * *

Two days later, Elspeth pulled her hood more closely about her face as she trudged through mud. Deep, disgustingly sucking mud. Poor Plum, trotting gamely at her side, was covered to his chest in the thick stuff.

Her woolen cape was completely soaked through from a downpour that had started several hours ago. Thankfully, the rain had slowed to a trickle, but the damage was already done. Her sturdy worsted wool dress was damp as well, and both of her feet were swimming in icy water inside her boots.

Really, it had been a most trying afternoon. She'd arrived in Dydle, the town nearest to Adders Hall, at a bit after one of the clock. The small inn where the coach stopped offered a lovely pork pie for luncheon, and she'd split one with Plum. Thus braced, she'd ventured forth to find a means of travel to Adders Hall . . . only to discover that there simply wasn't any. Horses were rare, and what carts there were—mainly of an agricultural nature— were in use. It seemed the people of Dydle preferred to walk.

As it happened, Elspeth was quite used to walking. Growing up in the Wise Women's compound, she and her sisters had shared a horse, an old gelding named Sampson who was usually commandeered by Freya or Caitriona, leaving Elspeth to wander the Scottish hills on foot.

Those meanderings had been mostly in sunny weather and of an easy length—perhaps a mile or two. This journey to Adders was only six miles but was hampered by the foulest of weather. The rain had started before Elspeth had lost sight of Dydle and had progressed to a downpour within minutes. The dirt road she was on had rapidly degraded into a stream of sticky, slippery mud. Her skirts were fouled to the knee, her hair dripped into her face, and each step was a labor, with her boots turned into mis-shapen mud balls.

She felt as if she'd been trudging along for hours—maybe days. The fields that had bracketed the lane had turned to a wood, making everything seem gloomy. Elspeth looked ahead, trying to see through the rain. Was there an opening in the line of trees up ahead at the right? She couldn't quite see. And then she stumbled, going down to her knees in the muck.

Plum came to lick her face as if in commiseration.

"Thank you." Elspeth stroked the dog and then dragged herself to her feet. It wasn't the first time she'd fallen, but her toes and her fingers were becoming numb, her skirts heavy with mud, weighing her down. She gasped and swiped the rain out of her eyes, watching the nearing turn.

Oh, thank Goddess! Crooked iron gates stood open where a carriage track broke off from the lane. Elspeth wrinkled her nose. She'd imagined a grand aristocratic estate. But the innkeeper had assured her that the big black posts were the sign of Adders Hall.

She sighed and turned into the track. The trees loomed closer, tall and meeting over her head. If this didn't lead to Adders, then she'd have to retrace her steps, but it seemed unlikely that there would be two such gates on the lane.

The track was rutted, and the puddles were therefore deceptively deep. Elspeth discovered this fact when her boot plunged into one, the water coming up to her calf. She winced and determinedly kept going.

Around a tall beech, the wood ended abruptly to reveal a field spread out before her, cows huddled under sparse trees. Did Mr. Greycourt keep cattle? Farther on, she could see a gray building, and the sight heartened her.

It took another half hour to travel to the steps of what

must be Adders Hall, though it wasn't at all as she'd imagined. For one, it was only a little bigger than a country squire's manor. Adders was built of worn gray stone, and the front portico had lovely Corinthian columns, but she could see two windows boarded up on the ground floor and another five on the upper floor, all to her left. The drive had once been properly graveled, but now tall weeds sulked in the rain.

Lifting her heavy skirts, Elspeth mounted the steps and knocked.

Then waited.

And waited some more.

She shifted from foot to foot. The minute she'd stopped walking, her toes had begun to freeze. Plum had grown bored and was sniffing the tall grass around the steps.

Another knock.

There must be someone inside—she'd seen smoke from one of the chimneys.

She had almost decided on going around to the back when the door was pulled open with a creak.

Before her stood a broad woman somewhere in her forties wearing a well-used apron. "Aye?"

Elspeth smiled as brightly as she could with rain dripping in her face. "Is this Adders Hall?"

"Might be." The woman looked at her suspiciously. "Who be asking?"

"Lady Elspeth de Moray."

The other woman gave her a slow inspection, from her muddy skirts to her sodden hood. She narrowed her eyes when she got to Plum. "That so?"

"Indeed," Elspeth answered cheerily. "I'm a friend of Mr. Greycourt's sisters, Messalina and Lucretia. They've told me so much about the library at Adders. I'm a bit zealous about books and libraries," she confided earnestly. "And since I happened to be in the neighborhood, I thought I'd pop in to look it over."

Her words seemed to have engendered a dead silence, broken only by the sound of trickling water from the eves above.

The woman stared at Elspeth, her face expressionless.

Then she inhaled. "Well then, best come in, hadn't 'e?"

*   *   *

It took Julian three days to make it to Adders Hall from Bristol. The roads were impassible to carriages, either flooded or washed away entirely or sunken into a morass of mud. He'd had to guide Octavia and the horse tied behind her around blockages again and again, so by the time he arrived at Adders, he was chilled and tired.

Julian rode around back of the hall, jumping down from the mare only when they made the stable.

Or what was left of the stable.

Adders Hall had originally been a hunting lodge—a place to play for the richest of aristocrats on his mother's side of the family. Therefore, the stable was a large building, built of stone, with many stalls and room above for the grooms' quarters.

Except there weren't any grooms.

Julian led Octavia and the spare gelding into the side of the stable still standing—the other half having fallen down sometime before he'd inherited the property. He took off both horses' saddles himself, rubbing them down briskly so they wouldn't catch a chill. He forked fresh hay into their stalls and gave each a bucketful of mixed oats and barley.

Then he clutched his wet tricorne to his head and ran to the back of the house.

God's balls, he was in need of rest.

The special kind of rest that he partook of only at Adders.

He banged on the kitchen door and was let in by Mrs. McBride, looking reddened and sweating from her cooking.

"Lord bless you, Mr. Greycourt," that lady exclaimed at the sight of him. "Whatever are you doing out in a storm like this?"

"Riding home, Mrs. McBride," Julian answered as he took off his dripping hat and went to the hearth to warm his hands. "Has she arrived?"

"Sir?"

"The woman," Julian snapped. He shouldn't be so impatient with Mrs. McBride—she'd served Adders for decades—but he felt his control on the point of breaking. "Did she make it through the lanes?"

Mrs. McBride narrowed her eyes at his tone, but all she said was, "She's in the library."

An odd place to show a hired woman, but he didn't care. "Thank you," Julian replied, throwing off his great-coat and exiting the kitchens. He needed a bath and a change of clothes, but the knowledge that his surcease was within his grasp drove him to the library.

He turned one corner and then another, rushing through his own house like a madman. Thank God there was no one to see his frenzy. If he knew, Augustus would have Julian by the neck.

Julian swept that dire thought from his mind and pushed the library door open.

Inside, the old room was dim, the high windows across

from the door letting in little light from the clouds without. One end had a fireplace, though, and it was lit, a roaring fire burning there. Julian started for the hearth, making for the figure he could see sitting in a chair before the fire, her back to him.

Julian was within a couple of steps when a short, dark form rose and commenced barking at him. He halted midstride, staring at the dog before him. The animal looked strangely familiar. Hadn't he seen such a dog with...

The woman rose from her chair and turned, metamorphosing from a prostitute into Lady Elspeth de Moray.

"What the bloody hell are you doing here?" Julian yelled to be heard above the dog's barking.

The animal abruptly stopped, looking uncertain.

Elspeth licked her lips, her usual sunny smile wavering. "Mr. Greycourt. Ah. Well, it's quite a story. You see, I—"

"No." He cut across her ruthlessly. "I don't want to hear your damned lies. Do you truly think me so half-witted?" He screwed his eyes shut. Was she spying for Augustus? Did it matter? He couldn't think. "Where is she?"

He snapped his eyes open in time to see her wary uncertainty.

"Who?"

"The woman," he growled through gritted teeth. "The girl who was supposed to be here. Where did you put her?"

"I don't..." Her brows knit and then cleared again, her expression very near to embarrassed. "Oh. You have a—a sweetheart you meant to meet here?"

He wanted to scream. To let all his urges and feelings roll out of him and thrash on the floor before her. "*No*. Not a sweetheart. A whore."

Silence enveloped the library as she stared at him, appearing dumbstruck.

"God damn it!" He whirled to go to the door. Perhaps she waited for him in his bedroom. A bold move, considering he rarely let the hired women in his house, and never in his bedroom, but he wouldn't quibble.

"Wait," she called from behind him, as if he would stop. "There's no whore here."

He turned. "What?"

She should've been frightened at his wild mood. She should've been disgusted at the word *whore*.

If anything, she looked *intrigued*. "There's only Mrs. McBride and me in the house, no one else." She tilted her head. "How was your whore meant to get here? The roads are impassible."

Julian almost retorted that he'd made it here on the roads, but she was right. The roads were impassible to any vehicle. A single horse might make it as his had, but Julian knew himself to be an excellent horseman. A girl off the streets would hardly ride a horse, let alone own one.

"How the hell did you come here?" he demanded.

"The mail coach to Dydle," she said with supreme dignity. "And then Plum and I walked the rest of the way here."

"And you brought your dog," he muttered. She was such a strange, unworldly creature.

She looked surprised. "Of course."

"Jesus," he muttered under his breath, and pointed sternly at her. "You stay there."

He strode to the door and into the hall. This couldn't be. He couldn't be stuck at Adders lustful and unable to relieve his desires. He was already on the cusp of losing control. How long could he last like this?

He stalked into the kitchen, where Mrs. McBride was swathing herself in multiple scarves. "You know what woman I meant. Is she here or not?"

The cook looked at him. "There's nobody here but my lady."

"No one." He collapsed into a chair, watching as the woman walked to the kitchen door. "You're leaving early."

"Aye, I am," she replied. "I'd hate to be caught walking in this storm after dark. Don't expect me tomorrow, either. There's no use trying to journey here with the roads as they are. You and my lady are on your own until the roads clear."

With that Mrs. McBride slammed the kitchen door behind her.

* * *

Elspeth looked at Plum as she sat in the library. "Should we follow him, do you think?"

The dog's only answer was to slump to the rug in front of the fireplace and turn over so his clumsy paws waved in the air.

Elspeth sighed, looking around. She was not even a quarter finished with the Adders library. After her arrival yesterday she'd spent most of the rest of the day washing both herself and Plum. She'd not even had time to look into the library until the evening.

At which point she'd discovered that, far from being the small room she'd expected from Mr. Greycourt and Messalina's description, the Adders Hall library was cavernous. Spiderwebs hung in sheets from the ceiling, and there was a pervasive smell of mold. Thousands of books lined every wall. Only two tall, narrow windows pierced the gloom. The fire helped—and brought warmth to the room—but Elspeth still had to light a half-dozen candles in order to see the print in the books.

When Mr. Greycourt had walked in, Elspeth had been looking at a small volume of poetry by an anonymous Elizabethan person. The pages were speckled, the binding rotting, but despite the book's condition, the sonnets within were simply divine. She wondered if this "anonymous" was a woman—how many anonymouses might be women.

But she was getting distracted again, perhaps because if she didn't distract herself, she would start thinking about Mr. Greycourt's prostitute. About Mr. Greycourt himself. About what he might do with a courtesan.

Would his gray eyes widen, his severe mouth open helplessly, his entire expression be unguarded in the throes of passion?

Elspeth swallowed. She shouldn't think of such things— at least not about a man who didn't even seem to like her. He'd been angry when he'd burst into the library earlier. She was quite obviously *not* the person he was looking for.

Well, that hardly mattered to her. What Mr. Greycourt did behind the door of his bedroom was none of her business.

The thought made her grumpy for some reason.

"Come on, Plum," she called to the dog. "No matter how angry he is, he can't keep me from supper."

So saying, she boldly left the library, skirts swishing as she walked down the hall to the kitchens. Mrs. McBride had proved to be a perfect companion yesterday and today. The cook didn't care what Elspeth did during the day, and she had made mounds of delicious food for both herself and Elspeth, among it the most wonderful apple pie.

Mrs. McBride had warned Elspeth this morning that she might not return tomorrow, but she'd assured Elspeth that there were plenty of victuals to be had in the kitchen.

Elspeth certainly hoped so.

She and Plum arrived at the kitchen to find it quiet, and for a moment she thought that they were alone. Then she saw Mr. Greycourt sitting at the worn kitchen table, his head in his hands.

Elspeth stifled a gasp. She'd never seen the proud man so vulnerable. She hesitated. Perhaps a retreat would be the smart thing. She could go back to the library until the kitchen was clear.

But that would mean leaving Mr. Greycourt alone.

Her heart squeezed. Somehow she couldn't make herself abandon him. Elspeth crossed to the hearth, where a pot hung near the fire. She lifted the lid, and a lovely warm smell of stew wafted out.

Plum came trotting over.

"Hungry?" she asked the dog.

Plum sat and licked his lips.

Elspeth tore a piece of brown bread into a battered old plate and poured a bit of stew on top, carefully stirring it until the meal was no longer hot.

She set the plate in front of Plum and then ladled out two bowls, which she brought to the table, gently setting one down in front of Mr. Greycourt and the other opposite him.

She brought the bread to the table along with a bit of cheese and a bottle of wine.

"Have something to eat," she said quietly to Mr. Greycourt. He still had his head in his hands, not looking at her. "I've got some wine and bread, and Mrs. McBride has made a stew. Beef, I believe."

Thick chunks of meat lay in the gravy, surrounded by carrots and onions and other vegetables. Elspeth blew on a spoonful.

Mr. Greycourt raised his head, looking weary. "What are you doing here, Elspeth? Are you a ghost sent to haunt me?"

She couldn't help but feel a twinge of hurt. "Whyever would you be haunted?"

"For my sins." He barked a laugh. "For my many, many sins."

She cautiously took a bite of the stew—delicious! "I've never seen you do anything sinful," she said as she uncorked the wine. "But even supposing you might be a very wicked sinner, why would *I* be haunting you?"

She poured them both wine.

He stared at her, his beautiful gray eyes almost despairing. "I don't know, but you seem uniquely suited to harassing me. Wherever I go, there you are, smiling and sunny, as if sent to draw me from my path. As if you could lift me from the darkness and lead me into the light."

Elspeth swallowed another bite of the stew. "And that's...bad, showing you light?"

"Very bad." He picked up his spoon and twirled it between his fingers. "I could get lost, lose my guard, wander into frivolity with you and your temptations."

"Hmm." Elspeth was doubtful that she made any kind of siren. Maybe he was simply exhausted from his journey. "Well, the only thing I wish to tempt you with now is that stew. Eat it, and it'll warm you."

She thought she heard him mutter, "Sorceress" under his breath, but he followed her instructions nonetheless, beginning to eat.

Elspeth felt a small sense of satisfaction at having

talked him into consuming his supper. He was so auto-
cratic, marching about like an ice man, imperious to all
physical want.

But he wasn't really, was he? Mr. Greycourt might
want to seem an automaton, but he was a man underneath
his cold exterior. A man who had needs. Didn't anyone at
all take care of him? Make sure he ate and slept and was
warm when it was cold?

She studied him as he sipped his wine. Mr. Greycourt
was usually so forbidding that perhaps most people simply didn't think he had any wants, let alone that he needed
attention from someone caring.

Perhaps she was the first to do so.

But then the memory of the woman he'd been looking
for when he arrived came to her, an unpleasant reminder.
He had his own life, and maybe this woman met his needs
all on her own?

Elspeth cleared her throat. "I'm sorry your woman
isn't here."

He glanced at her. "You shouldn't speak of such things."

"Why not?" she asked, honestly surprised. There were
so many rules in London for a lady—most of them restric-
tions on actions or words.

"Because—" he said repressively then shook his head.
"I beg your pardon. I had no business talking about the
women I hire. I can only blame my...tiredness from the
ride here."

"And your disappointment, I think," she said. He
looked at her blankly, and she added, "That she wasn't
here. Your woman. Your..." She wrinkled her nose. "Is
she really a whore or is she your lover or mistress? You
seemed awfully aggrieved that she wasn't waiting here.

More so than seems natural for what you call a whore. You must know her at least."

"No." He shook his head. "I contracted for her to be sent from...well, where she's from doesn't matter. Only that I don't know her. And"—he scowled—"this is not a suitable discussion for a lady."

Elspeth pushed her half-empty bowl aside and folded her hands on the table, setting her chin atop them. "Then don't see me as a lady if it's so hard for you. I'm really not a proper lady anyway. I grew up in the north of Scotland without lessons in drawing or dancing. I'm just me, Elspeth."

He looked at her oddly then, his gray eyes wide. Was it so hard for him to see her as just another person instead of a lady who needed to be coddled?

Elspeth smiled. "Do you want a bath after supper?"

"I..."

"Of course you'll need a bath." Elspeth hopped up. "I'd better start heating the water."

"I can do that," he snapped.

"And so can I," she replied. "Finish your supper."

He subsided then, eating the stew. But even as he did so, she could feel his eyes on her.

Elspeth filled a large kettle with water from the cistern and picked it up carefully.

"The pot is too heavy for you," he said from behind her. "I can do that."

She turned to look at him over her shoulder. "And so can I." She demonstrated by carrying the kettle to the fireplace, where she set it over the fire to warm. She repeated the procedure two more times. "There," she said after she had set the third pot. "It's not a lot, but you should have enough to heat a hip bath." She glanced around the kitchen. "If you have one here?"

"I don't understand," he said, not answering the question about the hip bath. "Why are you here? Why are you doing these things for me?"

"Well," she said, coming to sit across from him again, "I suppose someone has to do these things for you."

She smiled brightly.

His eyes narrowed. "And my first question?"

She met his gaze, saying nothing, and her heart began pounding because if he pressed the point...

Mr. Greycourt sighed. "What am I to do with you?"

"I don't know," Elspeth said honestly.

It suddenly occurred to her that they might be stuck at Adders for days, even weeks, until the roads were clear again.

She cleared her throat. "Erm. Perhaps in the meantime I could help you with your bath?"

His head jerked up as he stared at her incredulously.

"I meant," Elspeth hastily said, her cheeks heating, "filling a bath. With water. For you."

He shook his head, rising. "There's no need." He strode to the kitchen cabinet, pulling out a shallow copper bath from behind it. "I can do the rest."

"Shall I bring down a fresh change of clothes?" she asked, watching him fill the bath. "That is, if you have any here?"

"I do, but I'll find them myself." He glanced up at her, his eyes glinting silver in the candlelight. "You can retire now. Unless you mean to stay and watch."

For a fraction of a second, she contemplated telling him that she did want to stay. To watch him take off his boots and coat and shirt and breeches. To see him completely unclothed and then to witness him sitting in that small bath. The water would hardly come to his hips, certainly not covering, let alone hiding, his—his…cock. And balls.

She felt herself blush wildly.

"I'll just bid you good night, then," she said hastily. "Come here, Plum."

The dog got up slowly. He'd found himself a place by the hearth and was evidently loath to leave the warmth. Plum took a last lingering look at the fire before obediently trotting to keep up with Elspeth as she left the kitchen.

"Really," Elspeth muttered to the dog as they mounted the staircase to the next floor. "Must you tarry while I'm burning hotter and hotter? I can't think that's a kind thing to do to a friend."

Plum didn't answer, but he did wag his tail as they arrived at the bedroom she'd been using.

Elspeth pushed open the door and found the bedroom nearly dark. She suspected that at one time the room had been richly appointed, but the brighter rectangles on the walls were a testimony to pictures taken down, and the furniture was as sparse as in a monk's cell. A bed, a chair, and a small table with a broken leg, that was all. Still, the place was quite adequate for her needs.

Elspeth crossed to the fireplace and stirred the embers on the banked fire—she'd quickly discovered that Adders was a terribly cold house.

As she readied for bed, Elspeth considered Mr. Greycourt's arrival. He hadn't immediately thrown her out or forbidden her from searching in the library, which was a very good thing. Although, she reflected as she brushed her hair, Mr. Greycourt's leniency might be due to his wearied state. He might order her from Adders in the morning. But there was little she could do about that now—better save her worries for tomorrow.

As she climbed into the tall, narrow bed, she couldn't help her thoughts wandering back to the reason for Mr. Greycourt's visit. Did he meet his paid companions only in the country? If so, why? And what exactly would he do now that he'd been deprived of his chosen woman?

The last question jolted her into alertness.

Elspeth stared into the dark, imagining Mr. Greycourt in his bath—quite nude—terribly, horribly unsatiated. Wouldn't it be natural for a man thus deprived of another to satisfy him to...

A picture appeared fully formed and damnably detailed in her mind. Mr. Greycourt sitting in the shallow copper tub, his wet shoulders gleaming in the kitchen candlelight, his hand drifting lower over his stomach and between his legs... The details were blurry, but the thought was enough to make her shift restlessly, to send her own hand seeking between her thighs. Oh, she was so soft here! The silk of her thighs brushed against the backs of her fingers as she delved into her damp folds. Her little kernel was waiting, alert, slippery, and so sweet beneath her touch. A feeling of warmth stole through her as she circled that nub, imagining Mr. Greycourt touching himself.

Her palm lay on her maiden hair, and she realized he would have a bush above his cock, wouldn't he? Stark black like his hair, bold and curling, and a spike of pleasure shot through her. It was so naughty—picturing the hair on a man's bare, exposed body. She'd seen drawings of nude males—paintings, even—but they rarely had body hair. Perhaps hair was too basic, too animal, to be included in lofty ideals of artistic beauty.

But it was there nonetheless.

She had hair between her thighs, and Mr. Greycourt would have hair as well. He was just as human as she. He had needs. Felt pain and hunger and pleasure. How often did he touch himself? Did he do it on a schedule like a soldier—mannerly and businesslike? Or did he hate the idea of physical want, holding himself back, making himself wait until the need burst through his control?

She groaned softly, her finger moving faster.

And when he had lost all control, when he could deprive himself no longer, did he gasp when he finally touched himself? Touched his *penis*? It was wrong, wicked, to imagine such private things about someone else. She couldn't help herself, though. He'd bite his lip. Or maybe grit his teeth, the pleasure too overwhelming for starved senses. His long black hair would be unbound from that severe braid, falling recklessly about his shoulders, perhaps even caught between his lips as he lost control.

As he let himself free.

Warmth rushed through her, sweet, sweet oblivion, the sparks of her pleasure making her arch as she felt her own release.

Oh! Oh, that was lovely.

Elspeth rolled over sluggishly, her body turned to warm syrup, and settled, the image of Mr. Greycourt lax in his bath rocking her to sleep.

CHAPTER EIGHT

"The woman I love," Sabinus said,
"is called Christina."
And with that all Lady Long-Nose's hopes came
falling to the ground.
"She is shy," Sabinus continued, "and I wonder if
you might do me a favor?"
"Anything," Lady Long-Nose whispered.
"Can you become her friend?" asked her love.
                    —From *Lady Long-Nose*

Julian woke to an insistent knocking at his bedroom door
the next morning. He squinted, taking in the cold, dark
room, confused for a second as to where he was.

Then he remembered that he was at Adders. That he
was looking for his mother's secret book. That the girl
he'd hired hadn't arrived.

And he was stuck here with Lady Elspeth.

He groaned as the knocking started up again. Perhaps
this was a good sign. Perhaps the maid or the cook had
returned.

"Enter!" he called.

The door opened to reveal Lady Elspeth holding a tray.
Walking into his bedroom. With him in the bed.

Dear God. Could anyone be this innocent?

"It's night," he rasped. "What do you want?"

"It's not, actually," she replied with far too much cheerfulness. He noticed that the dog had followed her in. "Night, that is. According to the clock in the kitchens, it's already seven in the morning."

With that she threw back the curtains.

Julian shuddered, wincing away from the light, feeble though it was. "Seven of the clock is not a civilized hour of the day. Why are you awake? Why are you in my room?"

He thought he heard her laugh. He definitely heard the *chink* of china as she set something on the table beside his bed. "I'm awake because seven in the morning is a lovely time of the day—as is *six* in the morning, when I rose."

"*Six?*" he muttered, appalled.

"And I'm in your room because I've brought you tea."

He turned his head and found her beaming at him like a small, overly happy sun. "Oh God."

She cocked her head. "Do you always braid your hair?"

He blinked, sitting up. "It tangles in the night if I don't." What was he doing having a conversation with her in his bedroom about his toilet?

"It is very long," she mused, handing him a dish of tea. "Your hair must be beautiful when you let it out. Like Rapunzel's!"

He nearly choked on the tea. "Lady Elspeth, I—"

"Elspeth."

He looked at her.

"You called me Elspeth last night," she reminded him. He sighed. "*Elspeth.* I am not—"

"Well, no," she blithely interrupted, "you aren't Rapunzel. And you're certainly not the prince."

His heart contracted painfully.

She drew a chair next to the bed and sat down. "You're

more like a sorcerer living deep in the woods in a lonely castle all by himself. Perhaps with a magical raven as a familiar."

"You're babbling."

She looked hurt. She'd leave now—he'd driven her away—and he realized suddenly that he didn't want her to go.

"I beg your pardon," he said gruffly. "I should not have said that."

She inclined her head gravely. "No, but I forgive you. One shouldn't take anything said before the first cup of tea seriously."

He glanced at his cup to find it half-full. "Have you had your tea yet?" He drank the rest of his cup and handed it to her.

"Mm." She took the cup. "More?"

"Please." He watched her pour, her small, soft hands competent and sure. This was oddly domestic, sitting here, too early in the morning, with her.

With Elspeth.

She gave him the cup and then studied him, her face solemn. "I am sorry, you know. That Lucretia had to leave without bidding you farewell. And that we hadn't the time to tell you beforehand."

He glanced at her and then away. He'd been so angry that night at the ball. In fear for his sister, enraged that Mulgrave had gotten the best of him... "No." He cleared his throat before meeting her gaze. "I'm the one who should apologize. Lucretia needed to leave, and it was good that you found someone to take her." He hesitated. "Although I would like to know who this person was."

"A friend." She bit her lip. "I can't tell you more."

He nodded, though the answer left him greatly unsatisfied.

Elspeth clapped her hands into the silence, startling the poor dog. "What shall you do today?"

He glanced at the window. Gray clouds covered the sky, and rain had begun to spit against the glass, the day so dark it looked like evening instead of morning. "I have work to do. In the library."

"Really?" She sat up straighter. "Can I help?"

His first inclination was to deny her. To keep secret his plan and his thoughts as he had done with everyone for years. But what was the point, really? He no longer thought she worked for Augustus—the idea had been tenuous from the start—and she could help him. "I'm looking for a book."

She stilled as if caught off guard. "What sort of book?"

He grimaced. "A book hidden within a book, if my information is correct. My mother made some notations, but she wrote them inside a book to hide them. I'm not sure what it even looks like."

She tilted her head. "Why now?"

"What?"

"Well," she said slowly, as if thinking through an equation, "you've been master of Adders Hall for quite some time, haven't you?"

"Since my mother died," he replied gruffly.

She nodded, her smile entirely gone now. "So why decide to look now?"

He took a sip of his tea, watching her over the cup's edge. "I only learned about the book recently. From a former maid of my mother's."

She gazed at him, obviously waiting for more.

It was tempting. Very tempting. Just to open his mouth

and tell her everything. Spill his secrets and let them live or die in the light of day.

But caution had stood beside him so long, it had welded itself to his very soul.

He remained silent.

"Well," she said at last, "I can certainly help you search the library, at least. That is, if you don't mind." Her eyes were oddly intense.

He didn't entirely trust her. And she had some sort of obsession with libraries that he didn't understand yet.

She'd presumed too much, traveled here alone in some sort of outrageous quest. Her being here with him at Adders was far beyond the pale. He most certainly should rebuke her.

He should tell her that he didn't need her, didn't *want* her near him.

But that would be a lie.

He found himself saying, "Very well."

Her dimples made a reappearance as she smiled at him, her sky-blue eyes alight with excitement. Something in his chest squeezed hard, and he realized.

If anyone in this room was a sorcerer, it was she.

* * *

Elspeth surveyed the kitchen, hands on hips. She'd come down to discover what there might be for breakfast while Mr. Greycourt was dressing in his bedroom.

Her mind caught for a moment, snagged by the thought of *bedrooms* and *dressing* and Mr. Greycourt's long, nimble fingers.

Then she shook herself and reined in her thoughts.

Breakfast!

Mrs. McBride had made bread yesterday, and two loaves still stood in the kitchen cupboard, but Adders was chilly with the weather still damp and gloomy. Something hot was needed. She searched the kitchen, peering in bins until she found what she was looking for. By the time Mr. Greycourt arrived, she had a pot of porridge popping over the fire and Plum lying by the fire enjoying the heat.

He halted just inside the doorway. "Oatmeal?" His voice was not enthusiastic.

"Yes," Elspeth briskly replied, lifting the pot off the hook over the fire. "I know Mr. Johnson says the English only feed their oats to horses, but I grew up in Scotland, where we are canny enough to eat it ourselves."

He grunted and sat at the big, scarred kitchen table. Plum immediately got up from the hearth and trotted to his side to see if Mr. Greycourt had any food to give him.

Elspeth almost called the dog back. Mr. Greycourt had made it very clear that he didn't like dogs. But then she noticed he was caressing Plum's head.

She opened her mouth and then shut it again firmly. She had the idea that if she drew attention to the petting, Mr. Greycourt would deny it.

Instead she spooned the oatmeal into two dishes and added pats of butter to both. "There," she said as she placed the bowls on the table. "Doesn't that smell good?"

Mr. Greycourt, sitting across from her, looked dubious.

She pushed a little covered clay pot toward him. "Some like honey in it."

"Ah." He stirred a spoonful of honey into the oatmeal and took a bite, his brow clearing. "Palatable."

"Thank you." She felt a smile play about her lips. "Palatable" might not be the most enthusiastic of compliments, but if she waited for enthusiasm from him, she had a feeling she might grow gray hair first. She plopped a large spoonful of honey in her bowl. "I've always thought oatmeal the best breakfast on cool mornings."

He raised his eyebrows. "Do you eat it every day in Scotland?"

"No." She chewed thoughtfully. "Kippers are nice as well, as are boiled eggs, and scones with lots of butter are lovely."

He was still watching her, his gray eyes intent, his oatmeal seemingly forgotten. "I wasn't aware that the Dukes of Ayr were fond of oatmeal."

"Oh." She looked down at her oatmeal, stirring slowly as the honey disappeared. "No, I don't remember if Papa ate oatmeal, and I don't really know what Ranulf eats to break his fast." She cleared her throat. She'd have to ask him in her next letter. "But you see, after Papa died, we moved to the north of Scotland."

"With a relative?"

"Yes." She was careful of her words. "With Papa's sister, my aunt Hilda. She took Freya, Caitriona, and me to live with her. Lachlan, and of course Ranulf, stayed behind."

The parting had been hard, she remembered. She'd cried as their carriage drew away.

"Why 'of course'?" he asked lightly.

She darted a glance at him, but his face seemed without guile. "Well, they had to manage the dukedom, hadn't they?" Not to mention that the Wise Women didn't like the introduction of boys who were nearly men.

He stared at her a moment longer as if waiting for more information, but she merely took a large bite of the oatmeal.

Julian glanced down at his bowl. "Was she nice? Your aunt."

Elspeth swallowed hastily. "Aunt Hilda was marvelous! She was a bit gruff—she'd been burned in a fire, you see, and lost someone very dear to her—but she was kind and loving. She taught us to ride and to fence and to cook. Arithmetic, history, and geography. She read to us every night as we lay in bed, and she would lead us in discussions about all sorts of things—the metamorphosis of butterflies, poetry, the philosophies of Aristotle, Isaac Newton, and René Descartes, and the movement of the planets and stars." She stopped to take a breath.

"An unusual education for a duke's daughter," he said softly.

She glanced at him, startled. "Perhaps by society's standard. It seemed very normal when I lived there. We had a huge fireplace that we could all sit around at night, telling stories or reading from a book. When I went for a ramble, I'd climb the highest hill nearby, and if it was a clear day, I could see the sea. It was so beautiful." A sudden wave of homesickness swept her. She'd loved those hills.

And her friends and family who lived there. But most of them were gone now, she realized with a pang. Freya, Caitriona, Rikvi…

Mr. Greycourt's voice brought Elspeth out of her thoughts. "Is your aunt still there?"

Elspeth stared at him a moment before her eyes dropped to the table. "She died when I was twelve. I loved her very much."

All gone. All the Wise Women whom she loved and admired.

The ones who remained up in Scotland didn't hold the same values as she.

"I'm sorry," Mr. Greycourt said. "Who cared for you after her death?"

The Wise Women, of course, but she could hardly tell him that. "She had friends. Aunt Hilda, that is. They took us in, and Freya was eighteen by that point. Old enough to care for me as well."

There was a silence, and she wondered if Mr. Greycourt was suspicious of her vague reply.

But he said only, "That's good. I hope you were happy?"

"Yes," she assured him, for he seemed to need it. "I had a happy childhood."

He nodded and took another bite of the oatmeal before saying, "My sisters were sent to live with an elderly relative when my mother died."

She blinked, for he was telling her about his family without her nagging him to do so. "Were...were they happy as well?"

His face went blank, what little expression he'd been holding disappearing entirely. "I don't know."

"Didn't they tell you?" she asked softly.

He glanced up at her and then down again at his bowl. "No. I tried to write letters, but I was dissuaded from that immediately."

How had he been *dissuaded*? Her brows knit. "Were you not at this relative's house as well?"

"No." His mouth twisted. "My uncle felt that Quintus and I should be in London with him at Windemere House. Messalina and Lucretia were lucky—my mother sent them away right before she succumbed to her illness."

She took a sip of tea to steady herself. "And the Duke of Windemere *dissuaded* you from contacting your sisters?"

"Hm."

"That's terrible," she breathed, appalled.

"No, not at all." He pushed away his oatmeal only half-finished and stood. "I was seventeen—a man grown. And Quintus was there as well at Windemere House. I hardly needed missives from my younger sisters to survive."

"But...," she started. He was already walking away. She called to him, "But survival is a mere minimum in life. There is so much more!"

He halted at the kitchen doorway. "Is it? I wouldn't know."

And with that he left.

Elspeth scowled down at her bowl as she ferociously ate the remainder of her porridge. Surely, Julian didn't believe that. Surely, he had some happiness in life?

But as she thought about it, she wasn't sure. He wasn't close to his sisters. She'd noticed no friends around him. He really didn't smile...

She stood and stomped her foot, making Plum look up at the sound.

That was no way to live—hoping only for survival. Stupid man! Did he not understand that there was so much to enjoy in life? That there was more than duty and grimly marching through his days?

She gathered the dishes and brought them to the hearth. A pot was already simmering over the fire. Elspeth took it down, added cold water, and scrubbed the dishes clean.

He needed to understand.

But why was she so disturbed by Mr. Greycourt's philosophy of life? Did it matter to her if he was unhappy? If he had no one to love him?

It did. It really did matter to her.

She sat for a moment unseeing. She had a mission—a

direly important mission. But wasn't a person's life just as important?

Wasn't *Julian's* life important?

Yes, it was.

Elspeth blinked and realized she was still crouching by the kitchen fire and the pot of dirty water in front of her.

She rose, shook out the apron she'd pinned to her dress that morning, and threw the slop water outside.

It was past time she went to the library—if she wasn't wrong, both Julian and Maighread's diary awaited her there.

*   *   *

Mother had been quite ingenious to hide her notes within a book. Obviously, it had been overlooked by Augustus when the crates of books had been sent to Adders.

A shame her notes were equally hidden to him.

Julian sighed, looking up at the tall bookcases lining the room. They rose nearly to the ceiling, at least as tall as those in the library in Windemere. But there was no walkway at Adders, just a narrow, too-long ladder. He squinted. Would the blasted thing even hold him?

He heard the swish of Elspeth's skirts behind him, but he didn't turn. Bad enough that he kept remembering that one kiss—the coolness of her lips in the early morning, the flush of her face when he lifted his head.

The sight of her breasts straining against her stays under the poorly tied shawl.

He shook his head.

She cleared her throat behind him, a quiet *ahem-hem*, and truly whom was he bamming? He'd never be able to ignore her once she entered a room.

Julian turned to find her smiling hesitantly at him, which was patently wrong. Elspeth should never feel worried about her welcome. She wore a plain blue jacket made of ordinary wool and a tan skirt. Her skirt fell at her ankles more like a working woman's than an aristocrat's. A white kerchief was tucked in the bodice. He'd never seen a lady wear such a practical costume.

And he *wanted* her. Wanted to pull the concealing fichu from her pretty titties. Wanted to open his mouth over her nipples. Wanted to throw up her skirts and find her center.

Worse, he wanted her to command him to do so.

"Erm..." Her cheeks had pinkened. Did she know his thoughts? She drew a breath as if to steady herself. "I thought we should take Caesar's advice and divide and conquer." She cleared her throat again. "The library, I mean."

He dragged his mind back to his purpose. "You'll help me?"

"Of course," she replied. "And in return, I'd like to look for a book."

Ahhh. Now he might find out what she had been doing in all those libraries. "What book?"

Her eyes slid to the left. "An...old book." She brightened. "A family heirloom, in fact. Legend has it that the book is in the Greycourt libraries."

The book might be old, but the rest of her tale? Unlikely.

Cheek, assuming he'd help her steal an unnamed book from his library.

He'd waited too long to answer her, and now her smile had fled her face. He had grown used to that smile.

"Very well," he replied. "But I may have trouble looking for a book without description, title, or author."

"Oh." Her brows drew together as she thought. Probably deciding how much to tell him.

Behind her, Plum nosed open the library door and made his way to the hearth, heaving a heavy sigh as he lay down.

Elspeth came to a decision. "It's a diary. Handwritten."

Why would a diary be such a secret? Perhaps it had information that was detrimental to the de Morays, he thought cynically.

"And it came from the Greycourt estates in the north of England?" he asked. "In the box of books my mother sent me?"

"Maybe." She shrugged. "I only know it's in one of the Greycourt libraries."

"Very well," he said. "I take it you were searching for this diary yesterday?"

Her cheeks pinkened, but she said sturdily enough, "Yes."

"And you were only looking for a handwritten book?"

"Yes."

He'd expected as much. If she'd only glanced at the first couple of pages and seen a printed book, she could've easily missed his mother's writing. "Then you'll need to check the books you inspected yesterday in case one of them has my mother's writing. Which part of the library did you start in?"

"There." She waved to the right of the door.

"Very well. You research that area," he said. "And I'll begin on the opposite side." He pointed to the bookshelves on the right of the fireplace. "If we search clockwise, then we will cover the entire library."

"Very well," she said behind him.

He picked up a desk—a little spindly thing—and

brought it near the fireplace, setting it so that he could see Elspeth out of the corner of his eye. Then he took ten books from the bottom shelf and began his work.

It was tedious. The books were spotted and dusty, and there seemed to be too many books by obscure poets—obscure for a reason. He had to check every one, though. Bad poetry would be just the sort of book his mother would hide her notes in.

She'd loved Shakespeare's sonnets, and some of the more modern poets. As a boy, he'd had her read as he knelt at her feet, his head on her lap. And when he'd begun to write his own far inferior poems, she'd always praised him. Reading his poems to Father over and over again.

Julian shook his head. That had been long ago, before Augustus had come into their lives and Julian had realized that poems were a liability that could be used against him.

All that was in the past.

Across the room, he noticed that Elspeth was paging through the books that she'd already looked at for her diary. She was faster than he was, soon climbing the ladder for the higher shelves.

He frowned. She'd obviously already climbed that ladder to the highest rung to reach the books near the ceiling, but it was a daunting height. The thought of her missing a step . . .

He jumped from his seat, striding over as she touched the floor again, carrying a stack of books. "That's too dangerous."

She turned, blowing a strand of hair out of her face. "You needn't worry. I don't have a fear of heights."

Stubborn, stubborn woman. He glared at her, thinking, before he made up his mind. "I'll do it."

Her eyebrows raised. "What?"

He gestured to the ladder. "I'll take the books up and down the ladder. You look at them. You're quicker than I am anyway."

She blinked at him, her cheeks rosy from her exertion. For a moment, he was certain she would make an objection.

Then she nodded, her lips quirking. "We'll work together."

She sat on the bare library floor with her armful of books. He started to protest but caught himself. If she wanted to sit on the hard floor when there were plenty of chairs around, she must have her reasons. He didn't like it, but it was her choice.

They worked in silence for the next half hour, he estimated—for there was no clock in the room. That seemed to be her upper limit, though, for as he was descending with another batch of books, she sighed loudly.

"Do gentlemen often have illustrated books on the marital act?"

He nearly missed a rung. "What?"

He jumped the last steps to the floor and looked at her.

She had a rather large book open on her lap and was examining it with a considering moue. "There was a book like this in your uncle's house, and now here's another. Perhaps it's a family trait?"

He hoped he had nothing at all in common with his uncle.

Julian cleared his voice. "I didn't acquire the books in here."

"No," she said absently, turning a page, "but someone in your family must have."

This was a dangerous topic. He was already far too aware of her, sitting on the floor, her red-gold hair beginning to fall from its pins, her eyes sparking with interest.

He stifled a groan.

She peered closer at the page, a line between her eyebrows.

It cleared. "Oh. He's a satyr. That's his *hoof*." She shook her head. "I'm afraid these illustrations are not very good at all."

"You should..." His voice came out a croak. He cleared it. "You should not be looking at that book."

Her gaze was startlingly direct when she looked up at him. "Why not?" She leaned her chin on her fist. "If gentlemen want to engage in these actions, shouldn't a lady be aware of them? How else is she to understand her lover's needs? How else can she make intelligent choices?"

Her lover's needs. "I don't know what you mean." The hoarseness had returned to his throat.

She tilted her head. "I assume men choose which of these...positions most suit them. They must know of such books. How is it fair if a woman is not even aware of the possibilities? Should she simply rely on her husband's information?"

Yes. That was exactly what a gentlewoman should do. A lady was supposed to be innocent, unaware of the baser drives of her husband. Unaware of what Elspeth called *possibilities*.

But the thought...the mere thought of Elspeth examining rude drawings, learning from them what might be...

"What would you do with such information?" he asked

too abruptly. Too bluntly. A gentleman should never discuss such things with a lady—especially an unmarried lady.

Yet he had.

"I suppose…" She turned a page and raised her eyebrows at what she saw there. "I suppose I would have to study all the information available. Several sources, ideally, to be quite sure I had a complete knowledge of such things, even if the knowledge wasn't…practical."

"And then?" He could feel himself hardening. It was her certainty. Her calm acceptance that she was interested in such things.

In sex.

His cock jerked.

He licked his lips. "And then?"

"That depends." She smiled a secret smile. One that had been used by women ever since mankind had set foot on earth. "If I had a lover, I would tell him what I wanted."

"Just like that?" he asked, his voice lowered.

She nodded. "Just like that."

"What if he didn't want what you want?"

"Then he could say so, couldn't he?" She shrugged. "I suppose we wouldn't match. Wouldn't be compatible. In which case, I should have to find a man who was aroused by *my* needs."

Her gaze dropped from his face, trailing slowly over his chest and belly to pause at the falls to his breeches.

Where his cock strained to be released.

She stared, and he'd never felt anything so erotic. Just her, frankly observing him. She must be able to see the outline of his erection even as it pulsed with new blood. His libido laid bare to her for as long as she pleased.

Every muscle in his body tensed, restrained, unable to move unless she said so.

She sighed softly. "I'd search for a man who yearned for me and what I want. Who craved my touch. A man who put my pleasure above his own." Her gaze rose until she met his eyes. "Perhaps a man like you."

CHAPTER NINE

Now Christina was a lovely girl—pretty and shy.
Lady Long-Nose showed Christina how to dance and
ride, the proper etiquette for long official dinners,
and how to make friends with the
other girls in the court.
They became such good friends, in fact, that one day
Christina whispered to Lady Long-Nose that
she'd fallen in love with a man....
—From Lady Long-Nose

She'd never spoken so boldly in her life.

Elspeth felt liquid warmth between her thighs as she watched Julian. It made her want to squirm. To press her fingers against herself.

He was like a statue, a grave, beautiful Apollo, a god of music and poetry, who also held his sibyl at Delphi jealously to his heart.

Or so the myths said.

But what if it was the other way around? What if the sybil, a mere mortal, drew the helpless god's powers to her and made him writhe in ecstasy as she proclaimed the future?

Would that Apollo look like this just before he submitted to his oracle? Poised. Still. But almost quivering with strain?

She let her gaze wander back to his loins. She could see his member there, his penis, his cock, a solid ridge beneath the veiling cloth. Larger than she'd expected, but still frustratingly made indistinct by his clothes.

If she were to ask him, would he open his falls and let her see his naked flesh?

He jerked suddenly, as if awoken from a dream, and drew down the curtains of his face. "I must go. By your leave."

But he didn't wait for her permission. He simply left.

That she didn't like.

Elspeth pushed the book off her lap and growled. He should've waited for her word. Her command. He'd been excited by their discussion, she could tell. Why then would he leave before anything more could come of it?

Freya had told her that the rules in the world outside the compound were very strict. That women were either "good" or "bad," and the difference was based solely on whom she had sex with. For instance, a woman might have three husbands, which was "good," but if she took an equal amount of lovers when unwed, that was "bad."

Elspeth's jaw had dropped when she'd first heard this nonsense. The Romans and Greeks had had similar rules, but to still be practicing them in this enlightened age seemed bizarre.

But if Julian believed in strict adherence to these rules, then perhaps he considered it "bad" to talk about sex with her—she wasn't married to him, after all.

She scowled at the thought.

Stupid rules.

Stupid, pointless rules that left them both wanting.

Elspeth picked up the next book—a small copy of *The Compleat Angler*—really, why was this book so popular?—and began paging through it desultorily. Page after page of nearly illegible print. Obviously, this wasn't one of the better editions.

Then suddenly the pages were filled with scrawls in the margins, top, bottom, left, and right. Sometimes the writing was over the printed words.

She turned the book and squinted.

... my brother-in-law Augustus is poisoning me.

Elspeth's head jerked back in shock. This must be it, Julian's mother's notes. Who else would write about an Augustus? But Julian hadn't mentioned his mother being poisoned, had he? She'd died of an illness, unless he was hiding the truth from her.

If he wasn't ... then he didn't know how his mother had really died.

Elspeth bit her lip. What terrible information to give him. He already mourned his mother—how much more awful to realize she'd been deliberately murdered by his uncle.

She sighed and got to her feet, still holding the *Angler*. Julian would want to see this, even if it was terrible news. With this information, he had evidence against his awful uncle. Elspeth glanced to the door, hesitating. What would he do when he had his mother's notes? For one thing, he'd stop searching the library.

Perhaps he'd order her to stop searching as well. If she wasn't helping him to find this book, what reason would he have to help her find Maighread's diary?

She looked down at the book in her hand. Julian wanted—no, needed this book. She knew that. She was completely aware of how important the information within was to him.

But would it matter if he didn't see it right away?

After all, they were trapped here at Adders Hall. The roads were impassable.

She couldn't let him find his mother's words just yet.

Elspeth quickly stacked *The Prince* in the original Italian, *Gulliver's Travels*, and a copy of Euripides's plays in Latin on top of the *Angler*. She took a deep breath, picked up the stack of books, and walked sedately to the library door and opened it.

The hall was empty.

Her walk to the stairs was more hurried, and she kept a fast pace down the dark corridor to her borrowed bedroom. It was only as she approached the door that she let out a sigh of relief.

"What are you doing?"

She nearly yelped. Elspeth spun, the books clutched to her bosom, to face Julian in the hallway.

He was frowning at her. "I thought you wanted to search the library?"

"I do!" she replied far too loudly. She swallowed and continued more sedately, "I do want to search the library, but I found these books and thought they would be nice reading tonight."

"Indeed?" He arched a skeptical eyebrow. "What about the book of erotic artwork you were looking at?"

"I left it for you," she replied sweetly. "It is your book, after all, and I was loath to take it when you might need it."

A ruddy flush spread over his pale, cold cheeks. "Did you indeed?"

"Yes." She smiled. "But if you find you have no need of it, perhaps I'll borrow it as well."

"*Elspeth...*" Her name was a low rasp in his throat,

and for a moment all she could see was him, standing still for her in the library.

Then she came to her senses. "I'll return to help you in the library as soon as I can."

She slipped through the door and shut it behind her, leaning back against the wood.

There was silence from outside.

She turned her head slowly, pressing her ear against the door, feeling her heart beat against her breastbone. If she listened hard enough, could she hear his breathing? She could almost feel him standing on the other side of the doorway, separated from her by only inches of wood.

A scuff from the hallway and then the click of shoes walking away.

Elspeth let out her breath, vaguely disappointed that he hadn't forced the door and followed her inside. *Silly.* She had more important matters to attend to.

Pushing herself away from the door, she set the books on the small table beside the bed and then glanced around the room. There was no obvious place to hide the book. She'd heard of people squirreling away secrets in the stones inside the fireplace, but that sounded like a way to make the book go up in smoke.

She could put the book in the soft bag she'd brought with her to Adders, but wouldn't that be the first place Julian would search? That left the bed. She looked at it. The bed was the only large piece of furniture in the room. If she hid the book there, it would be found within seconds.

If there was nowhere to conceal the book, then she'd leave it in the stack of volumes on the table.

In plain sight.

*   *   *

An hour later, Julian looked down at Plum, panting gently by his side in the library. Elspeth hadn't returned. Which . . . was a disappointment.

He scowled.

She could at least take care of her dog.

"Come on, then," he said to Plum.

The dog stood at once, following Julian as he made his way back to the kitchen. He heard dishes clinking together as he neared, so he wasn't entirely surprised when he entered and found Elspeth bent over the hearth.

"Oh." She looked up and then straightened. "I was heating the stew for luncheon."

He nodded and crossed the flagstone floor to let Plum out. The dog took one look at the downpour and tilted his head up to Julian in a plea.

"You have to go out," Julian said gruffly. "Go on."

The dog glumly splashed outside.

"Thank you for tending to him," Elspeth said from behind him.

He shrugged, watching Plum come racing back inside again.

The dog shook, spattering him with muddy drops.

Elspeth giggled.

He turned and saw her holding both her hands over her mouth, her blue eyes gleaming.

"I'm sorry," she said, not sounding sorry at all.

"You are?"

For some reason, his words resulted in another round of giggles.

"Here," she finally gasped. "Sit at the table, and I'll serve us."

He complied, watching as she set the bread and cheese on the table and brought bowls of stew.

"I think you must like dogs," she said as she cut the bread.

He looked down at the stew, poking at a potato. "Perhaps."

"Only perhaps?" She glanced at him as she took a sip of wine.

He let his spoon drop, no longer hungry. "I had a dog as a boy. A terrier. He hated badgers. Used to chase them down their own burrows. I was always worried that a badger would kill him one day, but that never happened."

Julian bit into a slice of bread, not tasting anything.

"What happened to him?" Elspeth asked.

"I don't know. He disappeared after Augustus arrived at Greycourt. Aurelia had died, Mother was dying...I didn't have time to mourn a silly terrier." His voice had gone gruff by the end of the sentence. *Tom had been a good dog.*

A hand suddenly covered his on the table.

"I'm sorry," she whispered. "I'm sorry my brother hurt Aurelia, that your father died and then your mother, and your ghastly uncle took charge of your life."

He glanced up and saw to his surprise that there were tears in her eyes.

She swiped at them with her other hand. "I don't know why Ranulf did the thing he did. But I'm sorry you lost your sister because of him."

Except he hadn't. Julian blinked at the thought. Aurelia had been dead before Ranulf had come to Greycourt.

He opened his mouth.

Ranulf had been tarred black because of Aurelia's death and the rumors around it. If he told her, she wouldn't understand. *He* hardly understood the events of that night and why he'd had to betray both his best friends.

Julian shut his mouth. He could never tell her.

His guilt felt like an anchor sunk into the fleshiest part of his soul—heavy and unbearable and dragging him down.

They ate the rest of the meal in silence before returning to the library.

Plum at least looked relieved to lie on the carpet by the fireplace again. Julian was careful to put several more logs on the fire.

Then they returned to work.

Oddly, they worked together well, he placing the books to be examined on her right, she looking through each volume before placing them to her left, where he in turn picked them up to return them to the shelves.

Careful. Calm. Precise.

The room was infernally quiet, save for the turning of pages and the squeak of the library ladder. Julian should've settled into a bored routine. Instead he felt himself tighten. Needs, wants, the woman sitting at his feet, all combined into a terrible, waiting stillness. He could feel it in his chest, a stifled cry that if he let it go would continue on and on and on.

God, he wanted her.

More, he wanted her to tell him what to do. To lift all duty and expectation and fear from him so that he could float, entirely mindless save for her orders and pleasure.

Somewhere inside him, he was aware that he was putting these needs on the wrong woman. A woman both naive and, if he was right, a virgin. Elspeth would have no idea what to do with him.

But he couldn't help the fact that he was exquisitely aware of every movement she made. Of the curling strands of hair at the back of her neck. Of the scent of wild roses that seemed to linger in the air.

Was he going mad?

Julian closed his eyes. He was in control. He'd made it through more than a month of starvation in London. He was above his rude bodily urges. He didn't need release or pleasure. He could survive without.

"Are you all right, Mr. Greycourt?" came her throaty voice.

He opened his eyes and could think only how he wanted her to call him intimately by his Christian name. To order him into calm.

That...that wasn't possible. She was young and sweet. Any coarse thoughts concerning her were damnable.

Only a base villain would think of her in that way.

Helplessly, he looked at her plump, pink lips and her soft, dimpled hands and sensed that she was about to command him. To ask him to...

No. *No.*

"Mr. Greycourt?" she said quietly. Slowly. As if in anticipation.

He shook his head, attempting to drive the image from his mind. "Call me Julian."

His voice was curt, but she appeared unsurprised by his unseemly request. "Julian."

The sound of his name on her tongue was a delicious agony. "I'm fine."

"You don't look fine." Her brows were knit.

Jesus. He couldn't stand this anymore.

"I'm sorry," he muttered, turning away. "I should see to my horses."

He exited the room before she could respond.

* * *

Elspeth watched the library door close behind Julian, feeling restless, almost angry. If only he'd talk with her. Tell her what was bothering him. Let her...

She shook her head. No. She had more important things to think about.

See to his horses. An obvious excuse to get away from her, but it would take at least half an hour, surely?

Elspeth rose, shaking out her skirts.

Plum raised his head where he sprawled on his side near the fire.

"Stay," she said firmly.

He blinked and laid his head back down, but whether it was because of her order or because he liked the warmth of the fire more than following her, she wasn't sure.

In any case, this was her chance.

When Julian had found her in the library yesterday, she'd been thinking only of excuses so he wouldn't make her leave his house. It wasn't until later that she realized how silly she'd been. In between looking through the books in the library, she'd been stealthily searching the rooms in case the diary wasn't in the library. But she'd started at the far east wing.

She hadn't gotten to Julian's bedroom.

More fool she. Had she known that Julian would make a surprise appearance at Adders, she would've started with his bedroom. After all, wasn't the master bedroom the most likely place to hide something?

Elspeth gathered her skirts in her hands and ran down the hallway, stopping only to look in both directions before pushing open the door to Julian's bedroom.

The room was gloomy with only the light from the window. The bed was bigger than hers, the hangings probably once a rich wine red, though now they were limp and dusty, and it was obvious the moths had been at them.

There was more furniture than in her room. That made sense since he was the master of the house and presumably was in residence at times. She began with the desk near the window. It was an unfortunate Jacobean piece, heavy and overcarved and, frankly, ugly.

Elspeth pulled out drawers, both big and small, peering into recesses and probing the carvings to see if there were any hidden compartments. All she found was a broken quill, dried ink in a bottle, and a mouse nest at the back of one of the drawers.

She straightened, blowing a lock of hair out of her eyes. There was a bundle of saddlebags under the window, but Julian had just brought those.

She quickly searched the bedside table and the mantel around the fireplace.

How much time did she have remaining?

Elspeth didn't know, but she still had the bed to go. It was high enough off the ground that she could slide underneath it if she lay on her back. Julian's maids were not particularly thorough in cleaning. Elspeth sneezed three times in a row as she used her hands to feel about the boards and frame of the bed. Nothing.

She stood and brushed the dust from her skirts, wrinkling her nose. The headboard was of the same time period as the desk, so she crawled onto the bed and, kneeling on the pillows, began to feel around the carved faces. But again she found nothing.

Frowning, she sat back on her heels before climbing down once more and began looking under the feather mattress. There were two mattresses on the bed, the one below stuffed with horsehair. As she lifted both to look around under the head of the bed, she felt something hard between them.

Excitement shot through her. Sticking her hand under the feather mattress, she pulled out a square red book a little bigger than the width of her hand.

She opened the book.

At once she could see that it wasn't Maighread's diary, for the book was printed. She stared at it anyway. It was in a language she didn't recognize, but below the title was the figure of a blindfolded man kneeling at the foot of an equally nude woman holding a stick above her head.

The man's penis was erect.

A thrill like the plucking of a string went down the center of her body, landing in her cunny.

She turned the page.

The next held text, but the one after that depicted another nude man, this one bound to a cross laid sideways in the shape of an X. A fully dressed woman stood to his side with a flail. It might've been a scene of martyrdom save for the fact that again the man's cock stood tall.

In the next illustration, a tumescent penis filled the page, a sort of ring at the base, binding the flesh tightly.

Shouldn't that hurt?

She shook her head and looked further. There were many scenes of kneeling or prostrate men being whipped or flailed or beaten by women and men. Sometimes the naked men were forced to do humiliating things such as lick the shoes of a fully dressed woman. Often the nude men writhed as if they were in agony. Other times they shot their seed into the air.

But it was an illustration nearly halfway into the book that made her pause. It depicted a woman sitting on a chair holding her skirts above her knees. Before her knelt a man, his hands tied behind his back, his head buried between her thighs.

Elspeth couldn't help but squeeze her own thighs together. Something about the man's naked buttocks on his heels and the woman smiling down at him as she petted his head made her want to squirm. One couldn't see the man's face, only the back of his head between the woman's spread thighs. But the position made her think of what he might be doing so close to her quim. Was he kissing her there between her folds?

Was he licking her?

The door to the bedroom opened, making Elspeth start.

Julian Greycourt stood there, his black hair sternly bound into a braid, his light-gray eyes staring at her. "What are you doing?"

CHAPTER TEN

That book. Julian stared at Elspeth, sitting so casually
by the side of his bed, that damned red book open in her
hands. All his depraved desires were within that book.
All his guilt and shame. Everything that he feared, everything he had to hide from the world. Everything that could
destroy him if the wrong people knew.

And yet that book also held the entirety of his helpless
yearning.

Elspeth de Moray held his soul in her soft little hands.

"What are you doing here?" he asked again, and he
knew his voice sounded desperate.

She looked at him as if assessing him and said, "I was
searching for the diary in case it had been hidden here."

"That's not the diary," he snapped as she rose with the
book and took a seat on his bed. "How dare you—"

"Do you like such things?" she asked, and her eyes were no longer even on him as she carefully smoothed the page.

He didn't know how to answer. The question was so beyond the bounds of propriety that—

"I think you must," she mused. "Otherwise, why would I have found it between your mattresses?"

He licked his lips. "Another might have put it there."

"No." She gently shook her head. "The maids would have found it before now when they make the bed." She crinkled her nose and said almost to herself, "They must make the bed, even if they don't dust under it."

His mind had stopped working. He should be shouting, should be ordering her from the room. Instead he merely stood before her and felt his cock swell.

"No," she said again. "*You* put this book under your mattress. Close to you when you lay down on the bed. Within reach should you wish to peruse it in the night." She glanced down again. "It's nothing like anything I've seen before. I think…" She turned a page and her voice lowered to a whisper. "I think you must like it very much to keep it so close to you."

"I do," he said, and saying it aloud was like a dam breaking, the water sluicing out, unrestrained and roiling free. His shoulders relaxed even as he held his breath, ready for condemnation from her.

She only shot him a look from beneath her eyelashes before returning to the page.

Julian wanted to walk closer and see which page she was so intent on, but something held him where he stood. If only…

"Is it the pain?" she asked, a small line between her brows. "Is that what makes this book special?"

"Sometimes." He swallowed. "Sometimes it's merely..."

He trailed off. He couldn't say it. Not to her. He wanted suddenly to flee the room. Take his filthy needs with him.

But as he turned, she held up a hand. "No. Don't leave."

She didn't even look away from the book. As if she simply expected him to obey.

And he did, standing almost quivering before her.

She turned a page. "Do you require more than one person?" She flashed him another look. "Perhaps a man?"

She sounded utterly calm. Utterly unjudgmental.

"I..." Why couldn't he say the words?

"Tell me," she commanded. "Do you need more than one person?"

"No." He inhaled desperately. "I don't like to be the object of spectacle." Thank God, for his secret would certainly have been found out if he did.

"And a man? Do you require that?"

He closed his eyes. "Once...once I submitted to another man's prick. With my mouth. But I found I didn't enjoy it."

He opened his eyes. Surely *now* she would be appalled.

But she only hummed thoughtfully. "I see."

There was a silence broken only by the sound of pages turning.

Why was he still standing here before her? His cock was pressed against the placket of his breeches. He was exposed, stunned, without control.

She sighed softly. "Which illustration do you like the most?"

"There are several." He shook his head. "I should go. This is—"

"I think, actually," she interrupted in that low, throaty voice, "that you should undress."

He stopped breathing.

If she'd shown any hint of uncertainty, he'd have stridden from the room.

But her pretty sky-blue eyes were implacable. "Now, please."

He took off his coat, watching her as he dropped it to the floor.

She merely raised her eyebrows.

His waistcoat and shirt came off more quickly, followed by his shoes and stockings, which made him feel a bit of a fool, wobbling before her.

His cock throbbed.

When he reached for his falls, he hesitated and looked at her.

One corner of her curved lips twitched up. "Go on."

He swallowed and stepped out of his breeches.

He thought he heard a small inhalation, but he could no longer look at her.

The room was quiet as he unbuttoned his smallclothes, his hands brushing against his hard prick.

And then they fell and he was exposed before her, breathing in. Breathing out. His shoulders trembling with everything he needed.

"You're beautiful," she whispered. "I've wanted to tell you that since the first day I saw you in Windemere library."

He wanted...he wanted to preen beneath her gentle praise. To debase himself and let her kind words flow over his back, a salve for all his wounds.

"Come here," she called. "Kneel before me."

Slowly, he lowered himself to the floor.

"Right here." She pointed in front of her.

He shuffled forward, his cock tapping against his stomach, already beginning to leak. He kept his head down in submission so he was watching as her skirts began to rise over stockings, over knees, until they bunched on her sweetly curved thighs.

Then she parted her legs.

He stared at her pretty quim, her curling golden-red bush, her folds gently parted and glistening. For a second, he froze, rebelling. She was too pure. He couldn't do this to her, draw her into his depravity.

But even as his shoulders tensed, she laid her hand on his head. "Don't think." He saw out of the corner of his eye as she kicked off her slipper and bent to draw off a stocking.

Then she was wrapping it over his eyes.

"Don't think," she murmured again. "Don't worry."

He felt her tie the stocking behind his head.

Her hands cradled his face as she whispered, "Just lick me."

* * *

Her heart was flying, a swallow sailing high, soaring into the sun.

Julian knelt at her feet. His broad shoulders bowed, the long tail of his hair falling over his chest. He had very little hair on his upper body, but below his navel, a line of black hair led to his cock, flushed an almost purplish red, standing proud and thicker than she had expected. A drop of liquid trembled at the slit.

He raised his hands, broad but elegant, the fingers long and strong, and placed them on her legs, gently spreading them farther apart as he drew closer. All she could see now were his shoulders, the top of his head, her stocking blinding him, and his big hands on her white thighs.

"Lick me," she ordered, her voice breathy, and watched, rapt, as he bent his head.

A touch gentle and moist on the tender skin of her thigh. She could feel his mouth against her as he kissed his way to her cunny.

And then...

Oh, his tongue was hot. He licked delicately around the edges of her cunny, nudging between the inner and outer folds. Teasing. Making her tremble with anticipation.

"Further," she whispered, tightening her hold on his head, digging her fingers through the strung-tight locks of his hair. "Deeper."

He obeyed her words.

He moved his hands up to frame her center, and his thumbs held her open and apart as he licked firmly between her folds. The sound was obscene and sent a shiver through her.

Even as she shifted her hips in the tiniest movement, she wondered if he would need guidance to the perfect spot. But he licked upward with surety.

And then he stopped.

She waited, breathing. Was he disobeying? Had he come to his senses and decided he did not want this?

She could feel his breath, a warm caress against her wet skin, and then the tip of his tongue, almost tentative, licking around her pearl.

Oh, he knew what he did. He knew what pleasure he could bring her. And the teasing of that small, wet point, circling her flesh, enticing and yet never quite close enough, made her thrust against him.

Demanding more.

She felt his tongue flatten frankly against her, lapping at that part of her where all her pleasure centered. She gasped, throwing back her head. She'd touched herself there, but to have another do it, to have *Julian* do it, was unbelievably erotic.

She heard herself making foreign noises—a moan, a fractured gasp—and spread her legs as wide apart as she could, demanding he continue.

And he did, holding her hips still as he covered her with his mouth, still licking, still pleasuring her.

Oh Goddess. Oh Goddess, this was too terrible. Too wonderful. Her heart was galloping in her chest, she couldn't draw breath, and then it happened. A pulsing explosion, beautiful and complete, spreading outward in a warm wave to the very tips of her toes and fingers.

She lay there for unknowing minutes, simply feeling. Simply catching her breath.

And when she came to awareness again, she heard an odd sound. Moist. Rhythmic.

Suggestive.

Elspeth struggled upright to look down between her legs.

Julian knelt there like a Greek supplicant before a goddess, his head thrown back, his neck corded with tense muscle. He had removed her stocking and his face was one of agony, his mouth open and shining, his eyes squeezed shut. It was an expression that made her want to hold him, to console him in his extremity. And between his thighs, his fist worked, sliding and gripping his penis.

It was enormous now. Far bigger than any illustration she'd seen, scarlet with rage, veins entwining its length.

She watched, enthralled, as he bit his bottom lip, his

features twisting, until a spume of liquid burst forth from the tip, falling in pearly drops in her maiden hair and onto his thighs.

For a second, his head dropped, slumping between his shoulders, but then he looked up, and his expression was so vulnerable that her heart gave a pang. He looked boyish, his eyes wide, his mouth soft and uncertain, and he jolted to his feet as if he would run.

"No," she said softly, gently, as if instead of the arrogant, cynical Mr. Greycourt, he were a roebuck, poised to run from a clearing. "Stay. Stay with me. Please?"

She slowly held out her hand, half-afraid he would startle and bound away, and for a moment, he merely gazed at her, his gray eyes lost.

She curled her fingers, beckoning him to her.

He blinked and then came forward.

She took his hand and pulled him down to the bed, scooting over so he had room. He lay stiffly, not moving, until she pushed his shoulder, indicating he should roll over, his back to her.

Then she carefully wound her arm over his waist, snuggling. He was bigger than she, and she couldn't get both arms entirely around him, but it was near enough as she pressed her front to his back. She sighed a little, enjoying the nearness, feeling affection swell for this prickly man.

Julian relaxed, little by little, as if still waiting for something dire to happen. He was naked, of course. She hadn't pulled down the coverlet on the bed, but she was still dressed.

She curled her feet inside her skirts, throwing what she could over his legs. Then she hugged him close and lay her head against his bare back.

She could hear his heartbeat, thumping steadily, and she thought how nice this was, to lie together, silent in the midafternoon, his back rising minutely under her cheek as he breathed.

Thump. Thump. Thump...

* * *

Julian woke feeling refreshed, and for a moment he didn't know where exactly he was. The canopy above was familiar. He blinked and blinked again. This was his bed at Adders. He lay in his own bed, naked atop the covers, and there was a woman's hand on his stomach.

He stared.

Lady Elspeth de Moray's hand.

He sat up so abruptly the bed shook.

Elspeth was lying behind him, her cheeks flushed with sleep, her golden hair falling about her shoulders.

She yawned and stretched like a kitten and then tucked her fists back under her chin. Sleepy sky-blue eyes met his. "Aren't afternoon naps decadent?" she murmured. "I never feel so very boneless and warm at night."

For a moment, he could not answer—his mind had gone entirely blank—and when he did, his voice was hoarse. "I debauched you."

She hummed doubtfully. "I truly don't think so. After all, it was me giving the orders."

He felt the blood rise in his face. He was sitting here nude with his spend dry upon his thighs, and she lay there entirely composed and dressed. He took a breath. "You've lain with a man before."

"No." She watched him, her pink lips curving slightly.

"I haven't done more than kiss a boy once. He was the blacksmith's son and very handsome, though *not* very smart."

"Then..." He could feel his brows knit. "How can you do this"—he gestured to the bed they were in—"so naturally?"

"Books, I suppose," she answered. "There are many books about bedsport—so many! Some ancient, some quite recently printed. They come illustrated and not, and the illustrated ones vary. I've seen books with tiny colored paintings flecked with gold and others with quite crude drawings. Some books talk of coupling as if it were a heavenly rite. Others call it filthy, but still describe it in detail." She paused a moment. "But I only really have knowledge through books. Was I incorrect? Did you not enjoy what we did?"

"I...I did enjoy. Everything," he admitted. Good God, more than enjoyed. But then he pulled himself together. "Yet I've done a terrible disservice to you, Lady Elspeth. I am perverted. My desires are not like normal men's, they've been twisted out of shape. My touching you is an abomination itself."

She had her head cocked, observing him as if he were a strange volume found in an unexpected place in her library. "But I liked what you did. What *we* did together. You and I."

He shook his head, turning away to look for his clothing. "You don't know what is normal between a man and a woman. I've led you astray." He found his smallclothes and donned them before reaching for his breeches.

Behind him a great sigh came from the bed, and he couldn't stop himself from looking.

Elspeth lay indolently on his bed, an enticing Delilah

painted by Rubens, her eyes half-lidded as she watched him. "You keep saying that, but I assure you I don't feel led astray."

For a mad moment, he wondered if *she* was the one seducing, cutting away everything he knew to be true in the world, leaving him shorn and vulnerable.

Then he shook his head, dismissing such folly as he strode to the door with the rest of his clothing. "You are. I've corrupted you. Stay away from me, Elspeth."

He didn't quite slam the door shut, but it was close. Julian strode away down the hallway, feeling ridiculous that he'd been chased from his own bedroom.

He couldn't have stayed any longer, though. He'd been hardening even as they spoke. Her voice was so innocent as she talked about "bedsport" and her eyes so knowing. He'd found himself wanting to sink to his knees before her. To feel again that wonderful loss of thought as he worshipped her. To let her simply command him.

But he must not let his urges take control again. Bad enough that he'd shown her such sins once. To continue would be...

Would be...

He slammed his fist into the wall as he passed, letting the pain of his knuckles clear the lustful thoughts from his head.

He was almost running now, taking the stairs down in dangerous leaps.

Julian skidded to a halt before the library door, his chest heaving.

Control.

He needed to wrest back his control. Tie his desires tight to himself and cloak them in indifference. Could he do it now that he'd let himself free with her once? That indescribable bliss of submitting to her, of flying free without plan or thought or fear, had been heady. He'd never felt it with a woman he'd not bought for the night. For her to tell him she enjoyed it as much as he . . . was that not something he could let himself explore?

But no. What he wanted—craved—from her was not something a gentleman did with a lady. Had Elspeth been at all worldly, she would've known to be disgusted.

No. A man who had such abhorrent lusts turned to lesser-known houses of ill repute. To women who wielded canes and whips with eyes deadened by the world and circumstances.

Men like him didn't deserve a woman with kind blue eyes and a sunlit smile.

* * *

Stay away from me.

That was what Julian had said. *Humph.*

Elspeth scowled as she walked down Adders's upper hall, Plum trotting beside her. She could do that. She could continue searching the rooms that she'd not done before Julian had arrived. She could *stay away* from him for the rest of the day and tomorrow as well.

And his words wouldn't bother her *at all*.

Except that was a lie, and Elspeth really didn't like lying to herself.

His words had hurt her—more than they should have if she and Julian had simply enjoyed bedsport.

She halted before a door with a crooked knob.

Her head sagged. The thing was, she liked talking to him. He listened to her, even when she said something that didn't fit within his view of the world. And she liked listening to him. She had a notion he told her things that he told no one else. It made her feel warm. Soft. As if they were in a cozy space all of their own.

Except he obviously did not feel the same.

She yanked at the doorknob. There was a screech of metal on metal, and the door reluctantly gave. The room inside was dark and from the sudden itching of her nose quite dusty as well.

"Stay," she said to Plum, unsure if he'd obey, but the dog looked in the room and promptly sat on the floor outside.

Elspeth crossed the room to pull back the heavy drapes over the window. The fabric disintegrated in her hands, half of the curtains falling to the floor. Dim sunlight struggled through the dirty panes of glass.

Julian kept so much of himself hidden. She had to tip-toe around his walls, careful to not set off any concealed traps, because if she did, his words became cutting.

She looked around the room, which seemed to hold a jumble of furniture. There was a chest, and she knelt by it to lift the lid.

Or attempted to, anyway. The chest was evidently locked.

Elspeth blew a strand of hair away from her face and made a mental note to come back to the chest later. Nearby was a wingback chair with its horsehair stuffing spilling out from several tears. She dutifully felt about in the stuffing and surprised a nest of mice but found no diary. She searched the rest of the room—quite tediously—but found nothing save more mice.

By this time, Elspeth felt covered in filth. She glanced down at her sturdy dress and realized she'd have to sponge it off or risk trailing dust everywhere she went.

Which meant going down to the kitchens. She rose to her feet and stomped defiantly out of the storage room. If Mr. Greycourt was in the kitchen, it was only his own fault that he'd see her. After all, she couldn't *stay away* from their only source of food.

But the ground floor was empty, and the library door had been closed when she passed it.

The kitchen proved to be empty as well, which Elspeth should've been relieved by but was not. An old clock sat on a cupboard shelf, and she could see it was only four of the clock. Mr. Greycourt probably wouldn't have need to enter the kitchen before supper, which was hours away.

Elspeth stirred up the dying embers from this morning's fire and added more wood until it was well ablaze. Plum trotted over and slumped on the hearth. She hung a full kettle of water over the fire to warm.

She turned to the kitchen table and began undressing. Her cap was a sad gray, as was the apron pinned to her bodice. Her kerchief was equally dingy, but the jacket beneath wasn't entirely dusty—it just needed a good shaking out. Her skirt was the worst, but the quilted petticoat was also dirty around the hem. Her bum roll was fine, which was good because she had no idea how to wash it.

Elspeth wore only her stockings, shoes, stays, and chemise as she examined her poor wardrobe. The linens she bundled and set by the fire. They would need a proper wash. She shook the jacket into a dark corner of the kitchen. Properly she should do it outside, but just the thought of standing in the cold wind in her underclothes made her shiver. She'd just have to remember to sweep the kitchen when she was done.

Beating and sponging her skirt and petticoat was hard work, but they looked much better when she was done. It took another hour to wash her linens and sweep the floor. She was too tired to fill the bathtub, but she could wash her hair and face at least.

The warm water felt lovely on her cheeks, and she was just about to comb through her clean but wet hair when she heard a footstep behind her.

"What are you doing?"

CHAPTER ELEVEN

*Lady Long-Nose taught Christina all she knew
about poetry and beautiful words, but no matter how
Christina tried, none of the lessons seemed to
stick in her brain.
"Whatever shall I do?" Christina cried.
Lady Long-Nose knew what she must do, for Sabinus
would never love her. She gave Christina her own
letter and said, "Give him this."*
—From *Lady Long-Nose*

Julian was transfixed by the scene before him.

Elspeth wore only her chemise and stays, the light from
the fire behind her almost revealing her form. The curve
of her arse was tantalizingly close to being exposed. He
could see the press of her stays into her soft back, the way
her arms curved so gently from her shoulders.

And when she turned, her breasts were pushed into
beautifully plump mounds. Her chemise was embroidered
simply at the neck with blue flowers, and he followed the
thread with his eyes. Was that the pink of a nipple? Or was
he seeing things he wished were there?

"I'm bathing," Elspeth said.

It took him a moment to parse the meaning of her
words. He blinked. "Your hair is wet."

"Yes, it is," she replied kindly. "Wet and rather hard to comb." She gestured to the curled tangles.

"I could..." He cleared his throat, but his voice was still husky. "I could comb it for you. Before the fire."

She merely looked at him for a moment. "I thought you wanted me to stay away."

He had. He'd said that to her. "I..." His mind was a complete blank. *Don't hold me to my words*, he wanted to say. *Please let me in.*

She held out the comb, and he couldn't help but think she looked like some innocent Eve, newly born and unaware of her power, offering the apple.

He should walk away.

He meant to walk away.

His hand grasped the comb instead.

Julian took a breath and gestured to the hearth. "If we move closer, your hair will dry faster."

She nodded, and he dragged over two chairs.

She sat without further word, facing away as he took the chair behind her. He had to hitch the chair closer, spreading his legs to either side of hers, to comfortably reach the cascade of mane before him. Even then he hesitated. This was odd, surely. Elspeth sitting in her underclothes, the only sound the crackling of the fire and the soft snoring of the mutt. This was something outside the bounds of society—indeed outside his personal experience. To sit close to a woman without sexual intent—though the sensual tension was certainly high; to perform such a domestic act.

To comb her hair.

Elspeth made no move, said nothing at his silence and hesitation. She simply waited. Perhaps she thought of other things. The diary she searched for. Friends in London. Her dog.

But she shivered when he touched her nape, handling the mass of hair to bring it over the back of her chair. "Sit back," he said, his voice a deep scrape, as if he hadn't spoken for years.

She scooted until she rested against the back of the chair.

He took a breath and set the comb to her crown.

"No," she said softly. "It'll tangle more if combed from the top. Start at the ends and work up."

He nodded, though she could not see. The tips of her strands were heavy with water. He held them in his palm as he drew the comb through, water dripping to the floor. Did married men do this? Comb their wives' hair? Not in the ranks of the aristocracy, he was fairly certain. Ladies had maids to perform such services. Only a poor man might hold his woman's tresses and carefully sort the locks.

Or a man who dearly loved his wife.

Julian blinked, frowning at his work. He was not married. Or in love. So why did he perform this act? Was it a submission? A degradation, acting as her lady's maid?

But he did not feel degraded.

He felt...

Warm. Warm from the fire, certainly. Warm from the pulse of desire at the sight of her nape, gleaming in the firelight. Her body so close he could see the shadowed cleft of her bottom through the chemise. The soft, rose-scented skin of her shoulders. But warm in another way as well. Her acceptance of his presence. The relaxed, almost boneless way she sat, her neck exposed. As if she trusted him at her back.

As if she thought him a friend.

That was where the warmth came from. He wanted to lean forward and kiss her damp nape. Wanted to turn her around and take her lips. Wanted to pull her into his arms and hold her there, perhaps forever, a bright light for his coiled darkness.

"What do you think we should have for supper?" she asked, startling him from his thoughts.

He cleared his throat, making sure to keep his hands steady so he would not pull her golden hair. "What is there?"

"Wellll...," she said, drawing out the word as if thinking. "The bread, of course, though I fear it's gone hard. Some cheese. A sack of potatoes and one of onions. A small bit of ham. The eggs are gone, but we still have oats, thank goodness. Apples. Oh, and I found a lovely cabbage and two turnips this morning."

Julian's mind was entirely blank. "I suppose we could eat ham, apples, and cheese."

She hummed doubtfully. "The thing is, I don't think that's enough to fill both of us up."

"Then what do you suggest?" Red glinted in the soft locks he was combing, her hair curling around his fingers as he worked, like a happy cat napping in the sun.

"Soup." She bounced on the seat. "Hot soup is lovely on a dreary rainy day."

He cocked an eyebrow, even if she couldn't see it. "And you know how to make such a soup?"

"Yes?" She glanced over her bare shoulder at him, a skeptical siren. "Don't most people?"

He eyed her curiously. "Most common people, certainly. But most ladies? I very much doubt it."

"Oh." She turned to face forward again, hiding her expression from him. "Well, I learned cooking and other useful tasks when I was young, lady or not."

When she was young? Had Ran lost his family's wealth somehow? Why else would his sister—the sister of a landed duke—be forced to learn how to cook? But perhaps it was some sort of rustic education. A Scottish urge toward self-sufficiency even in the highest ranks of society.

That didn't sound right, either.

He cleared his throat. "What other things did you learn?"

"The usual." She waved a hand vaguely. "Geography, Latin, philosophy, arithmetic, Greek, history, and geometry."

Geometry?

She inhaled. "Cooking, cleaning, sewing—"

Those are feminine tasks at least.

"Hunting, trapping, swimming, and swordsmanship—"

What?

"How to shoot and how to ride a horse. Though"—she sounded wistful—"not how to ride sidesaddle as ladies do here. That looks rather more difficult."

She rode astride? He'd never seen a lady do such. It simply wasn't done.

He waited, but she seemed to have run out of accomplishments. "Anything else?"

"Oh," she exclaimed as if his prompt had made her remember something. "How to pick winkles at low tide. Though I suppose that's not really a skill. One simply waits for low tide and takes them off the rocks."

He blinked in confusion. "Winkles?"

She laughed. "Periwinkles. Sea snails, if you like.

They're lovely boiled in seawater. It was one of my favorite dishes growing up."

He'd stopped combing her hair, staring incredulously at the drying locks in his hands. "You enjoyed eating *snails*."

She turned almost all the way around then and smiled at him, her cheeks flushed in the warmth of the fire, her pink lips curved sensuously, her hair falling like a red-gold waterfall over her shoulder. She might've been painted by Botticelli, a Venus emerging from the sea.

"Yes, *snails*," she replied teasingly, oblivious to his thoughts. "Snails are delicious. One pokes them out of their shell with a little prick."

He felt a tightening in his loins at the innocent remark. How could she not know the other meaning to the word?

He muttered under his breath before he could censor himself, "I'd think a large prick would be preferred."

"I'm sorry?" she asked, her expression completely open.

How could this woman be the same one who had ordered him to perform such lascivious acts this morning? How could she leave him weakened and at her mercy and at the same time become excited by books and oatmeal and snails?

Why did Elspeth enthrall him so?

* * *

Elspeth stared at Julian, and for the life of her, she could not read his expression. Was it the winkles? Was he appalled at the thought of eating such common fare? She couldn't tell.

"I promise," she said softly, "not to put snails in the soup."

He blinked at that, his head tilting slightly, as if he were trying to see her in a dim light. His words, though, were dry as dust. "I'm most relieved."

She bit her lip to hold back a laugh, and his gaze went immediately to her mouth. "Would you like to help?"

"Help what?" he murmured, his gaze unshifted. His eyelids were half-lowered, giving him a drowsy, sultry look, as if the heat of the fire had melted him into a more unrestrained man.

She couldn't help the pressing together of her thighs. She wanted to lean forward and smell his heated skin. Wanted to open his shirt and lick his throat.

What had they been talking about?

"Soup." She stopped to swallow. "That is, would you like to help make the soup?"

He considered, and she rather expected that he'd decline. He'd been adamant about staying away from her before. And he'd had a cook to prepare his food for him. Perhaps he considered cooking beneath him.

She held her breath.

"Yes," he said in a low voice, surprising her. "I think I'd like to discover how to make soup."

Her smile couldn't be contained, spreading over her face, bunching her cheeks, proclaiming her happiness to all. "Oh, good." She felt her hair. It was nearly dry. "Are you done combing?"

"Ah." He looked at the hand holding her comb as if he'd forgotten it was there. "No, not yet. Nearly, though."

She turned to present her back and felt his fingers at the crown of her head, parting, sifting her hair. He was gentle as he worked the comb through her tresses. Her hair was fine and apt to tangle, and she'd been left in tears many a time when she was very small and a servant dressed her hair.

Julian was slow, thorough, as if combing her hair was an important job to him. Even with the heat of the fire, she could discern his warmth against her back and know it came from the man, not the fireplace. She held as still as she was able, luxuriating beneath his hands.

A creak from his chair alerted her that he'd shifted, but his breath against her ear was a surprise nonetheless. "Done now."

The scent of limes and cloves enveloped her, and she took a moment to come to her senses. "Oh. Yes. Thank you."

She gathered her hair and braided it swiftly into a simple tail over her shoulder.

Elspeth glanced from her own braid to Julian's, as ever neat and orderly down his back. "We match, don't we?"

"My tail could never be as beautiful as yours," he said, looking at her intensely. "Your hair holds all the colors of firelight."

She could feel a flush of pleasure spread up her cheeks. "Thank you."

For a moment, they seemed locked in time, her gaze caught with his.

Then Plum rolled over with a groan.

"Erm..." She blinked, feeling as if she were waking from a deep sleep. "Soup. Yes. We'd better start the soup."

She rose, smoothing out her crumpled chemise, which made her realize she was still in her underthings.

"If you could fetch some onions and potatoes from the larder?"

He gave her an odd look but went to the larder readily enough.

Elspeth hurried to the kitchen table and drew on her still-damp padded petticoat, tying it about her waist as swiftly as she could. Her skirt at least was dry.

She had only one arm in her jacket when she heard a masculine throat clear. "Would you like help?"

She yanked the jacket together in the front, knowing that her face must be red as a radish and her hair coming down again.

"No, no, I'm quite capable," she replied breathlessly.

And she was because her sturdy dark-blue linsey-woolsey fastened up the front, unlike a lady's gown, which either had laces in the back or had a stomacher to pin. A maid or several were required for a lady's toilet, and even though Elspeth *was* a lady, she was quite fond of dressing herself.

She finished pinning together the bodice and looked up.

Julian was watching her, a slight frown between his brows. "Won't you be cold away from the fire?"

She glanced down at her bosom. Without her kerchief the bodice was quite low, exposing almost everything above her nipples.

"I'm sure I'll be just fine," Elspeth replied, her voice higher. He'd already seen her in just her chemise, of course, but somehow having her skirts and jacket on made the same expanse of bare skin feel more exposed. "I'll just fetch the ham, shall I?"

She darted into the larder and blew out a breath. Silly! Ladies wore gowns much lower than hers at every London ball. She had no reason to be so shy before Julian

Greycourt. He was an experienced man and probably inured to women's breasts.

She pushed away from the larder door and found the remains of the ham hanging in a corner, as well as the turnips and cabbage, and then had a peek at Mrs. McBride's herbs and spices. Salt, pepper, and a sprig of dried parsley should do nicely.

She brought the lot to the table, where she found Julian frowning at the potatoes as if they'd given him a terrible insult.

"What shall I do?" he growled at the vegetables.

"Peel and chop, of course," Elspeth replied cheerfully. "But first can you half fill a large pot with water from the cistern?"

He went to find a pot without a word.

Meanwhile Elspeth found Mrs. McBride's knives in a cupboard drawer and took them out, testing their sharpness against the edge of her thumb. Nodding to herself, she brought them to the table.

Julian was back with the pot of water, and Elspeth hung it over the fire. "Now," she said, straightening, "do you know how to peel potatoes?"

He arched an eyebrow, looking the very epitome of an aristocrat, which she took to mean no.

Her lips twitched. "I'll show you." She turned to march to the table and sat, gesturing to the chair next to hers. "Sit next to me."

"You've taken to ordering me about rather easily," he murmured as he lowered himself to the chair. His broad shoulders brushed against hers.

His words made desire coil in her belly. She darted a cautious look at him. "You liked it before."

He scowled at a potato. "That was in the bedroom."

"And the bedroom is different?" He seemed to draw boundary lines around himself that she was supposed to understand, but they were invisible to her.

"Yes." The word was clipped, and for a moment Elspeth thought it would be the only answer. Then he grimaced and said with seeming reluctance, "What happens in private and in the bedroom is entirely different than the everyday." He shot a severe glance at her. "I am not some weakling to be ordered about."

"No," she replied softly, "you are not."

She was rather astonished, in fact, that he thought he had to make that point plain to her. He was one of the strongest men she knew. He guarded his family without them entirely realizing. Kept himself apart and aloof from his sisters even though she knew it must hurt him.

After all, as John Donne wrote, "No man is an island, / Entire of itself."

Elspeth shifted in her seat and asked diffidently, "I hope you don't mind me instructing you?"

"No, I..." His scowl was replaced with lips pressed together until he continued, "No. Just as long as you..." He seemed to search for the right phrase.

"Just as long as I don't hold you in contempt?" she asked softly.

"Yes." His glance was an edged ice shard. "That."

"Well, I don't," she replied gently. Then she picked up a potato. "The main thing to remember when peeling is to take as thin a piece as possible. Otherwise you end with a large pile of peelings and a very small potato."

She used a paring knife to deftly make a paper-thin slice and then handed the knife over.

Julian took it, and in silence, they both peeled potatoes, Elspeth glancing over every now and again.

"This one is green," he said, his nose wrinkling.

Elspeth suddenly wondered if he'd been a picky lad in the nursery—one who would refuse his egg if it was too runny. She could imagine him wrinkling a tiny aristocratic nose.

She cleared her throat. "Pare away the green part if you can, otherwise leave it out. It'll spoil the soup otherwise."

She indicated where he should cut on the potato in his hand, and as she did so, her fingers brushed against his. Her nerves seemed to light at the touch, her fingers almost tingling, and she snatched back her hand.

But he caught her hand, holding it gently in his own.

She swallowed, looking down at his larger fingers around hers.

"Thank you," he said, sudden and gruff, "for teaching me."

His grip tightened before he let her go.

She curled her fingers against her palm as if she could keep the feel of his skin within her grasp, and said huskily, "You're quite welcome."

They resumed their task, but Elspeth caught herself watching Julian out of the corner of her eye. He was such a strange, complex man. This afternoon she'd thought they'd never speak again, and now they sat comfortably side by side. Yet he was contained, a part of himself always hidden. If she asked, would he consider her a friend?

Did he have friends?

Or only women he paid for a night? What a lonely life his must be, if so.

Once the potatoes were done, they chopped the onions—rather tearfully—as well as the cabbage and turnips. Elspeth threw them all along with the ham into the pot and adjusted its position over the embers so that the soup simmered gently.

She turned to find Julian watching her, his gray eyes unfathomable in the firelight.

"I've tried resisting you," he murmured, his voice deep. "Tried and failed." He closed his eyes as if in despair. "Elspeth, tell me what I should do."

She walked to him and framed his face with her hands. "Stay."

And then she kissed him.

* * *

Her kiss started so innocently, a simple brush of lips against lips. But then she widened her mouth, and he couldn't withstand her temptation. He pushed into her mouth, deepening the kiss even as he felt her gasp.

She pulled her face from his.

He started to follow, but she placed a palm between them. "No."

She must have seen the outrage he felt because she smiled, a small, secret smile. "I'm hungry. Let's eat."

And then she walked away, her skirts swaying provocatively. Was she playing with him?

"Sit down," she ordered without looking at him.

And he obeyed.

The fire haloed her head in a golden glow as Elspeth bent over it. She might've been a magical being, her arts arcane, but then she turned, and her smile was quite human.

She set the table, bringing the wine, apples, bread with melted cheese, and soup, and then sat opposite him. "What do you think? Tell me."

The question was ambiguous, but he said only, "A feast fit for kings."

"You're mocking me," she said in her husky voice, smiling, "but you haven't tasted my supper yet. I think you'll change your tune."

He couldn't care less about the food, truly. All he wanted to do at the moment was sit and watch her.

"Eat," she said softly, gesturing at the food.

Julian examined the soup. Thick chunks of cabbage and potato with smaller bites of ham swam in the broth. He'd never been served such a plain meal, but the aroma...

His first spoonful was too hasty, nearly searing his tongue, but it was worth the salt of the ham, the homely but oddly satisfying cabbage, and the familiar feel of potato. The whole was exquisite.

"It's delicious," he said.

Elspeth looked up, her cheeks a deep pink from the fire and perhaps his compliment. "Oh, I'm glad you like the soup. It's simple, but sometimes the best dishes are."

He tilted his head in consideration. "I'll not argue with that."

He watched her smile to herself. Her hair was a nimbus, escaping her loose braid and curling about her face and ears. As she leaned over her meal, her breasts pushed dangerously against her bodice, swelling as if they might escape confinement entirely. Her skin was luminous in the firelight, the palest of pinks, shining like satin.

Julian could, if he tried, look at her without bias. See that she was plumper than was considered pretty. Shorter than was elegant. With a face that many would think ordinary. Someone who might be lost in a crowd.

But to him she was the sun in the sky, shining more brightly than anything else on earth.

He should be uneasy at such attraction. She was neither like the aristocratic ladies of London whom he encountered every day nor like the prostitutes he hired covertly on occasional nights.

Elspeth was a woman apart, unique unto herself.

"Have some of the bread and cheese," she said, pushing the plate nearer to him. "I tried toasting the cheese on top of the bread. I can't tell if both are better this way or apart."

He transferred a piece to the plate beside his bowl and sawed it apart with a knife and fork before taking a bite. The bread was crisp, the cheese salty and soft.

Elspeth was waiting anxiously for his verdict, her face serious. "Well?"

Julian swallowed. "Good."

She sat back as if satisfied, but she continued to regard him as he ate.

He glanced up after his next spoonful of soup. "What is it?"

She blinked as if recalling herself. "I was just wondering if your conflict is because it's me."

"I don't understand," he said.

She leaned forward as if on impulse. "You don't know the women you usually hire, correct?"

"Ah." He took a sip of wine before setting the glass down. "I don't know if we should—"

"Tell me."

He stared at her. "We're not in the bedroom."

"No," she said, selecting an apple. "We aren't. If you don't want to play, don't answer me." Her gaze suddenly caught his. "But I will be disappointed."

He swallowed. "I don't know them."

She nodded. "But you know me. You know the woman who orders you about. I'm a person."

Then he understood what she'd been driving at. "And you think it makes a difference to me?"

"It must." She held her apple out to him. "Please cut it."

He took it and wondered if she had thought about the symbolism. Of course she had. Elspeth was far more clever than he'd first given her credit for.

She watched him prepare her apple. "I think the reason you are so unsure of me is because you know me. When you open to me, it isn't to a stranger you'll never see again."

Too clever. He wasn't sure he wanted to know such things about himself.

He offered her the plate of apple slices.

She looked at it consideringly, her ruby lips drawn together in a moue. "Would you like some?"

"Yes," he said, feeling hot.

She took a slice, biting into it, making her lips slick. "Here," she said, holding the same slice out to him.

He took the offering and ate it as she watched. Her eyes seemed to darken.

Silently, she took another slice of apple and bit into it. This time he accepted the slice without her having to ask.

In this way, they shared the apple, eating it all, sweet and tart.

The fire popped.

"I do not understand you," he blurted like a callow boy.

Her mouth curved, glistening in the candlelight from the wine. "Don't you?"

He shook his head, unable to take his eyes from her. "Elspeth," he whispered, "what shall I do with you?

You blow your horn, and all my walls crumble to dust. I am left exposed and confused, racked with a terrible longing."

She smiled then, and in the candlelight, that smile was as old as the Garden. "Then let me comfort you and bring you peace."

CHAPTER TWELVE

The next time Lady Long-Nose saw Sabinus, he
exclaimed, "Oh, my lady, you'll never guess! Sweet
Christina has written me a letter so full of wit and
poetry that I've fallen even more deeply in love with
her. I believe such talent has never
before been seen in a woman."
Lady Long-Nose smiled and nodded and vowed to
never tell her love the truth....
                                        —From *Lady Long-Nose*

A light tremble ran through her body. Elspeth wasn't
entirely sure what an experienced lady was expected to do
in this situation, but she knew what *she* wanted.

"Come here," she said, her voice so low it was husky.
"To my side."

He rose at once, prowling around the table as if he
stalked her. He halted before her.

She tilted her chin to look him in the eye. "Will you
kiss me?"

He knelt between her legs, his head on a level with
hers, and brought his palms up to frame her face. She
leaned forward, her hands braced on his shoulders, and
then, finally, he kissed her.

She closed her eyes, feeling his mouth brushing over

hers, causing her lips to tingle. She'd never realized how sensitive her lips were. How ready to part and receive him. But he didn't take her invitation. He teased her, his touch so light over and over again until she thought she might go mad from the sensation.

She moaned, breathless, wanting, turning her face, pressing against him as if she could force him to go further.

He slid his mouth to beneath her ear, and the skin there was sensitive as well. She turned her face, giving him more access, and felt him nip her earlobe.

"You taste like honey," he rasped, his breath on her wet skin making her shiver. "I might devour you. Swallow you whole."

He murmured his erotic threats as he drew his lips down the cord of her neck, lighting the nerves there, making her press her thighs together. Could she come from just this? From only his words and his lips on her skin?

He widened his mouth and put his teeth to her tendon, but didn't bite. Instead he dragged his teeth against her, the touch so light she could feel sparks along the trail he made.

She swallowed, the movement pressing against his mouth, and he traced her throat with his tongue, sinking lower until he licked between her collarbones.

She arched her head back at the sensation, groaning aloud, and her voice broke when she said, "Please."

Only then did he retrace his steps, dragging his teeth over her jaw, until his mouth took hers again.

He devoured her, just as he'd warned, his open mouth startlingly hot. He licked over her bottom lip and into her mouth, his tongue meeting hers and battling, sliding, encouraging, until the room dissolved and she simply floated in the ether, her entire being focused on his lips.

Only his lips.

He dragged his teeth across her cheek, making her whine, and whispered roughly in her ear, "Come to bed with me."

"Yes," she gasped. "Yes."

Julian stood, even as she reached for him, and took her hand, tugging her upright. His gray eyes were darkened, the shards of ice in them glinting as he led her swiftly from the kitchen, up the staircase, and into his room.

"Elspeth," he groaned, suddenly stopping and pulling her into his arms again. "Tell me if this isn't what you want. Send me away and leave me, but do it soon because if we go a step further, I'll be unable to stop."

"I won't," she whispered, touching his cheek, making him turn his face to mouth at her palm. Her heart beat almost painfully. "I can't."

He made no comment to that, simply waiting.

"Do what you want," she ordered.

At that he stood and began unpinning her bodice. "You've driven me mad tonight, do you know that? Standing before the fire in only your chemise and stays." He helped her off with the bodice and her skirts. "Flaunting these beauties in front of me."

He lowered his face to her breasts, still bound in her stays, and she felt the faint scrape of his beard against her delicate skin. Her cheeks heated. Her entire body felt as if it were aflame, and she shuddered when he lewdly thrust his tongue between her breasts.

He groaned against her skin and whispered, "I hate these stays. I loathe them. They shall be burned as soon as I have them off you."

"Would you leave me naked, then?" she asked, her voice low. "For I wouldn't be able to wear my jacket without them."

"Yes," he said jealously, working at the strings of her stays. "You may wear only your chemise and what blankets I can find, and you'll sit in state in the library and order me about."

She laughed helplessly at the silly image, catching his face gently in her hands, interrupting his labor at the gussets of her stays. "Is that what you'll do?"

He stilled, watching her, his eyes almost calculating. "Yes, if that's what you want."

"I think I do," she whispered. For now, in this place apart from the rest of the world. It was a pretty dream, after all.

"Then let me finish," he growled, and attacked the strings once more, loosening them until he could draw the stays over her head.

He reached for her chemise, and she felt a small qualm for the first time. She knew her form wasn't considered ideal by those in society. She'd overheard the nasty words a few ladies whispered about her. It had seemed childish. After all, she didn't mutter about other women's heights or noses or teeth or anything else they couldn't help. Some women were thin and some wide. Why fret over how the goddess had made them?

But while such ideals were easy for her to know intellectually, it was harder when another was the judge—a man whose opinion she cared about. Would he find her unlovely?

So she held her breath as he raised her chemise, waiting.

She needn't have worried. The look Julian gave her nude body was almost reverent, and when he gathered her overflowing breasts in his hands, it was as if he held a treasure.

"Soft," he whispered, his thumbs caressing her skin. He looked up at her almost in wonder. "You're so soft all over."

Her lips parted in yearning. "You're overdressed."

He nodded jerkily and led her to the bed. "Lie down for me."

She sprawled across the bed, watching as he tore at his clothes, his eyes roving over her, from her mouth to her neck to her nipples. Down to her belly and over the fine hair at the juncture of her thighs. He reached for his falls and stopped abruptly, closing his eyes as if to hold himself together. Then he stripped breeches and smallclothes and stockings all at once before he got in the bed, crawling to her.

He locked eyes with her as he lowered his mouth, watching her expression as he touched the tip of his tongue to her left breast.

She swallowed and then had to close her eyes to feel the way his damp tongue licked over her breast, making her nipple dimple and come awake. She was breathing fast, her breast pushing up into his face, asking for more. And she jerked convulsively when he opened his mouth and sucked.

Oh. Oh Goddess, she'd never known this small part of her could send such strings of desire throughout her entire body, linking her breast to her cunt, making her grow damp. He suckled at her, and she wanted...wanted to squirm. To touch herself as he drew on her nipple.

He stopped suddenly, and she almost cried out at the loss, but then he moved to her other breast, sucking at that nipple as he played with the one left behind.

And that...that was exquisite, pulling sparks from both tiny points that seemed to rush over her body. She found herself grasping at his hair, and for a fleeting second, she wished he'd unbound it so she could slide her fingers in and hold him, trapping him against her so he'd be forced to pleasure her until they both unraveled.

She was moaning now, she realized dimly. Arching against him, her body begging for more, and then he took her hand and dragged it from his hair, pulling it down her body and over her mound.

He lifted his head and gasped, "Please. God, please, touch yourself as I pleasure you," before returning to her nipples.

The words, uttered in that crystalline accent with such obvious need, sent a bolt of sweet desire down to her center, making her clench her thighs and feel the wetness between her folds.

He sucked relentlessly, giving her no time to think, and almost compulsively, she teased her way through her curls and into that hot liquid. She found her point of pleasure and petted there softly for now. She was so close that the smallest movement might make her meet her crisis.

He switched back to her first nipple, roughly laving it with his tongue, and at the same time he took the other nipple between his thumb and forefinger and pinched.

She cried out, quaking with the sudden overwhelming pleasure, once, twice, a third time, her nerves all alight, her very being lost completely to the bliss, and then shuddered once more, almost delicately, a last shocking thread of exquisite feeling before slumping back, her eyes closed, her chest heaving with the aftermath of her orgasm.

It took her unknowing moments before she realized that he was pushing his penis between her thighs. Not penetrating her, but thrusting fiercely between, her liquid making the way slick.

She opened her eyes to watch.

He groaned above her as if in pain and glanced up at her, his face transformed into awful pleasure, teeth bared, the muscles of his chest and shoulders held in taut relief.

"Tell me," he begged, plunging eagerly into her thighs. She could feel that hard, heavy muscle demanding his release. "Tell me I can."

Her eyelids were heavy, her body lax and slumberous, and for a moment, her mood was cruel. She smiled at him, biting her lip, wondering if she should keep him here in this state of strained desperation.

"Please," he ground out, the word nearly unrecognizable. "Please let me."

Only then did she whisper, "Come for me."

He shouted, his entire body arcing up and back, his muscles stiff and frozen, his mouth open as if in agony.

And his cock pulsing, pulsing hot streams of his release across her thighs.

*   *   *

The clock on the mantel in Julian's bedroom chimed eleven times and then made an odd *clunk*, which, Elspeth supposed, signaled midnight. He'd told her sometime before—at breakfast? At supper? In the library? That the clock was broken, but it seemed to keep time well enough.

Well. Except for that *clunk*.

She should be getting up, dressing, and either going straight to her own bedroom or continuing to search the house.

But she was so cozy in Julian's bed. He lay snug against her back, a pile of blankets and coverlets over them, surrounded by darkness, only their breathing breaking the silence of the room.

Warm.

Relaxed.

Cocooned.

The outside world might be a hazy dream. They might be the only people on earth, together and perfect.

Julian was awake as well. She knew it from how his fingers tapped against her ribs every now and again.

She inhaled and asked quietly, "Is it that you need someone else's permission to feel pleasure?"

He stiffened behind her, the hand on her side curling. "I don't like talking about it."

She nodded, though whether he could see or perhaps feel it in the dark she didn't know.

For several long moments, the room was quiet, though his fist didn't relax.

He blew out a breath against the back of her neck. "Perhaps. I...don't think about it overmuch. Aside from fearing I'll be found out." His voice held self-loathing.

She frowned and turned to look over her shoulder, but of course she couldn't see him. "Why would anyone care what you do in bed?"

His hand drew away. "You mock me."

"No." She turned over fully, catching the hand he tried to withdraw. "No, I didn't mean to insult you, truly. I just don't understand."

She faced him now, their noses only inches apart, and still she could make out only the faint outline of his head.

She had no idea of his expression, but she could hear the bitterness when he said, "Society is only interested if the activities in the bedroom are not the usual, by which I mean a man with a woman, the man dominant and on top. Anything else is considered exotic or repulsive, and as a result, people are immediately deeply, obsessively curious. They enjoy discovering weaknesses. Passing judgment. Laughing with contempt."

Elspeth knew well enough the base desire to hold something over another's head. Most children felt the emotion and grew out of it, although some perhaps especially childish adults never left it behind.

Still… "They—*you*—consider what we do exotic? Repulsive?"

The word made her realize how hurt she was at the thought that he hated what they had done together.

"I…" His voice trailed away in the dark until he cleared his throat. "I don't mean what you have done, understand. But a man who needs to bow before a woman, to be humiliated, sometimes hurt, is not a man at all. He's a worm. The most disgusting creature alive. They would quite literally pillory me for it."

"Then they are wrong," she whispered heatedly. "Stupid and wrong."

"Are they?" His voice was weary. "I think I should feel the same if I wasn't cursed with this affliction. Often I do. I can't be proud of my submission. It's unnatural."

Her brows drew together. "But if you consider yourself unnatural and the act itself unnatural, I don't see how you can say I'm not unnatural, too. That I'm not disgusting."

"You aren't disgusting." His tone was harsh. "You're the most beautiful—"

"No." She set her hand over his mouth, stopping him. "There are only two possibilities. Either our acts are normal, you are normal, and I am normal, or the act, you, *and* I are disgusting. There is no in-between."

He kissed her palm, the simple gesture made powerful by the trembling of his lips, as if he tried to express all his longing in one act.

"I don't think of you as anything but perfect as you are," he whispered into her hand as he let her go. "But the things we've done in this room are aberrant. I know this. All of society knows this, and if they found out, they would ruin you and me with absolute glee."

"Who are these people?" she asked fiercely. "Who decides what is natural and what unnatural? What do they base this judgment on?"

"The Bible and what the majority of people think."

"Where does it say in the Bible that a man should not want to be submissive to a woman for bedsport?" she hissed. "The Bible tells us it's a sin for a man to spill his seed on the ground. Should we hang every male between ten and twenty?"

"No, of course not. That's—"

"It's ridiculous. They pick and choose what they want from the Bible," she interrupted loudly. "They know it, and I know it. And what about this majority? If most of the people of London don't eat oat porridge, but most of the people in Edinburgh do, then who is right? Is oat porridge inedible or edible?"

She felt his fingertips against her cheek. "I don't know," he whispered. "Your arguments are sound in the abstract, but they don't reflect the everyday. People do judge. People do gossip. People do ruin men—and women—on rumor alone."

Frustration made her blurt, "But can't you see—?"

His touch against her lips was featherlight. "If Augustus ever found out what I like in the bedchamber, he would have me disgraced and shunned within days. All your arguments and philosophical ideas will not change that one fact."

His words sounded like a door shutting.

She drew breath and caught his fingers within hers desperately. "Can you at least admit that, aside from your uncle's opinion and society's rule, what you want isn't awful? Your needs involve only the person you are with. You hurt no one. How can you be an abomination? Tell me you no longer believe such lies."

Elspeth waited, her breath caught in her throat, for his reply. For his voice in the night repudiating his self-loathing.

In the silence, she heard nothing.

Finally she drew breath, her heart breaking. "Julian..."

His lips touched her own, as fleeting as a dragonfly alighting. "Sleep with me, Elspeth. Let the night bring us peace."

And truly she would've continued protesting, but their space under the covers was warm and safe, and she'd had a tiring day.

She turned so that he could wrap his arms around her and draw her close to his solid heat, and despite herself, she was comforted.

But as she sank toward the dreams awaiting her, she couldn't help an irksome worry.

That Julian's thoughts about himself would bring disaster.

* * *

Julian woke to the faint sound of voices somewhere within the house.

Elspeth lay next to him, her pretty lips parted, her cheeks flushed with sleep. He wanted to stay here with her, his arms holding her, relishing her soft warmth, but of course that was sentimental foolishness. They were about to be discovered, and if nothing else, he needed to protect her and her reputation.

"Elspeth," he said quietly, cupping her face, "wake up. We're no longer alone."

She moaned and turned her face into his hand, and the sight made his heart clench almost painfully.

"Elspeth, please."

She opened her eyes then, blinking at the dawning light. "What is it?"

He removed his hand. Their ideal world was over, and it was time to return to reality. "I think the servants have returned. You must go to your rooms before they discover you here."

"But why?" she whined under her breath, her eyes closing again.

"No." He laid his hand on her shoulder and shook her. "You must wake up, Elspeth."

"All right." She frowned in what looked like irritation.

She must know she faced social disaster if found in his bed. "Come. Get up."

He rose himself, swiftly throwing on breeches and a

shirt and splashing his face with the ghastly cold water in his basin.

When he turned back to the bed, Elspeth had risen only as far as sitting on the edge. "Elspeth. *Now.*"

She glanced up in alarm, his growled words no doubt startling her, but she was wasting time. Did she want to be caught?

He pushed the thought to the side and pulled her up, making her stand as he threw her chemise over her head and piled her arms with the remainder of her clothes. It took only a moment to find the hall empty before he hurried her to the room she'd been using.

"Get in the bed," he ordered sternly as she stood just inside the room, blinking sleepily at him. "You need to make it look as if you've been here all night."

With that he closed the door in her face and straightened, listening. He could still hear the voices faintly below, which hopefully meant the servants hadn't left the kitchen.

Striding swiftly back to his room, he threw on shoes and a banyan—the house was damnably frigid in the morning—and took the stairs down at a sedate pace.

By the time he'd made the kitchen, the voices had died. No doubt they'd heard him approaching.

Inside, the room was almost stiflingly warm. The fire was roaring, with Plum blissfully snoring on the hearth. Two women swiftly rose from the table where they'd been enjoying tea.

"A good morning to 'e, Mr. Greycourt," Mrs. McBride said sturdily.

He nodded to her and the maid, whose name he'd forgotten. "Might I have something to break my fast? In the library, I think."

"Aye, soon as the fire dies down enough to be cookin'," replied Mrs. McBride. "But I can bring th' tea in two ticks."

Julian nodded. "I take it that the roads are clear?"

"Mostly," that lady replied, sending a stern glance at the other woman. "Told Alice that we'd best be gettin' back to Adders now that some of the mud has dried."

"Indeed," Julian muttered. Neither woman looked particularly eager to return to her labors.

He left for the library, thinking as he did so that he could've waited another couple of days for the servants' return. Sharing the house with Elspeth had become natural so swiftly. He'd thought he'd had days left with her. To let go of his duties and the outside world and simply *be*.

But that was over now, and no use bemoaning the loss. Julian squared his shoulders as he entered the library and took a seat before the table. He stared out the window at the gray skies and the black tree trunks, ordering his thoughts.

He needed to return to London, discover if Lucretia had gotten safely away, and see what Augustus's reaction had been. His uncle had never taken defeat meekly. Julian had to be ready to deflect whatever Augustus did next.

He felt a headache coming on.

He should discuss what to do with Quinn. Contact Hawthorne and Messalina to see if she was well. Be alert because Augustus would surely intensify his fixation on killing Julian. Perhaps Quinn should leave London as well. Find a safe place to hide while Julian somehow determined a method to stop the duke. Block the man from ever hurting his family again and keep everyone safe. Secure. Protected.

Julian sighed and laid his head back against the chair. It all seemed impossible. If only he had something to hold over Augustus's damned head. If only he had his mother's diary.

The door opened, and Mrs. McBride bustled in, laden with a tray. "I've eggs boiling on the fire, but I thought you could have this while you wait." She set the tray on the table and unloaded a steaming teapot, a teacup, a saucer, a basket of sliced bread, and a small dish of butter. "Made the bread just last night at home. Thought you'd be glad of it after being trapped at Adders."

"Yes, thank you," Julian said quite gratefully. "You are correct as usual."

The cook beamed before a too-innocent expression came over her face. "Will my lady be coming to breakfast? I saw she was still here."

Mrs. McBride gestured behind her to Plum, who had silently entered the library, his gaze intent upon Julian's bread.

"I don't know," Julian answered, busying himself pouring his tea. "Perhaps the maid should check?"

"Very well, sir," the cook answered a tad too neutrally.

Julian waited until the woman had turned her back to watch her leave the room. Mrs. McBride had always been loyal to him, and he was almost certain she wouldn't cause any rumors to spread about Elspeth, but he wasn't so sure of the maid.

He grimaced and then burned his tongue with the tea. Too late now. There hadn't been elsewhere for Elspeth to stay once she made it to Adders House. She could plead necessity if she had to, though most would then wonder why she'd made the trip in the first place to a bachelor's house.

God! Why was that diary so important to her that she'd risk social ostracism? Was she simply naive, or did she not care what others thought of her?

Or had she laid a trap to force him to marry her?

No. He was cunning and cynical and had the direst view of the world, but even he could not imagine Elspeth stooping so low. She simply was too genuine to do such a thing.

He sighed, trying his tea again. Of the two of them, he was the only one worried for her honor, and he supposed he'd be the only one attempting to save it.

The door opened, and Elspeth wandered in. She'd donned her gown and kerchief and put up her hair, though rather haphazardly.

"Oh, hullo," she said to him, and then ignored him to greet her dog. "Good morning, Plum. Did you have a good night in the kitchen?"

She knelt to rub the dog's ears briskly, which Plum seemed to find very pleasurable.

"What have you been feeding him?" Julian asked, telling himself he wasn't jealous of a hound.

She shrugged, attention still on Plum. "Oh, scraps I found in the kitchen. Eggs, some of the bread, and a carrot or two."

Julian wrinkled his nose and stared at the animal. "Dogs eat carrots?"

"This one does." She looked up at last, beaming.

It caused something to relax in him that she didn't hold a grudge for his rough waking of her. "Does Mrs. McBride know that you're up?"

"I passed a maid in the hallway," she said, sitting down, "and she assured me that Mrs. McBride would bring me breakfast in here."

He nodded, not entirely certain what to say next. He had a desperate urge to kiss her. To tell her she looked beautiful in the morning light. To whisper that he'd enjoyed holding her all the night long in his arms.

He could do none of that now. That was over. Instead he must play the coldly distant host, formal and reserved. Mrs. McBride might suspect something, but that did not give him leave to flaunt their intimacy before her.

It wasn't done.

No, it wasn't done.

"Are you all right?" she asked him, peering at him worriedly. "You look sad."

Did he? Obviously, he'd not entirely recovered his emotionless mask.

He shrugged. "Just considering how much of the library we've covered and yet haven't found my mother's book."

"Oh, of course." Her gaze shifted away from him and seemed to fixate on Plum, now lying by the fireplace.

He'd never taken second place in a lady's attention to a canine.

Mrs. McBride came in again, breaking the strange air of tension the room had somehow gained. "Good mornin', my lady. I've made you and sir some lovely boiled eggs, laid fresh this morning." She put down the eggs, propped in small wooden eggcups, two tiny spoons, salt, more bread, and a pot of jam, and then proceeded to refresh the teapot.

The cook scanned the table and nodded to herself. "There. That should be everything you need, but if you want more, you know where to find me."

"Thank you," Elspeth said brightly, already helping herself to the jam.

"Not at all, my lady," Mrs. McBride replied before leaving.

It hadn't missed Julian's notice that the cook seemed on far friendlier terms with his guest than with him.

He cleared his throat. "Now that the roads are passable, you should take your leave as soon as you can."

Elspeth paused, her knife in the air holding a generous blob of jam.

The jam dropped to her plate with a splat.

"But I haven't found the diary," Elspeth said. "I told you it was of the utmost importance. I have to stay."

"And I told you," Julian said, leaning forward, "that your reputation would be ruined if anyone discovered you here alone with me."

She rolled her eyes as if they were playing a game of charades and the outcome mattered not at all. "I don't care. You know that."

"*I* care," he ground out, attempting to keep his voice as low as possible. "I care about my reputation, and I care about yours. You need to leave."

Her lower lip trembled. "Do you want me gone so much?"

"Don't." He lifted his lip. "Don't pretend that this has anything to do with how I feel. If you stay, it'll be all but impossible to keep where you've been a secret. It's hard enough with how long you've stayed thus far."

"Then let me stay longer." She leaned across the table, all but putting her bosom in the butter. "If I'm already ruined, then what matters a day or two more?"

"Because I'm trying to keep you from destruction," he said in despair. "Can't you see that?"

"I can see, but I don't appreciate your work. I've no

need for a reputation, good or otherwise. I've never intended to remain in London."

"What?" His immediate, visceral reaction was denial followed closely by a sense of loss. Foolish. He'd never had this woman to begin with. "Where would you go?"

"Back to where I was raised," she said. "Away up in the north of Scotland. Where the Wise Women live."

CHAPTER THIRTEEN

*But Sabinus, having once read the beautiful words
Lady Long-Nose had written, demanded more
from Christina.
"I wish I'd never taken your advice," Christina
sobbed to Lady Long-Nose. "I can't write such poetic
words. Sabinus will find me out and hate me!"
Which is how Lady Long-Nose came to write more
heartfelt letters to her true love...
in the name of another....*
—From *Lady Long-Nose*

Elspeth could see Julian's expression close at her words, and her heart sank. She still remembered the words he'd said about the Wise Women at that bookshop on Bond Street: "strange women who wanted to be thought witches."

His mouth pursed with what looked like impatience. "That's a story they tell children at the border. That the Wise Women will come and snatch you away to use you in their cooking pot."

She winced at the description. "Those tales are spread by our enemies, but the Wise Women are real enough. I'm one of them."

He stared at her. "You're saying that you're a witch."

"No." She shook her head. "We're not witches—at

least not the kind you mean. The ones who consort with the devil and can fly and eat little children's bones. Those witches aren't real, as I'm sure you already know. They're just the superstition of fearful people. The Wise Women are a group who have lived and worked together for centuries."

His eyes narrowed. "In secret, you mean."

"Yes." She darted a swift glance at the door and kept her voice low. "We've had to be secret for over a millennium. Most people do not understand women living without the guidance of men. Many would kill us if they knew."

"If you live entirely without men, then how do your women not die out? Are they immortal in some way?" His voice held the trace of mockery.

"Of course not," she chided. "Didn't I just tell you we were real? Flesh-and-bone women, not some fairy tale. There are those women who seek the company of men or even decide to live with a man. A few—a very few—trusted men live within our compound. And once in a while, a woman comes to us who wants to join our numbers. If she is in earnest, then she is allowed inside."

He grunted. "You just told me that you didn't need men."

"No," she said softly. "I said we lived without the *guidance* of men, not that we abstained from them entirely."

"At least we males have a use for something," he muttered sourly.

She wanted to laugh at his disgruntlement, but somehow she stifled the impulse. "Yes, men are quite useful for the getting of children, but I suspect those who choose them for partners value them for more than that."

He sighed. "Even if I believe this"—he waved his hand in the air—"*story* you're telling me about Wise Women, how could you possibly be part of a band of rebel Amazons when your father was the Duke of Ayr?"

"Ah." She poured herself another cup of tea and one for him as well. "That is a tale. You see, the Dukes of Ayr are in many ways tied to the secret of the Wise Women. Centuries ago, one of my great-great-great-however-many-grandfathers married a Wise Woman." She glanced at him over her teacup, amused to see him scowling. "She was my great-great-great-however-many-grandmother, and both her daughters and her *sons* were brought into the secret of the Wise Women. Since then, the dukes in my family have helped and many times married Wise Women. All daughters of the de Moray family are either honorary members of the Women or decide to join them permanently."

Julian's eyebrows had risen during her recitation. "Ran knows about this secret feminine society?"

"Of course."

"What about Lachlan?"

She tilted her head in confusion. "Why would we keep Lachlan in the dark? Even if we tried, it would be impossible."

He sighed and pushed his plate away from the edge of the table, crossing his arms on it instead. "This is where you came by your more unusual ideas, I take it?"

She smiled kindly. "Unusual to you. Not at all unusual to the Wise Women."

"I take your point," he said thoughtfully, staring at the table before him. "Where you come from, you have no need of a virtuous reputation."

"No." She shrugged.

"And you intend to return to the Wise Women," he said, his voice flat.

"I . . ." She took another sip of tea, buying time to think. Well, she'd already told him most everything else. "I'm afraid I can't. Not right now, at least."

"Then where do you intend to live?" he demanded.

Oh, she knew where his questions were leading. "In London for the nonce."

His voice became hard. "Then your reputation does matter, no matter what ideas you were brought up with. You'll live among London society and London's rules. They will crush you if you step even a toe out of line."

"No." She held up her hand to stop his harsh words. "You don't understand, I—"

She was interrupted by the door opening again.

Mrs. McBride gave them a keen look, perhaps having heard Elspeth's raised voice from the hallway, but her words were prosaic enough. "Shall I collect the dishes?"

Elspeth inhaled and put a smile on her face. "Not just yet. Perhaps in another half hour?"

"Yes, my lady." The cook's tone made it plain that they were taking an awfully long time over eggs and bread.

But the cook left nonetheless and closed the door behind her.

"*Elspeth*," Julian immediately hissed.

"Just listen," she snapped back, albeit in a quieter tone. "The reason I cannot return to the Wise Women now is because there is a civil war there. The Wise Women for centuries have held it as their mission to help other women in the wider world. Women who are beaten by their husbands. Women carrying a child they do not want or can't bring home. Women entangled in London's laws and attitudes."

There was a silence. Julian's eyebrows had drawn together. "Who agreed to escort my sister?"

Elspeth swallowed. His tone was too even. Her next words might make him hate her forever. "She's called the Crow, the messenger for the Wise Women. She travels all over Britain, and she's very experienced at keeping people from noticing her."

She waited to see how he would react.

He pinned her with a look. "And you trust her?"

"Yes," she said, trying to infuse all her faith in the Crow into one word.

He looked at her a moment more, then nodded once. "Go on. Tell me about your Wise Women."

She took a deep breath and began again more slowly, "As I said, for longer than anyone living can remember, we've helped those in need. But now there is a faction within the Women who would like us to turn our faces away from women in distress and lock our doors to the outside world. Permanently."

He turned his hand in a circle as if to indicate *and?*

Elspeth inhaled. "There are many of us—my sisters and others—who cannot abide by this idea, but the Hags, the ruling body of the Wise Women, are now united against those of us who wish to continue helping the women outside our compound. Most of us have been pushed out of our home."

His eyes softened. "Is that why you came to London?"

"Yes," she admitted. "I worked in the Bibliothaca, our library—a vast resource of our history and knowledge and the literature and knowledge of other people. I was apprenticed under the Bibliothacar, the keeper of the Bibliothaca, and should've succeeded her, but the Hags put another woman in my place, and I was forced to leave with my sister Caitriona. I chose to come to live with Freya in London while Caitriona took another path."

"But—"

"*But*," she said hastily, wanting to tell him everything before he lost patience, "I came to London to search for Maighread's diary. She reformed the Wise Women and wrote our laws. We have only a bastardization of the original laws that leave our mission much too open to interpretation. It's said that Maighread wrote down our history, how the Wise Women came to be, and with it the original laws. Don't you see? If I can bring back this artifact, I can persuade the Hags that their ideas have strayed from the path of the founders. I can bring the Wise Women back together."

She stopped abruptly, out of breath, and looked at him anxiously.

She couldn't read his expression.

"Is that what you're searching for in my library?" he asked slowly. "This diary that will somehow convince your Wise Women?"

His skeptical tone was hurtful, but she nodded, never taking her eyes from his. "Yes. You see why I must remain here?"

He pursed his lips, staring down at his hands as if to tell the future. "How could such a book have come into *my* library? I doubt the Greycourts had any dealings with your Wise Women."

She noticed that he hadn't agreed with her.

For a long moment, he sat, his hands clasped before his mouth, and she couldn't tell what he thought. Then he shook his head slowly, and her heart plummeted.

Until he spoke. "Very well. You can stay here another three days."

*   *   *

He was a damned fool enslaved by lust and Elspeth's hopeful face.

Later that afternoon, Julian reflected on his decision to let her stay. They were working in the library together, Elspeth busily paging through books as he climbed the ladder to fetch more for her. He'd known even as he'd said the words that he wasn't letting her stay out of sympathy for her cause or even pity for her pleading eyes.

No, his agreement was entirely self-serving. He wanted her, as his commanding mistress, as the soft, warm woman in his bed, and, oddly, as the friend who talked and argued with him.

And that just made him a doubly damned buffoon because he could not touch her now.

As if to make his point, the maid—Elsie?—entered the room and inquired if they'd like tea.

Elspeth sat back, swiping a lock away from her face and leaving a dust mark on her forehead. "Oh, that would be lovely! Thank you, Alice."

The maid dipped a curtsy and smiled, revealing two missing teeth.

His servants had never smiled at him.

Scowling, Julian descended the ladder and stalked closer to her. "A break so soon? We'll never find your diary—or my mother's book—if you keep stopping."

She looked up, her face shining despite the grime. "Work goes much easier with breaks—especially tea breaks." She sent a distracted glance at the door. "I hope Mrs. McBride sends some of those scones she was baking before luncheon. They smelled heavenly."

"Scones." He stood over her, frowning at the dust in her hair.

Elspeth leaned back on her hands. She was sitting rather disgracefully with her legs crossed before her.

He'd never seen any but a man in such a position.

She arched her neck back and looked up at him, and though her position was inferior to his, he had no doubt he wasn't the superior. "Why are you in such a bad mood?"

He opened his mouth to reply—what he wasn't sure—but Mrs. McBride returned with both the tea and a generous plate of scones.

"Oh, wonderful!" Elspeth exclaimed, and then glanced ruefully at her hands. "I'd best go and wash up so I don't drink dirt with my tea."

She was up and out of the room before he could think of a reply.

Mrs. McBride was slowly unloading the tea and scones onto the same table where they'd broken their fast, Plum at attention near her. "She's a lively one, isn't she?"

Julian looked at her suspiciously. "I beg your pardon?"

"Lady Elspeth." The cook jerked her head to the door to indicate whom she meant, as if there were any other lady lurking about. "Don't mean any offense by it. She just seems a bright one. Makes the hall feel happier."

He cocked an eyebrow like a supercilious fop. "You're ascribing emotion to a building."

She set her hands to her hips. "I think you understand me well enough, sir."

And with that shockingly blunt statement, she left.

Julian brooded. Now the servants were rebelling against his authority.

The problem was, he did know what Mrs. McBride meant.

Even Adders Hall with its dingy walls, falling-apart

furniture, and gloomy rooms seemed to have come awake with Elspeth here. She smiled. Often and easily. No wonder the servants liked her within minutes of meeting her. They probably dreaded the thought of how this house would be when she went: cold, lonely, and crabby.

Or perhaps that was he.

Quick steps came from the hallway, and Julian drew out his handkerchief and was studiously cleaning his hands by the time Elspeth came back in. Her face bore the signs of a wash, but if she'd tried to tidy her hair, there was no evidence of it.

Julian had encountered ladies and paid companions with perfectly tamed hair, their lips and cheeks painted exquisitely. He'd seen a fortune's worth of diamonds and emeralds drip from earlobes, necks, and wrists. And yet Elspeth, with her flyaway hair and wearing a plain, worn gown, was the most enticing woman he'd ever seen. Maybe it was the sunshine smile she was wearing.

It had to be the smile.

In any case it was obvious that he'd lost his wits somehow.

As a result, his voice came out sharper than he'd meant. "Don't grin so much. The servants will suspect."

She looked at him with amusement as she sat. "Suspect what? That I'm happy?"

He growled under his breath. This was a losing battle. "I'll send one of them to hire a coach and driver when you're ready to leave. I don't like the thought of you on a stagecoach with strangers."

She poured him a dish of tea. "Won't that make the people in London more suspicious, if I arrive back in a coach you've rented?"

He scowled down at his tea, stirring sugar in vigorously.

"Don't tell anyone who rented the coach. I'll pay the driver to keep silent."

"Very well," she said slowly, giving him an odd look.

"All this is for your own good," he said grumpily. "You need not treat it as a joke."

She looked at him for a moment longer before reaching for one of the scones. "How often do you live here at Adders?"

He peered at her suspiciously at the change of topic, but she seemed concerned only with spreading as much butter as possible on her scone. "About half the year, taken altogether. It's cheaper than London, but I daren't stay away from my sisters and Augustus's machinations for too long lest he make a move I can't counter in time."

Her brows knit as she spooned jam onto her scone. "You've told me how much your uncle hates you—and indeed your whole family—but I don't understand. What could you have possibly done so young that he keeps his rage over the years?"

Julian helped himself to a scone. "There doesn't seem to be a reason other than pure, wicked spite." He frowned as he took a bite of the scone. Currants. Horrid. "Augustus told us often enough when Quinn and I were trapped in Windemere House that he hated his brother, my father, so in some way, his ire seems to have been passed down. But I don't know why. Father never made mention of a rift with the duke. I'm not even sure Father *knew* his elder brother hated him so much. Perhaps Augustus held some sort of jealousy toward my father, and it festered as time went on. Or perhaps my uncle was born with a bilious heart."

"It's hard to understand people who hate without reason," Elspeth said rather thickly through a mouthful of scone. She stopped to take a sip of her tea. "Their hatred brings them no joy—quite the opposite, usually—but they refuse to leave it behind."

"I've never thought about his hatred in that way." He shrugged. "It simply is."

She nodded. "I suppose that's much more practical."

He paused, wanting to acknowledge that her philosophical musings were interesting by themselves, whether practical or not.

But as he hesitated, she nodded at the uneaten scone still on his plate. "Do you not like it?"

She had a bit of jam by the corner of her mouth, and he couldn't tear his eyes away from it. "Currants. I can't stand them."

"Really?" Her eyes widened in what looked like honest concern. "What, not at all? What about in oatmeal?"

"No, that's worse." He shuddered at the thought. "They swell in the water and become mushy."

"But that's why currants are put in," she explained solemnly. "Or raisins."

He wrinkled his nose. "No."

She tilted her head as if he were an odd specimen in a scientific display. "Dried plums?"

The dog perked up at his name.

"Oh God," Julian protested.

She laughed then, throwing her head back without any decorum. "But you've slandered poor Plum!"

"Have I?" Julian gave in to impulse and reached across the table to swipe the jam from her mouth.

She blinked, watching him, as he licked it off his thumb.

He met her gaze. "Sweet."

Her eyelashes fluttered as if he'd caught her off guard,

and suddenly his chest seemed stifled by longing. Bloody hell. He'd sworn he wouldn't do this.

Julian cleared his throat and looked down, only to find the dog sitting patiently by his side, its head cocked and its eyes trained on his leftover scone. "I thought he didn't like me."

"He doesn't really know you, does he?" she murmured softly. "Go on. Give him your scone and see if he likes you better."

Julian glanced at her severely. "That's bribery."

Her lips curved. "That's friendship."

He didn't agree at all with her philosophy, but he found himself offering a broken-off piece to Plum anyway.

The dog took the bit of scone politely, without even the scrape of his teeth.

"At least he doesn't bite," Julian muttered, feeding the rest of the scone to Plum. He ran his fingers over the dog's head, tousling Plum's silky ears and scratching his neck.

When Julian looked up again, Elspeth still watched him, her eyes soft. He caught his breath. He still felt the beat of lust low in his belly, but there was also something else, entirely innocent, that made him want to take her hand and simply stare at her for hours, maybe eternally.

He tore his gaze from hers by will alone and stood. "I need to see to Octavia."

His exit from the library was rudely abrupt, but it was necessary he leave her at once.

He wasn't sure he could restrain himself if he stayed.

* * *

Elspeth ate another scone, but she barely tasted it and fed the crumbs to Plum.

Ought she to leave Julian alone? Probably. Tending to his horses was obviously an excuse to get away from her. Perhaps to release personal needs. He was a secretive man, and she respected that. But he was also her lover. The man she'd shared want and pleasure with. And she had found that, although some women undoubtedly could have congress with a man without changing inside, she could not.

And she knew that she should find him.

So she did.

Outside, the rain might've stopped, but the wind was sharp and chill. Elspeth trudged over the rutted ground to the stable—or what was left of Adders's stable. It was a low stone building, more than half of the structure fallen.

She looked at the ancient lintel in trepidation before pulling open the door.

Inside, it smelled of damp stone and rotted straw and, under those, horse and manure. Obviously it had been many years since horses were stabled here regularly.

At one end she saw—almost to her surprise—that Julian was indeed tending to his horse. Julian's lantern glowed, lighting him and Octavia. The mare was tied in the aisle, a second horse in a stall behind her. Octavia snorted at her entrance, watching her warily. The man didn't even raise his head from his work—shoveling old straw and manure into a wheelbarrow.

Elspeth hesitated but then decided she needn't have come at all if she were to be a coward. She walked to Octavia and halted an arm's length away.

The mare's ears flicked forward in interest.

"Aren't you lovely?" Elspeth crooned to her. "I'm sorry

I didn't think to bring you a treat. That was quite remiss of me."

Plum had stopped by her feet, but now he ventured close to the horse. Elspeth watched. Octavia could hurt the dog should she wish.

The mare merely lowered her head, snuffling curiously at Plum.

Plum licked her nose.

Octavia jerked her head back but then lowered it to blow at the dog and then shake her head as if in horsey laughter.

Plum immediately went into a play bow—the first that Elspeth had seen him make.

She laughed. "Silly. How do you expect Octavia to play with you? She'd run you right over if let loose."

Julian sighed from the stall, and Elspeth glanced over to see him leaning on the pitchfork, watching her. "Octavia has never been as serious as her name," he said. "And she likes dogs."

"Does she?" Elspeth asked in delight.

Plum was now darting forward at the horse's legs, pretending to attack before retreating just as swiftly. Octavia watched bemusedly before stamping her hoof at the next attack, sending the dog into spins of excitement.

Elspeth knit her brow, concerned that the horse would accidentally stomp on the dog, but Julian reassured her. "You needn't worry. Octavia knows to be gentle."

Elspeth nodded, stepping closer to the open stall. "She seems quite an intelligent horse."

Julian glanced at her sardonically as he began shoveling again. "Have you met many stupid horses, then?"

"Not many," Elspeth allowed. "But there *was* King

George. He was an old gelding at the Wise Women's compound, and my sisters and I learned to ride on him. He was scared of birds. And cats. And the moon."

"The moon?" Julian muttered under his breath. "You're making that up."

"I'm not," she replied indignantly. "He couldn't be ridden on clear nights. He'd take one look at the moon and simply refuse to move. We found Old Bess atop him one morning, still arguing with him at sunrise. She'd meant to visit her brother who lived in the village, but King George had refused to take her."

He grunted.

She chose to take that as encouragement. "He'd been orphaned young, King George that is, and Old Bess said that was why he was so daft. She used to swear at him in the most terrible way, but then she wept for him bitterly when he died. Took to her bed and refused to get up for a month. We all thought she might die there, but eventually someone told Bess that her brother meant to marry again, and she got up just to go scold him for being an old fool. He was seven and eighty, but he was her *younger* brother, so she felt protective."

She watched as Julian labored with the manure and straw. He'd stripped out of his coat and waistcoat, even though the stable was chill, and wore only his shirt, his sleeves rolled past his elbows. The muscles of his forearms flexed as he moved, the shirt sticking to his back with sweat, and really the sight was most fascinating.

Elspeth licked her lips, warmth creeping through her limbs. She truly hoped she wasn't blushing or—or exhibiting signs of what she felt. He wouldn't feel the same at the moment. She worked to repress her longing, the memories of his face frozen in agonizing pleasure, his mouth open helplessly, the tendons of his neck standing in stark relief...

Oh dear. She seemed to only be making it worse.

"I think all older sisters—and brothers—feel protective of their younger siblings," he said, interrupting her heated thoughts.

Elspeth blinked. "I beg your pardon?"

He didn't seem to notice her distraction, almost as if he were talking to himself. "It's an older brother's duty to care for the younger family. His duty no matter what. He has to protect his brother and sisters, or he's no man at all."

"My brothers don't protect me," Elspeth said.

She felt rather as if she'd broken into his own musings when Julian's head shot up. "What?"

"Ranulf and Lachlan." She shrugged. "I don't think they even worry about me or my sisters. I'm not sure I would want them to, truthfully. I'm quite capable of seeing to my own protection. And if I need help or want comfort, I have Freya and Caitriona."

Julian was frowning. "You don't think Ran would help you, should you need it?"

"I think he might," Elspeth admitted. "Although it would be hard for him after being a hermit so long."

Julian shook his head, turning away. "This discussion is moot. I cannot change what is in the past."

Elspeth watched his shoulders bunch under the shirt. "No, of course you can't change the past. I'm not sure what that has to do with Ranulf and his isolation, though."

"Nothing. Nothing at all." He pushed past her with the full wheelbarrow and out of the stable. A moment later, he was back, the wheelbarrow empty. Julian dropped it to the ground with unnecessary force.

He was so angry, and she wasn't sure why. She was fairly sure it wasn't she. Perhaps the reason Ranulf was in seclusion angered him? She was ashamed then at the thought. Of course he'd be angered remembering his sister's death.

"I'm sorry I brought Ranulf into the conversation," she said softly.

Her apology didn't help. If anything, his shoulders were more tense now.

"Julian?" she asked.

He shook his head almost violently. "Never mind. Let's go inside."

She agreed at once, but she couldn't help studying his back as they trudged to Adders. What was she missing?

CHAPTER FOURTEEN

*Who knows how long such a strange contretemps
might have continued—Christina meeting Sabinus
to give him letters written by Lady Long-Nose, only
to have him demand more, thus forcing Christina to
return to Lady Long-Nose so that lady had to write
again—if something hadn't intervened.
Unfortunately, the intervention was Sabinus being
kidnapped and taken to the fairy court....*
—From *Lady Long-Nose*

Late that night, Julian threw yet another accounts book
across the library. The book hit the fireplace mantel and
ricocheted off to fall where Plum was lying asleep. The
dog bounded up and gave Julian an accusing look.

"What of it?" Julian snarled. "I don't know why you're
here with me instead of with your mistress."

Plum ignored him and moved to the other side of the
hearth, presumably because, in his dog mind, it was safer.

Julian sighed.

His frustration had risen to the point that now he was
frightening innocent animals.

What was he to do if he never found the book Mother
had written in? He'd pinned his hopes on the damned book
since he'd found out about its existence. If he couldn't act

against Augustus with some sort of blackmail material, some secret the duke was hiding, then...

Then he'd have no recourse left.

Messalina was safe with Hawthorne and his men. Lucretia, God willing, was far from London with the Crow woman and presumably safe for now. But that still left Quinn exposed. His brother was a man quite able to defend himself in a physical altercation, but a shot from a hidden sniper?

Julian remembered Westminster Abbey and that bit of stone chipping off the statue before he'd even registered the sound of the shot.

No man could guard himself from a bullet.

And in the future? When Messalina or Lucretia or Quinn had children? What then? Would they all be held hostage to his uncle's whims?

Julian let his head drop to his hands. He mustn't give up hope. He'd find a way—somehow—to stop Augustus. If nothing else, he'd kill the old man. Perhaps he'd have time to flee England. Perhaps he'd hang. But in either case, his family would be safe without his uncle. They'd be disgraced, unable to mingle in society for at least several generations with a murderer for a relation, but they'd be alive.

Julian felt something wet touch his cheek and jerked his head out of his hands. Plum sat beside him, head cocked inquisitively.

Even Elspeth's dog felt sorry for him.

Julian reached out, offering his fingertips, and Plum poked his head under Julian's hand, begging for a pet.

"Where's your regard for Elspeth?" Julian muttered under his breath, Plum's fur soft under his fingers. "You can't let your guard down just because I seem harmless now. How do you know I won't turn on your mistress?"

The dog merely groaned, his body leaning heavily against Julian's side. An animal could be so easily swayed by honeyed words and a gentle hand. Elspeth needed a better guardian. She might be able to defend herself against an open attack, but she too could fall to a bullet.

Or to betrayal.

The thought sent a sharp ache through his chest. He could almost see the pain and confusion Elspeth would feel if she learned he'd lied about Ran murdering Aurelia. She'd turn away from him. He'd never touch her again.

He couldn't bear the thought.

Plum grumbled under his hand, and Julian realized he'd stopped petting.

"So greedy," Julian said absently as he resumed scratching behind Plum's ears.

Elspeth wanted to be independent. She wouldn't care for his protection. Once she'd finished searching Adders's library and returned to London, would he even see her again?

Better that she didn't, a cruel voice in his head said. He was dangerous to be around, a man twisted by his past sins and his unnatural desires. He had ruined her brother and her family in an unforgivable act.

Julian closed his eyes.

He was her enemy. Even if she didn't know it.

Plum suddenly stretched out his legs before him, bowing his back before standing upright again and shaking. The dog seemed to give Julian a significant look before trotting to the closed library door and sitting expectantly.

Julian glanced at the clock. It was well past midnight. "Yes, all right. It's past time for you and me to retire."

He let the dog outside at the kitchen door, offered him water, and then climbed the stairs, Plum's nails clicking against the hardwood floor. The upper hall was silent, no light beneath Elspeth's door.

Julian hesitated, but Plum impatiently scratched the door.

"Shush," Julian ordered the dog. "Don't wake her up."

He let the dog into the darkened room, the light from his candle barely reaching the foot of the bed. For a moment, he stood there, listening to the dog settle until all he heard was Elspeth's gentle breaths, sighing in and out. Somehow the scent of wild roses lingered in the air, and he imagined the nape of her neck, the skin humid from sleeping, vulnerable and waiting for him in the bed if he walked closer. She would be warm and soft, drowsy and pliant, and if he lifted the covers to crawl next to her, he'd smell her, the scent of Elspeth distilled in her warmth, calling to everything male inside him.

Julian shook his head, stepping back silently, and closed the door gently as if locking away a treasure.

He stood there, his forehead resting against the door, trying to hear her breathing.

But the door had blocked both the sound and the scent, a barrier firmly between them.

He sighed, lifting his head. He'd lived three-and-thirty years without hearing Elspeth sleeping. He could survive another night. And another. And then another. All the days of what remained of his life, one night at a time, alone.

A scrape came from the stairs, and Julian turned to see a light ascending.

Julian just had time to step several feet away from Elspeth's door before Vanderberg came into sight.

The valet smiled, the candlelight casting weird shadows over his face. "I've found you, sir!"

* * *

When Elspeth walked into the kitchen the next morning, it was to the sight of a golden-haired man chattering animatedly to Mrs. McBride as the cook chopped potatoes.

He immediately jumped up from his chair and bowed. "Good morning, my lady. Would you like for me to serve you breakfast in the dining room?"

Elspeth raised her eyebrows. Up until now, she'd had her breakfast in the cozy kitchen or in the library with Julian. She hadn't even been aware that there was a dining room.

The man looked abashed, perhaps taking her pause as a reprimand. He bowed again. "Oh, of course! I haven't introduced myself yet. William Vanderberg, Mr. Greycourt's valet, at your service."

Elspeth darted a glance at the cook and saw her shake her head minutely before Elspeth smiled at the valet. "Thank you, Vanderberg. I would indeed like my breakfast, but in the library, please."

"As you wish," he chirped, bowing again.

Elspeth eyed the man. His constant bowing seemed a bit excessive. She smiled at Mrs. McBride and turned to make her way to the library.

There she discovered Plum, already sitting next to Julian as the man absently scratched the dog under the chin with one hand while he paged through a book with the other.

He glanced up and tossed the book aside. "Bound pamphlets describing men condemned to execution at Newgate. One of my ancestors must've had a macabre mind." He looked away. "Where would you like to sit while I bring you the books?"

"By the window, please," Elspeth said, pointing to a chair in the sunlight. "But I haven't had my breakfast yet. Your—"

The door opened to reveal Vanderberg holding a tray.

"I'm playing footman today," he said cheerily as he walked in, setting the tray on the small table before turning to Julian. "Would you like some more tea, sir?"

Julian shook his head, his eyes on another book. "No thank you, Vanderberg."

The little man—for he couldn't be much over five feet—nodded and left the room.

Elspeth went to sit at the table, and Plum got up, coming to lie at her feet, although she wasn't foolish enough to think it was she that drew the dog. The ham on her plate gently steamed next to a mound of shirred eggs.

She took a bite, eyeing the dog. "You've somehow seduced my dog in the night." She cut off a tiny piece of ham and surreptitiously fed it to Plum under the table. "Were you plying him with scraps all last evening after I went to bed?"

"No," he said shortly, not even glancing up from another book. "But I see you have that bad habit."

Her eyes rose at his dispassionate tone. Was he trying to put her off conversation with it?

Ha! More fool he. Elspeth had grown up with two older sisters who used to hide from her when they tired of her chatting. Not that it had saved them. She'd always found Freya and Caitriona in the end.

"It's so nice to see the sun out," she murmured now. "Do you have a garden somewhere? I'd think Adders would be perfect for one of Mr. Brown's romantic scenes. All you'd need is a hermitage right there." She pointed to a small hill in the distance, nearly hidden in the trees.

"A hermitage," he said, his voice flat.

"Mm." She swallowed a bite and took a sip of her tea. "Caitriona says they're quite fashionable on grand estates. Apparently, English lords and ladies hire hermits to live in their hermitages. Picturesque, you know."

He blinked as if coming out of a daze. "No, I'm afraid I don't know. I don't have either the money or the time for such ridiculous pastimes. I can't believe it's even true. Where did your sister hear about such things living way up in Scotland?"

"Newspapers, mostly, on gardening and land management," Elspeth said brightly, remembering Cait, her brows furrowed ferociously behind her spectacles as she bent over some paper. Elspeth felt a sudden pain in her chest. When would she next see her sister? She didn't even know.

She sighed and continued, "You wouldn't believe how boring gardening papers are to read. I only tried once. But when Caitriona would tell Freya and me what she'd learned, it was always interesting." She shrugged and cut off another bite of ham for Plum. "I was amazed by what the nobility got up to in England."

He gave her a dry look. "As opposed to the Scottish nobility being raised to become Amazons."

She grinned at him, delighted. "Oh, is that how you see me?"

He glanced away. "Not exactly."

The urge to poke him was nearly overwhelming, but she refrained out of a suspicion she might not entirely like what he'd say.

Elspeth inhaled. "Well, you must admit some of the mores of polite society in London are quite puzzling."

"Such as?"

She waved her fork vaguely. "Valets, for instance. Oh, and lady's maids. Whyever would you want to employ someone to dress you? It seems rather awkward."

He was silent a moment before replying quietly, "You mean Vanderberg, I take it."

"Well, not specifically," she prevaricated. "But in general, yes. For instance, did you arrange for him to meet you here? And if so, how have you managed to dress yourself in the meantime?"

"I have no trouble dressing myself," Julian replied dryly. "A valet is most useful in London, helping to dress for parties and balls. And I didn't ask for him to come here. He must've been confused."

Elspeth returned thoughtfully to her eggs. In truth, she was quite curious about the valet, turning up as he pleased at his master's home. She might be new to the English ways and not fully understand quite a lot of them, but she rather thought such independence in a servant was frowned upon.

"And I don't find being dressed by a servant uncomfortable," Julian said. The corner of his mouth kicked up in a cynical way. "You might tell me that's because I was raised with servants, and you'd probably be right. But in any case, Vanderberg isn't like other valets. He came to me when I was fifteen. My father hired him when he was only sixteen. He'd worked under another valet in the house of a friend of my father, but I was his first proper situation. He'd been with me for two years before that awful summer." He inhaled. "And Vanderberg stayed with me. Even when I went to London to live with my uncle. Even when I've not always had the funds to pay him properly."

She thought about that as she poured herself another cup of tea before saying carefully, "You said once that you didn't trust any of the servants who lived at Windemere House. That they were in your uncle's pay to spy for him." She glanced up. "But you trust Vanderberg?"

He pressed his lips together. "I'm not so naive as to think that any man is above bribery, and I suppose Vanderberg has more cause to need money because of me. Nevertheless, I trust him. He knew secrets about me when we lived at Windemere, and he never betrayed me."

"And here?" She sipped her tea before setting the dish down and looking at him. "Does he know the secrets you keep at Adders Hall?"

He stiffened, his voice clipped when he answered, "I've never told him explicitly, but he's an intelligent man. He must know that what I do is illicit at least." He watched her carefully, his gray eyes clear. "You need not fear him. I've made pains to tell him that you're only here because you are a friend of Messalina and were stranded in Dydle. Of course, that story wouldn't help you if word gets out in society that you stayed with me alone for several days. But I have confidence Vanderberg won't talk. He won't betray you."

Elspeth looked down at her empty teacup. Julian had made the consequences clear to her should people in London find out about their sexual activities at Adders Hall. Yet she couldn't help thinking, *But what if it is* Julian *who is betrayed?*

CHAPTER FIFTEEN

Christina was inconsolable. "A beautiful man like
Sabinus will be a jewel of the fairy court.
They will never let him go."
"Still we must try," Lady Long-Nose said briskly.
"Perhaps we can ransom him with gold or jewels."
At that, Christina wailed all the louder. "Where can I
get a ransom? We don't even know how to
find the fairy court." . . .
— From *Lady Long-Nose*

Elspeth sat before the fire late that afternoon, still searching through dusty tomes, her fingertips growing grayer and grayer. Plum lay beside her, a warm weight.

Julian was on the ladder, and she paused to look up at him. They hadn't spoken in the last hour. There was no need to; the remaining books in the library were growing fewer and fewer.

Above Julian's head, the last shelf in the library was half-empty. He gathered the remaining books in his arms and clattered down from the ladder.

He had dust in his coal-black hair, as if playing an old man in a traveling theater company.

She looked wearily at the books he laid on the small table beside her. "Do you think we'll find the diary—diaries—in there?"

He glanced from the small stack of books to her, his expression softening. "Perhaps we will."

His words were supposed to be reassuring, but they both knew the search was a lost cause. The books on this side of the library were mainly folios, too large to be diaries of any sort.

But Julian sat in an armchair near her and paged patiently through one of the folios. Elspeth took another and began blindly searching. There was no reason for her to stay once the library had been searched. She'd already looked through all the remaining rooms. Maighread's diary, if it ever existed, patently wasn't at Adders.

But Julian's mother's book was.

Elspeth winced, glancing up through her eyelashes at him. He looked so tired—almost defeated. But he would have the book he looked for. It was right now up in her bedroom. She could get it now for him if—

Elspeth stared down at the book in her hand, carefully tilting it so Julian couldn't see the page. A hollow had been cut into the book. And within lay a plain brown book without any markings save those made by damp.

Julian stood suddenly, tossing down the last book. "It's not here." He strode to the fireplace, his back to her. "God what a waste."

Elspeth's fingers shook as she pried the little book from its hidey-hole, taking a quick look inside. On the inner cover was a faint hand, *MAIGHREAD'S BOOK*. She caught her breath, holding it so she wouldn't make any sound.

"I'd look for secret compartments in the house or priest holes," Julian said, his back still to her, "save for the fact that my mother's family has never been Catholic."

"I'm so sorry," she said, guilt spreading like a poison along her veins as she hid the small diary in her pocket.

She shoved the book it had come from into the stack of volumes on the floor.

He turned to look at her, his face agonized. "I've been such a fool."

She blinked, feeling an arrow through her heart, and looked down guiltily at her grimy hands. Was hiding his mother's book worth this pain? But if she gave it to him now he would know she lied and be angry with her. He'd send her away. Was wanting a few hours more with him so awful? "I don't believe you a fool to want to save your family."

He scoffed.

She licked her lips. "Do you think me a fool?"

"No." He frowned at her. "What do you mean?"

Elspeth shrugged, standing. "Well, if I'm not a fool, then my opinion must count, and I think you are a very brave man." She looked at him. "Not a fool."

He was silent.

Elspeth felt despair. "How many years have you fought the duke while guarding your family at the same time? With no respite, ally, or place to feel safe? Julian, I don't see how you can remain sane."

"Perhaps I'm not," he said quietly. "This fight, as you call it, has infected every thought in my mind until there is no other thing there. But you are wrong when you say I've had no respite." He looked up at her, his eyes piercing. "You. You've smoothed balm over my wounded head. You've brought me peace, if only for a little while."

"Then I'm glad of it," she replied softly, knowing she didn't deserve his trust. An awful heavy feeling lay deep in her gut. Because Julian was no longer a stranger to her. She could see now the man beneath his icy shield, alone and shivering but still intent on his mission, pushing forward even as his soul froze.

She wanted to be his warmth. His fire.

"I don't think," Elspeth whispered, "that I've ever been so intimate with another human being as you."

He winced, glancing away.

"No," she said, gently. "I don't mean physically. I mean in the spirit. This has been..." She searched for the right words. "A time apart from the world. It seems almost a fantasy of my mind, you and me together as merely man and woman. I think I may always treasure this time with you."

He swayed as he stood before her, and she made up her mind.

"I need to wash my hands." She went to the door with Plum trotting at her heels, pausing before she touched the doorknob. "Wait for me here."

She didn't look to see if he complied. She walked down the hall, breathing calmly, and entered the kitchen.

Cook and Vanderberg sat at the table gossiping, but the valet immediately rose. "Can I help you, my lady?"

"I just need a basin of water and some soap," she told him.

He nodded and went to the cistern as she let Plum out the back. Something moved in the gloom outside, back against the trees. Elspeth caught her breath, her senses suddenly alert.

The figure turned and disappeared.

"Is she out there?" Mrs. McBride asked casually.

Elspeth looked at the cook as Plum came back in. "Who?"

Mrs. McBride shrugged. "A woman. Saw her this morning and again in the afternoon. Don't know what she's doing, lurking about."

"How . . . how do you know it's the same woman?"

"She's got a twist to her mouth," the cook said. "Ugly thing."

Elspeth shuddered. It must be the assassin sent by the Wise Women. Who else could it be? How long had the woman been there, watching Elspeth?

"Here you are," Vanderberg said, setting a basin of water on the table in front of her. "Are you all right, my lady?"

"Yes." She tried a smile but it failed. "That is, I'm quite tired, I'm afraid."

She took the soap and plunged her hands into the water. Her fingers felt filthy with more than just dust no matter how she washed, but she dried them at last.

She knew both the cook and the valet were watching her as she left silently. Plum had decided to stay in the kitchen, of course. That was, after all, where the food was.

Julian looked up when she came to the door of the library, and she studied his face, trying to memorize it.

Tomorrow she must leave. Walk away as if nothing had happened to her body and heart. She wasn't altogether sure she could do it—return to London and normal life. Life without this intimacy and trust with him.

But that was on the morrow, hours away. Tonight, they were still together, and she couldn't fathom wasting their time.

"Will you come with me?" she asked. "Now. To my bedroom?"

His eyes widened, and she could see his brain turning over, beginning to think of all his objections.

"No," she said sternly. "Don't think. Don't pause. Come with me now."

And he did. Obediently standing and following her from the library.

Elspeth half thought they might meet Vanderberg on the way, but the house seemed empty, as if they were still the only inhabitants.

When they arrived at her room, Julian hesitated again, looking at her door almost as if it were a trap. At the same time, Elspeth could see the tension in his shoulders, the way his eyes kept darting to her mouth.

"Come inside," she whispered. "Come be with me, Julian."

She pushed the door open and went in, never looking back, as if expecting him to follow her without protest. Her heart was pounding, though, with expectation, but also prepared for disappointment should he balk and leave her there alone.

But her lover trailed her as if in thrall.

Elspeth felt a shiver of pure *want* in her belly. Somehow the thought of having power over this proud man made her desire him more. She wanted to strip him and lay him bare in body and soul, his attention only on her, his needs subject to her whim.

She bit her lip at the mere thought.

"Take off your clothes," she said, taking a seat on a chair to watch him.

He lowered his eyes, his hands moving to shrug off his coat, but she stopped him.

"No," she said, soft but firm, "look at me, please. I want to see the expression on your face."

He inhaled sharply, and she couldn't help but notice that his cock was straining against his breeches.

She suppressed a smirk.

He began again, carefully pulling off his coat and folding it to place it on the table. His eyes had darkened as she watched, his cheeks flushed, but his mouth nearly defiant. Did he want to test her will? His fingers moved to the fall of his breeches.

She shook her head. "The waistcoat and shirt first, please."

His lips twitched as if in irritation, but his hands moved to his waistcoat buttons.

She watched as he slowly peeled off waistcoat and shirt, but she couldn't help a small yawn.

His eyes narrowed at her. "Do you find me boring?"

"You? No," she said with a twitch of her lips. "But I did not say you might talk."

His mouth twitched as if he wanted to reply but he remained silent.

Her smile grew. "Your stockings and shoes next."

He threw her an irritated glance but moved to obey her.

Elspeth could see that his cock looked to be at full length now, straining against the placket of his breeches.

He straightened when he was barefoot, watching her for instruction.

"Good," she said in approval. "Tell me, are you uncomfortable?"

His jaw jumped. "Yes."

"*Very* uncomfortable?" she asked, examining what she could see of his groin. He looked enormous.

He didn't reply, and she glanced up to see him glaring at her.

She pursed her lips. "Answer me, please."

"Yes," he ground out.

She smiled sweetly and stood. "That's better. Now come undress me."

He stalked to her, standing a full head or more taller than she. He was powerful, looming, looking barely restrained. But he *was* keeping himself in check. As if he were a high-tempered stallion, able to crush her, but bowing before her hands on his reins.

The thought made her feel liquid.

She tilted her head to watch his face as he unpinned the bodice of her dress, spreading and opening the two sides to reveal her stays. His dark brows were drawn down, as if he were mastering a difficult but important task, and a flood of affection suddenly washed through her breast. His body, his demeanor was so different from the one he showed the rest of the world every day. Had anyone else ever seen him so open, so vulnerable?

Well, yes, a nasty little voice in her head replied. Julian had dallied with paid mistresses for years. Presumably he did with them exactly what he was doing with Elspeth now.

The thought was a sour one. Perhaps that was why her voice was sharp when she ordered, "My skirts next."

He shot a glance at her from under his brows but obeyed easily enough, untying skirt and underskirts.

She praised him, then, when he dropped to his knees to take off her shoes. "You've been so good for me," she whispered, stroking his head. "So obedient."

He didn't reply, but she could see the tension leave his shoulders.

When he stood again, his eyelids were drooping as if she'd given him a glass of wine laced with some sleeping potion.

"My stays," she whispered. "Will you unlace my stays for me?"

He moved as if under a compulsion, his hands coming

to rest against her breasts as he loosened the strings. She could feel each movement of his fingers, sure and precise, and shivered from the warmth of his hands brushing against her. Soon she wore only her chemise.

She stilled his right hand and brought it to her lips, kissing his fingers. "What do you want now?"

He swallowed, his Adam's apple sliding along his strong throat. He stared at her breasts. "I want to take this off you." He met her gaze, and she could see that he wasn't as tamed as she'd thought him. Somewhere deep inside those icy eyes, a flame burned. "I want to see you naked."

Her lips curled. "As you wish."

He pulled her chemise off in a trice.

"On your knees," she whispered. "And mind you don't touch yourself. Have I told you how I like to see you there before me? Your back bowed, your head lowered, to me, a lass you might break in two if you wished."

He frowned at that, even as he dropped to the floor before her. "I'd never hurt you."

"Perhaps not," she said softly, her hands on his head. "But if you wished to do so, you could. The thought of all that strength compliant to my whims makes me wet."

He inhaled as if drinking in the scent of her cunny, right in front of his face.

"Oh, Julian," she said almost reverently, "make me fly."

He set his big hands on her hips and lifted her right leg to drape over his shoulder, a position she'd not thought of before this night. Then he pulled apart her folds with his thumbs and drove his tongue straight inside her.

She moaned, the sound loud in the room, and was going to say something, but he did it again, and thought seemed to flee her mind. She was bucking against him, grinding herself into his face, and he was mouthing and tonguing her through it all. He lapped hard and fiercely against her pearl, driving her nearly out of her mind.

For a second, she glanced down, wanting to see him at this work. His eyes were closed, his brows drawn, and his cheeks sheened with some substance. She realized with a thrill of pure lust that it was *her* essence he had smeared on his face. Her liquid, her scent. She'd marked him as if he were a stallion, saddled and reined and bridled and hers.

She threw back her head at the impossible thought, breaths coming fast in her throat as he kissed and sucked and fucked her with his tongue, driving her, driving her, until she made that leap, as profound as a dive off a cliff into the sea, her entire body seizing with the spasms of her orgasm. She coiled over him, his hands bracing her, the only thing keeping her from falling as she panted hard, stars flickering before her eyes. For one long moment, she didn't even exist, she merely floated on warmth, drifting through the aftermath of her pleasure.

Then she lifted her head and looked down at him as he lazily mouthed her cunny. "It's your turn, I think."

* * *

Julian was aching, he was so hard, yet he didn't want to move until Elspeth gave him the order. He knelt at her feet, worshipping her sweet pussy, heady with the scent of her, a goddess meant to be paid obeisance. He felt serene here, without thought, pain, or anxiety. Without care.

Simply existing in her presence.

"Come," she said, swinging her leg off his shoulder. "Come to the bed."

He stood and followed her, aware that the restriction on his stiff prick made moving awkward. She climbed in the bed and motioned for him to do so as well.

Then she lay on her side and examined him as he knelt before her. "I feel cheated somehow," she said. "I've never touched your cock."

The words brought blood both to his cheeks and to his straining prick. He wanted—suddenly needed—her to touch him.

"Come closer," she commanded.

He could do naught but obey, presenting the obscenely bulging placket of his breeches.

She trailed her hand down along the outline of his prick, so lightly he should never have felt it, yet he did. Her fingers left a trail of lightning behind, charging him with lust so that he couldn't help but groan.

Her lips twitched slyly, her gaze never leaving his breeches. She reversed the course of her fingers, playing idly along his length until she came to the button of his falls. Her eyes flicked up to his, sky blue, and if he weren't intimately aware of what she was doing, she would look a girlish innocent.

She flicked open his buttons, letting the flap fall but doing nothing else to remove his breeches. His cock promptly thrust through, hampered only by the fabric of his smalls.

"Poor, poor thing," she crooned as if reassuring his prick. "You must be so unhappy caught up in all this."

She slipped her fingers into his placket and found the second slit of his smallclothes. He felt her hand wrap around him, cool in contrast to his enflamed prick, and she drew him forth.

He swallowed, watching her, wanting to thrust into her hand, to demand attention or at least to take control of what she did, but he remembered her earlier admonitions and let go of the urge. She was in charge. He'd given over the reins, letting her decide what he was permitted to do.

The relinquishing of control should have made him angry or tense or uneasy. He thought other men might feel something like that. But to him, it was a peaceful thing not to have to think. To know that he was helpless to her and in turn that she guided him. He'd always felt that when he'd paid for his expert companions, but with Elspeth there was something else. A final level that gave until he slowly spun in a state free from worry. Merely waiting, obedient and aching.

She was examining him now, curious and unknowingly provocative. First stroking over his length too lightly and then sliding his foreskin down, touching one finger to the drop of liquid at his tip. He felt as if he might go insane from the gentle touches on his heated length. She stared for a moment and then brought the glistening bead to her mouth, tasting and then screwing her face up and drawing back her head like a kitten tapped on the nose.

The sight made him desperate. "Elspeth," he whispered. "Please."

"Hmm?" she murmured absently, and then glanced up at him. She must've seen something in his expression, for she seemed amused. "Oh, very well."

He thought he might have surcease. Might finally be able to reach his peak. But then she drew away from him, lounging against the pillows.

Did she mean to torture him further? She looked like a reclining Venus, all plump curves and pinkened skin, her nipples rose against the white of her breasts, the fine red hair over her mound damp and gleaming in the candle-light. Her juices were evidence of the pleasure he'd given her. She was a wanton, waiting for a personal servant to bring her grapes and wine so that she might watch him at leisure as he fought to keep from spilling.

"Now," she said, tilting her head as if for a better viewing angle, "you may touch yourself."

The order made his heart stutter. One thing to finish himself in the heated aftermath of loving her as he'd done that first night. Another to kneel before her and frig himself as she watched calmly. It was humiliating. Subservient.

He felt desire pull his balls up tight, and his prick jumped before he even took himself in hand.

She laughed lightly, breathlessly. "I think he's eager, don't you?" She looked him in the eye, smiling, a siren beyond even the gods' imagination. "Go on."

He held her gaze as he grasped himself, immediately pulling fast and roughly, the beat of his lust pulsing in his belly and his balls. He wouldn't last long. Not if—

"No," she said sternly. "Not so quickly. Gently, please."

He nearly growled. "But I—"

"Want to spend?" She lifted a mocking eyebrow. He nodded mulishly. "No doubt, but *I* want to savor this. I want to watch every little change in your eyes and in your cock. And I'm the one in charge, am I not?"

"Yes," he hissed, doing as she said, slowing his movements, touching himself lightly.

God, she was forcing him to tease himself.

"That's right," she purred, making herself more comfortable. "If only you could see yourself. I should have brought you to a room with a mirror and made you stand before it. Watch yourself as you work. Or perhaps I should invite other ladies to see you. We might have tea, all in our silks and lace, tittering behind our fans as you stand there, your chest flushed, sweat upon your brow and your cock. Your beautiful, magnificent, *hard* cock. I should charge them for a touch. Or better yet a taste. I'd let them each have one lick as you stood before them. A tiny sip to let them know exactly what I have in my possession."

Bloody hell. He could imagine the scene, him naked in a mill of overly dressed women, sweating and straining as she made him perform for them. The thought alone was—

"Slowly," she admonished. "Slowly, I said."

He glared at her. Did she think him an automaton? Without feeling or sense? He couldn't hold himself back. It was impossible.

As if she knew what he thought, she quirked her lips and said, "You can do it. I know you have a will of iron. Surely you have possession over your body?"

He gritted his teeth, trying to blank his mind, touching his prick with only fingertips, each stroke an exquisite agony.

She spread her legs wide, letting him see the dark coral of her pussy, plump and wet with her desire, the lips open so that he could see everything.

He couldn't tear his eyes away, watching as she reached down and fingered herself.

He gasped, squeezing the base of his erection to stop from spilling at once.

"You seem very close," she mused. "So hard and heavy and such a deep red, nearly purple, isn't it?" She flicked her eyes to his. "I think you should take your hand away, just let me look for a moment."

He didn't know how he did it, but he obeyed. Kneeling, trembling, on the very precipice, his prick an obscene stand.

She did look, her gaze examining his straining erection, a smile curled at her lips. "Are your nipples sensitive? I've always wondered why men have them. If I sucked at one as you did mine, would you feel it?"

She waited expectantly for an answer, and he forced himself to nod jerkily. He must not think of the image his brain conjured from her words, but it slipped into his mind without his permission: Elspeth, spread over him, her head at his chest, delicately sucking at his nipple.

His cock pulsed with his desire, his entire being pounding with the same beat of *want*. Sweat was trickling down his back as he waited for her permission.

Her command to come.

"Please." His voice was nothing but a slurred plea. "Let me come to climax. *Please*."

"Mmm." Her head was tipped back, her eyes closed, her mouth opened helplessly.

He watched as she stiffened, her feet pointed, her hand clutching at the sheets, and shivered for a long, long moment. He groaned under his breath, wanting to touch her, touch himself, to simply let go and follow her in release.

Her body went limp, and she smiled, her eyes finally opening. "You've been so good. You didn't touch yourself, did you?"

He shook his head, past the ability to speak.

"And I think that must be becoming painful," she

murmured thoughtfully. "I think…yes, I think you should touch just the tip. Very delicately, if you please."

He swallowed, skimming his fingertips on oversensitive skin. Just that little touch was sending shudders racking through him as he tried to hold off. Hold on…

"You're so beautiful," she whispered, "trembling on the edge. I wonder how long I could make you stay balanced there? How long you'd let me."

He watched her through half-closed eyes. "As long as you wish."

She nodded. "The perfect answer. You deserve a reward. Stroke yourself."

All it took was one downward fist, and he was coming, splashing against the sheets without care, so hard his body shuddered as if he were in the throes of death. Gasping, jerking as his penis continued to spurt the aftershocks of his spend. He'd never felt such an intense release in his life.

He came to himself, still trying to catch his breath, feeling as if he'd been through some sort of metamorphosis.

As if he wasn't the same man as before.

* * *

The next morning the bed was empty.

Julian knew he shouldn't feel disappointed. No doubt Elspeth had left before the maid could discover them. But he'd hoped to see her again this morning. Perhaps to kiss her. Perhaps more.

But that time was past now.

Julian dressed swiftly and exited Elspeth's bedroom. At least they'd have breakfast together before she left. He'd have a few more hours with her.

But when Julian made the library, it was empty. He frowned. Was she still in the kitchen?

In the kitchen, Vanderberg sat at the table with a pot of tea, chatting with Mrs. McBride.

The valet rose swiftly on Julian's entry. "I'm sorry, sir, to not wake you, but Lady Elspeth said you wished to sleep further."

Julian waved aside his explanation. "Where is she?"

Vanderberg looked uncertainly at Mrs. McBride.

The cook straightened where she was kneading dough. "If you mean my lady, she left before dawn."

"Left." Julian blinked stupidly at the staring servants.

Then he turned and rushed back up the stairs.

Elspeth's room was exactly as he'd left it, the bed unmade, the rumpled sheets tossed back. He'd been too eager to find her, he hadn't really looked around the room. Now he saw that her bag was missing, along with the few possessions she'd brought with her—the comb she'd kept on her nightstand, the scatter of hairpins next to it, and, of course, Plum.

He should've realized at once when the dog wasn't there to meet him at the bottom of the stairs this morning.

She'd truly gone.

He went to his own bedroom out of some sense that said to check all the possibilities. It was empty. No dog. No sweet woman looking at him with sunshine in her eyes.

He was turning to the door when something out of place caught his attention. A book lay on his washbasin, sitting primly next to his razor.

Julian reached it in two steps and saw a folded piece of paper atop the book. He smiled as he opened it. She'd left

him a farewell note. Then he began to read, and his brows
drew together.

Dearest Julian,

*I thought it best to catch the early coach in town
so as to not cause a commotion. I enjoyed greatly
my time with you at Adders. I think you'll be
interested in this book. I found it the first night. I
hope you can forgive me for keeping it from you
until now.*

—Elspeth

Julian slowly lifted the book, turning the pages until
he found the first line in his mother's handwriting. She'd
had it all this time, lying to him. Gaily letting him fruit-
lessly search for it.

Elspeth had betrayed him.

CHAPTER SIXTEEN

*But before Lady Long-Nose and Christina could
form a plan, a tall, lean fairy appeared before them.
He had the coldest silver eyes Lady Long-Nose
had ever seen.
He said, "The Fairy King has read the letter written
by Sabinus's true love and would like to
meet her. Now."
Christina looked at Lady Long-Nose
in utter horror....*
—From *Lady Long-Nose*

"You'll leave tomorrow morning," Freya said. "Kester has a carriage ready to take you to Scotland, and he's hired guards for you as well. Everything is arranged, except you're not listening to me, are you?"

Elspeth started guiltily. "I am. Truly I am."

She'd arrived back at Harlowe House only that afternoon, after two days spent returning from Adders. It was now evening, the curtains pulled against the dark sky as they lounged, just the two sisters, in Freya's sitting room, warmed by the lit fire.

Elspeth rather thought she might never want to leave the room, even if Freya was planning just that. After all, she couldn't go back to Whispers now that she'd betrayed

Messalina's brother, and she wasn't at all sure she should take Maighread's diary to Scotland now that she'd finally found it. Wasn't that ironic? She'd accomplished her mission, discovered a treasure lost for decades if not centuries, held the hope of the Wise Women right in her hands, and she couldn't move.

"Elspeth?" Freya called her back to the present. "Something's wrong, I know."

Something was wrong indeed.

"I don't know what to do now," Elspeth said blankly. Plum shoved his big head into her lap, and she absently stroked his head.

"Do?" Freya sounded exasperated. "You only need to worry about how you will present the diary to the Hags when you return." She frowned. "It won't be easy. They obviously don't want to see Maighread's writings."

Yes. Yes, that was absolutely what she should do, what she'd always planned to do, but now the problem was... "What was it like when you married Kester?" Elspeth asked slowly.

Freya turned to stare at her. "What?"

She could feel the heat of a blush moving up her cheeks. Freya was looking at her as if she were mad now. "How did you know you were in love with him?"

"Know?" Freya wrinkled her brow. "Well, Kester listens to me, for one. He's interested in my thoughts and opinions, even if he doesn't agree with them."

"There must be more than that," Elspeth said a bit desperately.

"Yes, naturally," Freya said dryly, "but I don't think you want to know about our bedsport."

Elspeth merely looked at her.

Freya stood and walked over to a cabinet in the corner of the room. She opened it and removed a decanter and two glasses before returning to the settee and pouring them both a drink.

"Brandy," Freya explained, answering the unspoken question as Elspeth sniffed at her glass. "Ladies aren't supposed to drink it, hence the cabinet."

Elspeth took a sip and sighed at the warmth in her throat.

"We didn't get along at first," Freya said. "I thought he'd helped cripple Ran, and, too, I wasn't best pleased that he didn't remember me." She snorted and took a sip from her glass. Her expression softened. "But in the end, we discovered each other. I wouldn't trade what we have together for anything in the world."

Elspeth frowned at her glass. "What do you mean by 'discovered each other'?"

"Well...," Freya said slowly, "I suppose I mean that we discovered who each other is. No, that's not quite it." She thought a moment and then looked up. "Do you remember those roses that Caitriona used to have in her garden? The great, puffy ones that have layers of petals that open when they bloom?"

Elspeth nodded.

Freya turned her glass thoughtfully. "Imagine that the outer petals of the rose are all of society—everyone you don't know. And that the center where the pistil lies is you."

"I can never remember which part the pistil is," Elspeth confessed.

Freya gave her a look. "How many times did Caitriona explain this to you? The pistil is the part in the center that becomes the rose hip when it's pollinated." Her sister set aside her drink and cupped her hands together. "These are the outside of the rose, the petals that guard against the world that doesn't know you at all." She slowly opened her fingers. "Inside are more petals—they represent your acquaintances. The people whom you greet on the street or whom you might talk to at a ball. They know you, but they probably couldn't tell you that strawberry tart is your favorite pudding."

"Ohhh," Elspeth said, "I'm beginning to see." Though she still wasn't sure how the rose pertained to love.

"I hope so," Freya said. "But remember that there are even more petals beneath those." She let her hands drop as she smiled at Elspeth ruefully. "I can't demonstrate with my hands, so imagine that rose with all the petals curled each within the other. The third layer are your closest friends and family. The people you live with. The people you grew up with. They know you better than the outer two groups of petals, don't they?"

Elspeth nodded. Rings within rings, each smaller than the last, each closer to oneself.

"These people know you very well," Freya said. "They know what you like and dislike, they know the type of person you are. But there's a last ring." She wrinkled her nose. "No, not a ring. Perhaps the stamen sitting next to your pistil at the very center of the rose." For some reason, her cheeks pinked as she smiled privately. "That is the person who knows you best of all. The person who knows your mind and your soul and your heart. That is what Kester is to me."

For a moment Elspeth said nothing as she considered Freya's words.

Julian knew her. Could he be the man at the center of her rose? She rather thought he might be. She caught her breath. But if that was so, she'd already ruined their relationship. She'd selfishly taken his trust and trampled it without thought.

"Elspeth?"

She didn't realize she was crying until she heard the alarm in Freya's voice. "I betrayed him," she sobbed.

Freya was always quick. Perhaps too quick. "Julian Greycourt?"

Elspeth nodded. "He was there, at Adders, and we became close. Very close."

She felt Freya's arms wrap around her. "I don't approve of him, you know that, but I'm sorry."

"I need to apologize to him." Elspeth knew it—had known it since she'd left him—but her resolve was certain now.

She could feel Freya nod. "Perhaps you should clarify what happened that night at Greycourt. I haven't shown you the letter we received from Ran while you were gone. He seems determined to remain a recluse. I'd like to change that if we can."

Elspeth felt worse. How could she forget her oldest brother in all of this? "If I can only—"

Her words were interrupted by a shot that would've taken Elspeth's head off if she hadn't chosen that moment to lie down on Freya's lap.

Freya swore horribly and stood, looking like an Amazon as she shook a long knife down from her sleeve and threw it at the woman standing just inside the door to the salon.

There was a shriek and then a horrible silence as the woman slumped to the floor.

Belatedly, Plum barked.

Elspeth shakily stood and looked at the stranger and realized that she had a scarred lip. The knife was lodged in the woman's throat and by the amount of blood she was quite dead. Elspeth gulped. "That was a very good throw."

"Wasn't it?" Freya grinned viciously before tutting. "They always forget that they only have one shot with a pistol."

Kester came running into the room. "What?" He looked down at the body. "Who?" He knelt and pressed his fingers to the assassin's throat before shaking his head. "She's dead, whoever she is." He looked up. "Are you all right, darling?"

"Of course," Freya said. "She meant to kill Elspeth." She cocked her head, examining the body. "I don't think we'll have to worry about her anymore. That is…" She looked at her husband. "You will help me dispose of her, won't you?"

Kester sighed. "Naturally. Whatever my wife wants. Though I do wish you could advise me in advance next time you decide to murder someone in your salon." He sounded put out, but Elspeth couldn't help noticing the small smile that he sent Freya.

If only Elspeth could regain Julian's trust so easily.

*   *   *

The next day Elspeth saw Julian again.

She was sitting in St Martin-in-the-Fields with Kester and Freya and the Holland family, watching as Arabella Holland married the Earl of Rookewoode. The bride was lovely in a pink gown with lace at the elbows and over-skirt, and the groom cut a dashing figure in silver velvet.

"So romantic!" Regina Holland exclaimed, rapt, while observing her sister. She turned to her fiancé, who was seated beside her. "Mr. Trentworth, we really must marry on a sunny morning. See how the sunbeam halos them as if in a painting?"

"Yes, indeed," Mr. Trentworth murmured for perhaps the fifth time since they'd been seated.

Normally Elspeth would be watching the wedding with interest. She'd never been to one in London, or indeed outside of the Wise Women. But she found she couldn't make the effort to pay attention. Everything seemed gray even in the sunlit church.

There was a clatter from the back of the church, and Elspeth turned to see what it was. Most of the people behind her were watching the wedding, of course, though there was a florid man who'd already fallen asleep, his chin resting on his chest. No one else was looking around so perhaps—

The ramble in Elspeth's head stopped, for she'd met Julian's eyes. He was seated at the back of the church all alone save for his brother, and he was glaring right at her. She swallowed. Even with the cold light in his eyes she felt longing for him rise in her breast.

Elspeth faced forward, conscious of all the people around her. But when she cautiously glanced, no one seemed to pay her any mind. That at least was a relief. She'd looked for Julian since she'd returned to London. Looked and not found him. Messalina had given her the address of an inn where Julian was staying with his brother, but he hadn't been there. She just wanted to apologize to him. Even if there wasn't ever anything else between them, she must tell him how sorry she was. Why hadn't she given him the book when she'd found it? At the time her reasoning had seemed sound, but now she knew she was a fool.

Now she saw only the justification of a selfish woman.

Elspeth pressed a handkerchief to her eyes, hoping that Freya wouldn't notice. She needn't have worried.

"He looks so self-satisfied," Freya muttered, frowning. "Like he's doing her a favor by marrying her."

Elspeth blinked and glanced at the wedding couple.

Arabella nearly glowed with joy, and she looked at her husband as if he were a god and she some supplicant. As if she would die for him gladly, she was so in love.

The earl was smiling at his bride, but his expression was indulgent and, now that Elspeth was looking, just a bit smug.

Her sister was correct. There seemed to be an imbalance in their regard for each other.

But did she truly understand how a woman and man in accord might look at each other? She'd spent only a few days with Julian. It had felt momentous, a seismic change to her very being. But had it been the same for Julian? Did it matter when he stared at her so coldly now?

The thought was a jolt straight through her heart, that she'd almost had the center of the rose, so precious, so rare, but she'd crushed it between her fingers instead.

The audience rose suddenly, and Elspeth stood belatedly. The bride and groom were already retreating down the aisle. The new Countess of Rookewoode beamed delightedly. The earl grinned as if he'd finalized the purchase of some long-coveted land. Once seen, the disparity in their emotions was impossible to forget. The realization made her impossibly sad.

The wedding guests began to slowly file out of the church, the crowd jostling a bit. For a second, Elspeth saw a woman's face, oddly familiar, over Kester's shoulder. Then a gentleman moved, and she was gone.

Elspeth frowned to herself. It almost looked like—

"Are you all right?" Freya asked at Elspeth's side.

Elspeth nodded but then shook her head. "I thought I saw someone from the Wise Women."

"Who?" Freya was immediately searching the mass of people.

"Deidre Dungrave," Elspeth said slowly.

Freya's eyes snapped back to her. "The Nemain?"

"I think so." Elspeth nodded slowly. She continued to look around. Did she have another assassin after her? She found it very hard to care.

Freya swore under her breath.

Elspeth leaned into Freya as they made the doors. "What do you think it means?"

"I don't know," Freya replied. "The Crow said she didn't know where the Nemain was."

"Could she still be loyal to the Hags?" Elspeth asked. "Could they have sent her?"

Freya bit her lip. "I hope not."

"What are you whispering so conspiratorially to Elspeth?" Kester bent to ask.

"My—our—other life," Freya replied significantly, since Kester knew about the Wise Women.

He nodded. "Can you break long enough to attend the wedding breakfast?"

Freya took his arm, leaning close to her husband. "I suppose we'll have to, won't we? Now take us to the carriage, please. I don't like Elspeth being out in the open."

Kester nodded. "Right away."

The ducal carriage was only around the corner, but it took several minutes to get there, as they had to make their way through not only the wedding guests but also the common people who had gathered to catch the coins thrown out by the earl's servants. Elspeth could feel sweat rolling down her back the entire time.

They arrived at the carriage and got in before Kester

knocked on the roof to let the driver know they were settled.

Elspeth waited for the carriage to pull away before saying, "Perhaps she's doing other work for the Hags."

"Maybe," Freya said thoughtfully. "But I don't think so. Not after the Hags declared that they'd separated from the outside world."

"Dare I inquire what you are talking about?" Kester asked with uncharacteristic diffidence.

"A possible second assassin after Elspeth," Freya said bluntly.

Kester winced. "The more I hear about the Wise Women, the deadlier they seem."

"Only sometimes," Freya said, patting her husband's hand.

Elspeth frowned out the window. She'd not yet made plans to return to the Wise Women's compound with Maighread's diary. Part of her hesitation came from the fact that she'd like to have others backing her when she returned. The other part, she had to admit, was pure procrastination.

The thing was, she rather liked living outside the compound. It was a strange world to her, it was true, but she had so much freedom. There was no one to decide the course of her life for her. She could move as she wished, talk to people as she wished, see things as she wished. She loved living in London. And a small, reckless part of her whispered that if she was here instead of the far north of Scotland, then perhaps she could attempt a reconciliation with Julian.

As unlikely as that might be.

The carriage stopped.

"Shall we?" Kester said, descending and holding out his hand to Freya and then Elspeth.

She stepped down, shaking out her skirts before looking up at Rooke House's edifice. It was classical, but there was also a hint of the baroque in the extravagant curls decorating the cornices and the grand tympanum over the entrance.

Inside, the house was lavishly appointed in the baroque style with wildly carved tables, chairs, and mirrors and, naturally, a painted ceiling.

"Why is it always naked babies?" Elspeth wondered.

"What, dear?" Freya asked distractedly.

The guests were being ushered into a dining room lined with portraits, presumably the earl's ancestors. A life-size sugar swan surrounded by flowers and sweetmeats was the centerpiece of the long table.

"Messalina and Hawthorne are over there." Freya waved and then moved toward the head of the table. "Pity we can't sit with them. You're too high ranked, Kester."

Elspeth looked around. If Julian was at the wedding, surely he'd attend the breakfast? But she couldn't see him. Her spirits sank.

"I'm going to visit the necessary," Elspeth murmured to Freya.

"Be careful," her sister whispered. "I don't see Deidre, but that doesn't mean she's not here."

Elspeth turned and sidled to a discreet door in a corner of the dining room. She entered a small room reserved for ladies to refresh themselves in. Fortunately, there was another door across from the first, leading into a small corridor.

Elspeth slipped out.

Perhaps Julian had decided to skip the breakfast. Or

he might be somewhere with other male guests. Gentlemen had so much more freedom to do as they pleased on occasions like this. They might even be toasting the groom.

Oh, this was a fool's errand.

But she couldn't stop herself. Just one more chance to talk to him, to see his gray eyes and know his attention was on her.

Love was a terrible affliction.

Elspeth tiptoed down the hallway, hoping she wouldn't meet anyone. She was peeking around the corner to see if the next hall was occupied when she felt a hand on her shoulder.

She was pulled into a dark room and spun around.

Julian glared down at her. "Was everything you said to me a lie?"

* * *

He'd been angry since he'd seen her at St Martin-in-the-Fields, sitting so primly, her glorious hair standing out like a beacon in the crowded church. No, even before that. Since he'd discovered her letter at Adders. It was a creeping, grudging, despairing anger.

How could she?

The room was dark, but he could see the whites of her widened eyes. "I'm so sorry, Julian."

He tightened his grip on her shoulders. "Why?"

"I…" She cleared her throat. "That is, I have lied to you, I suppose, from the moment we met, but that was because of Maighread's diary. It was—is—important to me." She licked her lips and said in a whisper, "Perhaps too important, since I prioritized it over you."

"You could've trusted me." He felt like shaking her. Why apologize now, when it was too late?

"I should have," she agreed readily. Her eyes looked so sad, but could he trust them? "That was my mistake. But... but surely you've lied to me as well, by omission if nothing else. You're keeping secrets from me."

"That was before," he growled, knowing he was exposing himself to her. "Before we were at Adders together, before I told you about my family and how close we were to danger, before I knelt at your feet."

She bit her lip but carried on bravely in the face of his wrath. "And Ran? I think I deserve to know what happened that night. Did you help beat him? Did you stand back and let others do the work for you?"

He reared back as if he'd been slapped. The guilt nearly overwhelming him. His voice was low and harsh as a result. "You're trying to draw attention away from your own lies."

"Oh," she gasped. "I never—"

"Did it mean nothing to you?" He felt as if his chest were being torn asunder. "Did *I* mean nothing to you?"

"Julian," she whispered, so sweetly, so softly, "I'm sorry. I should never have hidden your mother's book. But you see, I needed to find Maighread's diary, and I wasn't sure if you'd let me stay once your mother's book was found. My search was just as important to me as yours was to you."

"Was it?" he growled. "Are your sisters in danger?"

She inhaled, her eyes wide in what looked like shock, and for a moment said nothing.

He was glad. He wanted her to be shocked, to realize the injustice she'd done him.

"No," she whispered, his domineering goddess brought low. "Your sisters are more important than the diary. I was a fool. But Ran—"

"No." He shook his head. "Not here." They were no longer at Adders. That dream had shattered.

"I'm sorry," she said again. "I thought…"

"What?" he replied bitterly. "What did you think?" He could hear footsteps hurrying by in the hall outside and more distantly the murmur of voices from the dining room. They had stayed too long here.

Julian grabbed Elspeth's hand, dragging her to the door.

"Julian, wait," she protested, far too loudly.

"Hush," he hissed. "We need to return to the party."

"No," she protested. "Can't we stay here just a little longer?"

Too late, too late, too late. Everything they'd had was fallen to ruins. He opened the door gingerly. Thank God, the corridor was empty. "Go."

He could see her mutinous expression in the light. Even now, as his heart beat with trepidation, he wanted to pull her into his arms and kiss her until she saw reason.

Until she stopped her lies and kissed him back.

But that moment was past. He had no right anymore to her.

Elspeth stepped into the hall and was gone.

Julian waited a moment more and then walked in the opposite direction. He was almost to the dining room when he nearly ran into Leander Ashley, the Earl of Rookewoode.

"Greycourt," the newly married man exclaimed. "Just the man I wanted to see."

Julian pulled himself together. "Congratulations again. Your bride is lovely."

"She is, isn't she?" Rookewoode grinned. "But I want to talk business with you, if you don't mind."

"Won't your countess miss you?"

Rookewoode waved away the concerns of his new wife. "Just for a moment. She won't mind. Come to my study. It's just here."

The earl indicated a room down the corridor. Inside the curtains were pulled and the fire was lit.

Rookewoode leaned against what looked like a Jacobean desk, heavy and solid. "Now. I've had a word with Lord Admiral Swanson, and the old man turned the color of the inside of a blood orange when he read your mother's words. He might look aside for many things Windemere had done, but murder—murder of his brother's wife—is quite another matter. Thought Swanson might drop from apoplexy right there, and then where would our plans for him to spread the word be?" The earl made a wry face. "But the old boy rallied round and proceeded to rant and curse Windemere for the next hour. Never heard such words. But of course, he was in the navy."

"Good." Julian nodded distractedly. His mind was still on Elspeth. On their parting. On the innocent way she'd glanced at him in the church. But she *wasn't* innocent, perhaps had never been. It had been his own blind stupidity to even think so. She'd maneuvered him with the seasoned ability of an old card sharp.

"You don't look enthused," the earl interrupted his thoughts, eyes much too intelligent. That was the thing with Rookewoode—he acted the careless rogue right up until he surprised you with a sudden word or act of perception. "What's bothering you, Jules?"

Julian shook his head. "Nothing to do with this matter."

"You know we have him," Rookewoode said. "Your uncle can't escape from the charge of murder in your mother's own handwriting. He might never be brought before Parliament, but he's ruined."

The thing was, Julian did know. He was on the very cusp of finally winning against his uncle, yet all he could think about was Elspeth and her betrayal.

Of losing her.

Julian straightened. He'd never had Elspeth. That had been a fallacy of his own imagination. She'd been using him for her own interests the entire time.

He looked at Rookewoode seriously. "Thank you. I don't know if I could have pulled this together without your contacts."

Rookewoode shrugged. "You just would've taken a bit more time. The end would've still been the same." But the earl grinned, looking quite pleased with himself.

"Shall we return to the breakfast?" Julian asked. "They'll be wanting to toast you and the countess."

"Already started before I left," the earl replied cheerfully. "But yes, let's return. Shouldn't want to disappoint the aged female relatives." He mimed an exaggerated shiver of horror.

The dining room was loud when they entered, people talking to their neighbors. The bride's face lit up when she saw Rookewoode, and he grinned at her as he sauntered over. Julian made his way to his designated seat somewhat farther down the table from the bridal couple. He caught Kester's measuring eye as he sat, and Julian looked hastily—guiltily—away. Elspeth was right. She did deserve the truth.

*   *   *

Elspeth was poking at a piece of seedcake the next afternoon when Freya asked, "What happened at the wedding breakfast yesterday? You haven't told me a thing, and I'm quite frustrated."

They sat in Freya's salon, the sun coming in the windows, Plum pretending to sleep while Daisy batted at his ears, trying to get the other dog to play. A whole tray of cakes and tarts and savory little pies sat before Elspeth and Freya, and it all should've been perfect.

Except Julian had dismissed her, and Elspeth had no idea how to fix it.

Or if she even could.

Her shoulders slumped. He'd been so angry at the breakfast yesterday. It all seemed hopeless.

"Elspeth?"

She glanced at her sister. "Yes?"

"What is it, dear?" Freya nodded to the plate. "You've destroyed that poor seedcake, and I don't think it's done a thing to you."

"It isn't my favorite." Elspeth wrinkled her nose at the crumbs on her plate and set it aside.

"And the haddock this morning for breakfast?"

"Well, *fish*."

"You love fish." Freya gave her a stern look. "Last night at supper you didn't touch the ham and potatoes, and you refused a slice of apple tart. *Apple tart*, Elspeth."

Elspeth sighed. The problem with sisters was that they were much too observant. And didn't mind sticking their noses into other people's business.

Freya bit her lip. "Darling, something's troubling you. Please tell me."

And cared far too much.

Elspeth tangled her fingers together in her lap. "I'm afraid I've done something you'll find quite foolish."

Freya tilted her head and waited.

And waited.

Maddening. Freya had always had the ability to make Elspeth talk.

"I've fallen in love with Julian Greycourt."

Freya dropped her teacup.

"Oh dear," Elspeth exclaimed gratefully, "I should call for a maid."

"No." Freya halted her with an outstretched hand. "Leave the spill for now. Let's talk some more."

Elspeth sat back down a little sulkily.

"Sometimes when a woman beds a man, she becomes caught up in the emotion of the act," Freya said very carefully. "Could that perhaps be the case here?"

"I enjoyed very much what we did in bed." Elspeth closed her eyes, carefully pushing away the memories. "But that's not why I love him. Julian is such a proud man. He cares very much, perhaps too much, for his family. He loves intensely, and I rather admire that. He likes so many things—books, dogs, sweets—and yet he hides his likes because he sees them as weaknesses. He doesn't know how to peel potatoes, but he tried for me. His words can be so sharp they cut, but inside he's so soft and caring, that he's the one in the end who bleeds." She opened her eyes and looked at her sister helplessly. "I love him. And I think he might've loved me."

Freya hummed. "But?"

"But I apologized, and he will not accept it." Elspeth felt her voice go thick with tears. "Trust is perhaps the most important value to him, and I broke it."

A sob shuddered through her, and suddenly Freya was beside her, wrapping her arms around Elspeth.

"I shall gut him," Freya snarled, "for making you weep."

"No," Elspeth gasped, pressing the handkerchief that her sister gave her to her eyes. "You can't. I love him, and it's my fault, truly, that he's angry at me. I lied. And I hid something important from him so that I could stay at Adders longer, looking for the diary."

"I refuse to believe that you're the villain of this piece," Freya said fiercely.

"I'm certainly not the heroine." Elspeth looked up at Freya's ceiling, trying to stop the tears. "I don't think there's any villain or hero. It's just that he doesn't feel the same as I. He doesn't love me in return and"—a sob caught her, making her voice break—"and I must live without him. And Freya, I don't know *how*."

Her emotion overwhelmed her again, the sorrow and tears making her gasp. This ache in her chest was unbearable. Why should she feel such pain when weeks before she'd not even talked to Julian? Couldn't she simply pretend she'd never met him, never talked and laughed with him, never felt his mouth on hers?

But love was like an infection of the heart—once settled, it couldn't be cleaned out, sinking in without cure, taking hold, until the entire body throbbed with it.

Until she might die of it.

Elspeth wasn't sure afterward how long she stayed in Freya's arms, racked with tears and sorrow, but she had begun to still. To sit limp with itching eyes and flushed cheeks.

Then the door flew open.

Messalina rushed in. "I came as quickly as I could. I didn't find out until just an hour ago at Lady Greenhill's salon. I..." She stopped short, her eyes widening as she saw them. "Oh, you've already heard. I'm so sorry."

"Heard what?" Freya asked. "What are you sorry for?"

Elspeth sat upright, the sodden handkerchief still pressed to her nose.

Messalina was watching her with pity in her eyes. "That my brother is rumored to have... unusual tastes in the bedroom. That he seduced you, Elspeth."

CHAPTER SEVENTEEN

*"What shall I do?" Christina whimpered. "What if
the fairies keep me as well?"
Lady Long-Nose turned so that the fairy could not
see her lips and whispered, "You must go. Sabinus's
life might well depend on it. Here." She thrust one
of her letters into Christina's hand. "Give this to the
Fairy King should he demand more poetry."
At this Christina began to wail, "Please, you must
come with me!" . . .*
—From *Lady Long-Nose*

Quinn had spied Lord Mulgrave leaving London in the
wee early hours and it was that news that preoccupied
Julian in the afternoon. They hadn't heard anything from
Lucretia, either good or bad. Julian was cautiously opti-
mistic that that meant she hadn't been caught. But then
why would Mulgrave quit London? To search for her himself? Hardly a reassuring thought.

As he walked through London, Julian debated with
himself whether to set off after Mulgrave himself or even
send Quinn. Which was perhaps why he didn't realize
something was wrong until he arrived at Opal's Coffee
House.

Heads turned as he entered. Several leaned close to
their neighbors to murmur something.

A man smirked at him.

Julian shook off the feeling of being talked about. It wasn't the first time that tongues had been set a-wag by his stained reputation. Augustus had seen to that when he'd first brought Julian and Quinn to London and made sure that everyone knew about Ran's beating and blamed him.

Julian got his tankard and brought it to a table in the corner. Archway was already seated by the hearth nearby, but he rose as Julian sat.

Archway didn't look over as he fussed with his hat and stick, but Julian heard his murmur. "Not here, not now. Money is money, but I cannot be seen with you. Your peculiarities should've stayed behind closed doors."

Julian didn't turn as the other man left. Didn't blink or otherwise show that he'd heard anything, but his senses were suddenly alight. The hissing of the whispers near him, the giggle from across the room, a laugh cut off.

Peculiarities.

This was his worst fear made real.

He could hear a pounding in his head, the racing of his blood, the animal desire to flee when cornered. But fleeing only prompted a predator to chase.

Julian made himself take a sip of coffee, the liquid tasting like boiled slops. He slowly opened a newspaper and feigned reading a column, though he had no idea what it said. He could do this. Wait it out for ten or fifteen minutes. Show them he wasn't afraid.

But he couldn't help the trickle of sweat down his spine. Had to constantly tamp down the temptation to look up, to see how many were watching him.

Another sip.

He could do this.

He *would* do this.

He was a Greycourt, and however sullied that name, he bore it proudly.

So Julian sat and sipped, though his stomach was acid, and when his tankard was done he slowly folded the paper and rose.

Everyone. It was everyone watching him, from an elderly man in a full-bottomed wig to the boy who ran errands for tuppence, sneering in the corner.

Julian didn't pause or hesitate or make any sign at all that he was aware of the combined stares. He placed his hat on his head and strolled leisurely toward the door.

He was nearly there when a man with yellowed teeth muttered, "Like it on your knees, do you?"

Julian turned and looked down with eight generations of aristocracy behind his cold stare. "I beg your pardon?"

"I said...," the man began, but trailed off under Julian's icy gaze. "Nothing," he muttered, turning back to his table.

Julian stood watching the man a moment longer to make his point plain and then drawled, "Indeed."

Outside, the wind was whipping around corners and spitting rain that stung his face as he turned toward Windemere House, for there was only one person who had the power to disseminate the rumor so fast.

How had the duke known?

Julian had always been as discreet as possible, to an almost obsessive degree. He hid his identity if he could and held his affairs at Adders instead of London. Made sure the women he purchased were by reference only and were paid well. There were only three servants at Adders: the maid, Mrs. McBride, and Vanderberg.

The only time he'd broken his rules was with Elspeth.

That...that had to be coincidence. Yes, she'd lied about

the book and had left him cold in the bed they'd made love in. But to betray him in this way was so low he couldn't fathom Elspeth doing it. She was too kind, too sweet. But if it wasn't she, then that left only servants who had been with him for years—Vanderberg and Mrs. McBride for decades.

It must be Vanderberg. The valet was in London, had seen Elspeth at Adders, and certainly, after all these years, had had more than a hint of what Julian did in the country.

The thought brought him pain—more pain. The coffee-house had been like fighting through a battlefield, and he hadn't even met his prime enemy yet.

There was no one else the traitor could be. If not Vanderberg, then who? Mrs. McBride or the maid, whatever her name was, both of whom never left Dydle?

Or Elspeth.

If Elspeth had betrayed him in this way, he would never recover.

Julian shook his head. Windemere House was in sight, and he must armor himself. It didn't matter in the end who had betrayed him.

He couldn't trust anyone.

With that thought firmly in mind, Julian knocked at the door to Windemere.

Johnson opened the door, and when he caught sight of Julian, his mouth twisted in a nasty sneer. "What do you want?"

Julian didn't bother answering. He shoved the butler aside and walked in.

"'Ere now!" Johnson shouted behind him, but Julian didn't stop.

He took the stairs two at a time, striding down the hall to his uncle's study.

He shoved open the door to find Augustus in consultation with a man in a bobbed wig and half-moon spectacles.

The other man jumped, but Augustus merely smiled, leaning back in his chair like a self-satisfied lizard fat with slugs.

"You mustn't mind my nephew, Doctor," the duke said. "He's of a nervous disposition and prone to unnatural urges."

The doctor sucked in his breath, peering at Julian over his spectacles. "This is ... ?"

Augustus nodded with sickening pity. "The one you've heard about. Yes."

The doctor coughed and stood. "Then I'll bother you no longer, Your Grace, since you have ... erm ... family matters to attend to. I'll leave my instructions with Her Grace's lady's maid. The duchess most likely merely ate something that didn't agree with a lady's delicate stomach. Better in no time, I'm sure. With your permission?"

The duke nodded graciously as the doctor bowed himself out the door.

Julian deliberately took a chair, carefully arranging his hat and cane on his knees before looking at his uncle. "You think you've won. You haven't."

"No?" Augustus laughed. "It certainly seems like victory from my point of view. Your embarrassing perversions are known by all in London. Soon in all of England. This bit of gossip is delicious! The nephew of a duke who enjoys licking the feet of women? Who can't even get a stand without being humiliated?" He tutted. "Why, boy, if I'd known you'd liked that sort of thing, I would have beaten you bloody when you lived with me. I think we'd both have enjoyed that."

The words were nothing more than what Julian had expected. What he'd imagined for years in his own mind. They hardly mattered now. It was almost a sort of relief: his secret was in the air, no getting it back, no stopping it. There was nothing he could do or say or even hope for to ameliorate the disaster.

It was almost freeing.

And with that thought, Julian relaxed and smiled at the old man. "Stories. Simple stories. My reputation is ruined, yes. I won't ever be able to wade through society's waters again, but it's a small loss, I think." He shrugged. "After all, I can do other things with my time. Read. Travel. Oh, and do business. Because a man's ability to do business is about money, not personal matters."

Augustus grinned, steepling his fingers on the desk. "Of course. But it's almost impossible to do business without money to invest. Something of which you have very little."

"True." Julian bowed in mocking admiration. "I quite forgot how wise you are, Uncle. I think, though, you've forgotten one other thing a man needs to have to do business."

"Do tell me your thoughts on business, Nephew. You must have many, considering how little you've done over the years."

"Well, yes," Julian said lightly, "that has been what I've made pains to make you believe."

Augustus stilled.

"But as to your question..." Julian felt a savage smile widening his lips. "I think you'll agree that a man's reputation is vital for business. If a gentleman were, for instance, to poison to death his sister-in-law, and the truth came out...?"

The duke choked, and for a glorious second, Julian thought he might have an attack of apoplexy. Then the old man got out, "What? What have you done?"

He wasn't even able to pretend disinterest.

Julian spread his hands wide. "I've spent the last week talking to your business partners. Showed them notes that my mother left, detailing how you killed her. I'm surprised you haven't heard that *your* secret is out as well."

Augustus stared wildly for a moment before spitting, "Mary. Your bitch of a mother was far too sly."

Julian rose. "My mother was never the word you called her, but she was a remarkably clever lady. Yes. She realized what you were doing and left me the evidence to find. Really, it's she who is the author of your downfall."

He turned to leave.

"Wait!" Augustus shouted.

Julian glanced back to see his uncle half-risen from his seat and leaning heavily on the desk, his face suffused with red rage. "Yes?"

"Whom have you told?" the duke demanded. "Who knows?"

"Everyone," Julian enunciated. "I've explained exactly what you did to all the gentlemen who ever did business with you. Even the ones you no longer do business with. After all, a man's reputation is the first currency in business. Without it?" Julian shrugged. "You might as well be penniless."

He closed the door quietly behind him.

*　*　*

Julian made his way to Whispers that evening, glad of the shadows. After this, he'd leave the city, help Lucretia, and find somewhere to lick his wounds. But first he'd confront her.

He ran up the steps to Whispers and pounded on the door. It opened to reveal Hawthorne.

"Where is Elspeth?" Julian asked.

Hawthorne raised his eyebrows. "The library."

Naturally.

Julian took the stairs two at a time. He wanted this over. Done. And then he'd somehow forget her sunray smile and laughing eyes.

He opened the library door to find Elspeth alone, sitting on the floor, and for a moment, his heart contracted. She looked just as she had at Adders.

Only they'd left Adders behind.

"Did you do it?" he demanded.

Elspeth jerked her head around to stare at him. "Do what?"

He squatted near her so he could properly see her eyes. "Betray me. Again. Told all of London the secret I entrusted to you."

She blinked rapidly. "I—"

His upper lip curled. "To think I felt guilt for not telling you that Ran did not kill Aurelia."

"You what?" She looked shocked.

He nodded. "She was dead before he ever got there. I saw her body."

He could see outrage rising in her eyes. "You told the world that he was a murderer, and you knew better? All along?"

"Yes."

She slapped him, turning his face with the force of her blow. "Ran is a recluse because of your lies! How could you betray him like that?"

He looked back at her, leaning so close their noses nearly touched. "How. Could. You?"

"I didn't!" she bellowed. "I never told anyone about Adders. Why would I?"

"I don't know," he replied. "Pure wickedness?"

Her head jerked back. "Is that what you think of me?"

He hesitated, perhaps for only a second.

But she caught it. "You don't."

He looked away. "I know you betrayed me. I just can't make myself believe it."

"Come here," she said.

And he couldn't—he could not—tear himself away from her gaze. He came to her.

They sat together simply breathing for a moment, and he had no idea where to go from here. He was so tired.

She licked her lips. "Tell me what happened the night Aurelia died."

He laughed, a curt gust of air. "I don't know, not entirely. I thought perhaps my mother's notes would tell me. That she knew how Aurelia died and implicated my uncle." He sighed. "I think, in the back of my mind, I was searching for information that would somehow make me less guilty."

Why would she ever want to touch him again knowing he'd kept the truth about Ran from the world? He should leave her alone.

But she grasped his hand, and somehow, though her hand was half the size of his, he couldn't move away from her.

"You need to explain," she said gently. "What happened?"

"You must already have an idea," he replied impatiently. Did she think he enjoyed talking about that night?

She shook her head. "I vow I don't."

He closed his eyes. "Your brother was beaten nearly to death for the murder of my sister, and I didn't do anything to help him."

"Why not?"

He gave her a weary look.

She jerked his hand gently. "Truly, Julian. I've heard the de Moray version. That Aurelia lured my brother to your home, where she died, and he was beaten for it. Now I want to hear yours."

"I think the Greycourt story is already well known," he said bitterly. "Augustus made sure of that."

She nodded. "But I've never heard your tale. Not from your lips."

For a moment he only stared at the motes drifting in a sunbeam. This was folly. The whole world knew the skeleton of the story. Why give muscle, blood, and skin to the entire horrible night?

Perhaps this was a penance. A final confession of his sins.

"They were in love," he said, remembering that summer. Every memory was in sunshine until that night. "My sister and your brother. He was only seventeen, Aurelia barely sixteen. We all knew Ran would propose someday. When we were out of school, he, Kester, and I. They'd get married, sometime in the future, unite our families and estates, be happy."

Aurelia *happy*.

He closed his eyes to steady himself and continued, "But Father died suddenly that summer, of a fit, and he'd made Augustus our—my sisters and brother and my mother—guardian. The duke came at once, smiling and acting the part of the kindly uncle, and then he betrothed Aurelia to an ugly old man."

"But that part has never made sense to me," Elspeth said, tugging at his hand again, presumably to draw his attention. "Why make another betrothal when she already had an understanding with the heir to a dukedom?"

He shrugged. "Pure hatred? Augustus fattened on our family's grief and anger. Aurelia was alarmed, of course, but she thought we could talk Augustus out of the match. Make him see reason. As the weeks went by and the date of the wedding was set, she grew increasingly frantic. The duke left for a couple of days, and when he returned, he brought the man he'd contracted Aurelia to."

Julian grimaced and glanced at Elspeth. "Not only old, but smelly as well. The poor man had ulcers on his legs, and the smell of rot preceded him into the room. We were sitting at supper, simply staring, dumbfounded, at the suitor Augustus wished to make Aurelia's husband. I should've said something then. I should've stood and demanded Augustus leave the house and take his selection with him."

He breathed in, remembering, retracing his actions, and knowing he might've saved them all.

"What happened?" Elspeth asked, her voice soft.

"Aurelia confronted him instead. While I was thinking, trying to find the right words to make our insane uncle abandon this horrific travesty, Aurelia stood and yelled at Augustus. Told him exactly what she thought of him and that she'd be dead before she married that elderly man."

"She sounds very brave," he heard Elspeth say, "and very young."

He raised his eyebrows. "She was only five years removed from the age you are now."

"I think, though, that we were raised very differently,"

she said quietly with a sad sort of smile. "And though my childhood was provincial, it was perhaps less sheltered than your sister's."

He stared at her. Only a fortnight ago, he might've argued that living most of one's life in a secret compound was the very epitome of being sheltered. But maybe he would have been wrong. Elspeth might have strange views on society, but she was exceedingly practical. "What would you have done in her place, then?"

She shrugged. "Probably hesitated to speak, just like you. I would've let myself seem meek and cowed, and later I'd have packed what I could carry and left in the night."

He couldn't help thinking that Aurelia might be alive if she'd burned less brilliantly.

Julian shook his head. "Augustus was furious that a girl barely out of the schoolroom should say such things. He berated my mother to her face and swore at our dead father. He seemed on the precipice of violence. I thought he might kill Aurelia then. But instead he had her dragged to her room and locked her in." Julian swallowed. "That was the last time I saw my sister alive."

Elspeth had tears in her eyes. "I'm so sorry."

"Don't be." He shook his head, impatient with his own verbal circling. He'd meant to tell her the truth.

Julian focused his gaze on their entwined hands. "I told Ran, almost immediately, and Kester, too. Ran wanted to storm Greycourt, but I persuaded him to wait. Augustus had brought with him a dozen or more men who obviously were not mere servants. I wanted to avoid conflict. I was worried what Augustus meant to do. I passed word to Aurelia that Ran meant to save her so she wouldn't try to escape on her own." He stopped to shake his head. "It should have worked. Ran and Aurelia should have been away well before anyone knew."

"What happened?" Elspeth whispered.

"I don't know exactly," he said, "but when I went to Aurelia's room that night, the door was already open. Augustus stood just inside, and behind him Aurelia lay on the bed bloodied and unmoving. Dead."

She squeezed his hand but said nothing more.

He closed his eyes. "I should've called the footmen—*our* footmen. I meant to, but Augustus advanced on me, his eyes bloodshot. He told me to think carefully about what I would do next because my mother, remaining sisters, and brother were in the house. With his men."

"He held them hostage against your behavior," she breathed.

"Yes. Augustus told me Aurelia had died trying to escape—that she fell from the window somehow." He shook his head. "I didn't know whether to believe him or not. I was sobbing over my dead sister, and...I don't know that I thought out anything after that."

"How could you?" she murmured.

"Augustus knew about the planned elopement. I followed him outside, into the stable yard behind the house and gardens where Ran and Kester were meant to meet Aurelia and me." He inhaled, feeling his chest tighten as it had that night. "There was a signal I was supposed to use—a lit lantern draped in a red fabric to tell Ran and Kester that it was safe for them to enter the grounds." He swallowed. "Augustus ordered me to make sure Ran came, or he'd have his men kill the rest of my family, starting with the youngest—Lucretia. So I did. I made the signal and betrayed my best friends."

*   *   *

Elspeth watched Julian's drawn face as he confessed to her what he considered his sins and wondered if he'd ever told this story to anyone else. No, she thought not. He'd held this terrible, soul-destroying secret inside himself and let no one know.

"Stop," she said, laying her hand on his cheek. "I don't blame you for any of this. I refuse to."

His expression didn't ease, but his face pressed against her palm as if seeking warmth.

Or absolution.

"I could tell no one," he said, his voice rasping. "Augustus virtually imprisoned us at Greycourt. Aurelia was buried in secret. Mother was overcome with grief for Aurelia. She never rose from her bed again and died the next week. Messalina and Lucretia were sent to an elderly male relative to live. Quinn and I made to watch as our uncle pillaged the house before he dragged us to his carriage and set off for Windemere House. By the time we made London, the news had spread through the entire town: Aurelia had been murdered by Ran, and he'd lost a hand from my family's vengeance." His lips twisted. "Some even said I'd cut off his hand myself."

She winced. "That must've been horrible."

"Yes, it was," he said unemotionally. "But I deserved it. My inaction led to the injury to his hand and thus the infection that took it."

Elspeth looked him in the eye. "Nothing you say will make me believe that a seventeen-year-old boy, under the threat of his family being killed, was in any way responsible for the beating your uncle ordered. The duke is the one responsible for everything that happened, and making you believe that *you* were the one that injured Ran is part and parcel of his evil."

He sighed, his head dropping to lean against her shoulder. "I don't know what to do."

"Can we be friends again?" she asked. "I want you to look at me as you did at Adders. As if you know me. As if you want me."

"I do want you," he said quietly. "I've always wanted you, will always want you, but we're no longer at Adders. Everything has changed."

She closed her eyes against tears. She wanted to wail like a child. Why must things change? Why must he push her away when all she wanted ... all she wanted ...

"Won't you at least kiss me?" she whispered, unmoving.

"Elspeth ..." He sighed. "We can't. Not anymore."

"Why not?" she asked. "We're alone here."

His eyes screwed shut. "I told you I can't."

"Should I ..." She licked her lips, hesitating because she wasn't entirely sure. "Should I order you?"

"Dear God, that's not what I mean." He laughed, his voice cracking, as he flung himself flat upon the floor. "You don't understand. I've made you the talk of the town, dragged you through the worst sort of scandal, and even beyond that ..."

"What?" she asked. "Tell me what to do. Tell me how to make it right again."

"Beyond the scandal and London and all of society's damned rules ..." He took her fingers between his, and for the first time, she saw what he looked like defeated. "This. This thing between you and me. It isn't something that can be forced or even seduced. I'm different from other men. You've known that from the beginning. Something inside me was made strange and odd and different. I can't rise without the command, the stern hand—"

"Then let me be the stern hand," she pleaded, tears in her eyes. "Let me take charge."

"*But*," he said, squeezing her hands gently, "*but* I can't obey a mistress if I can't trust her."

She stared, uncomprehending.

He brought her fingers to his lips, kissing each one, almost in apology. "I care so much for you, Elspeth. Your smile alone is enough to live by, and you've brought me great joy." He smiled sadly. "But darling, I don't trust you."

CHAPTER EIGHTEEN

*The fairy's cold eyes flicked to Lady Long-Nose, and
he said, "You may accompany Sabinus's true love."
At once, the world seemed to turn upside down, and
they stood now in the center of a strange copse of
trees. No bird sang, no creature stirred, and worst
of all, nothing had color. The fairy's clothes had
changed to silver armor, and he wore upon his
head a crown of human finger bones....*
— From *Lady Long-Nose*

Freya watched Elspeth as she packed the next morning in
the room across the hall from Freya's. "Aren't you being a
bit hasty, darling?"

"No," Elspeth replied. She didn't want to talk, didn't
want to think. She just wanted to leave.

Her heart was broken. It had always seemed like an
overdramatic expression—a heart breaking—but that
was exactly how she felt. As if something within her was
broken and could not be repaired.

And now she was crying again.

"I really will gut him if you ask," Freya said in a dis-
tressingly sober voice. "Just tell me."

"Don't kill Julian." Elspeth sniffed, patting her eyes.
"He doesn't deserve it. If anyone deserves to be gutted,
it's me."

Freya scowled. "I really don't see how that's possible."

"It's because I betrayed him," she said.

"How?"

But Elspeth had started tearing up again, so she just waved her hand.

A knock came at the bedroom door. The maid peeked around the door and said, "Your Grace, there's a visitor—"

"Leave us," came an imperious voice from the hallway, and Deidre Dungrave walked into the room.

A knife suddenly appeared in Freya's fist. "What do you want?"

Deidre merely raised her eyebrows at the knife and said, "Calm down. I'm not here to hurt either of you. Quite the opposite."

The Wise Women's Nemain was a tall woman with pale-blond hair and startling green eyes. She held herself as if physically fighting Freya would be no trouble at all.

"May I sit?" she asked, sounding a little amused.

Freya gestured to a chair—with her knife hand. "Please."

The Nemain nodded and sat gracefully. "I've come to tell you that Eve has been tasked with your death, Elspeth de Moray, and I will protect you from her."

Elspeth exchanged a glance with Freya, who looked cautious.

"Eve?"

"Oh," Deidre said, sounding almost embarrassed, "you don't know her. Eve is a little shorter than me, has brown hair, and has a badly stitched scar on her face just here." She motioned to her upper lip. "She was supposed to be my replacement." Deidre's voice was disdainful.

"I don't think we need worry about her," Elspeth said.

Deidre's brows snapped together. "Why not?"

"Because I killed her," Freya said matter-of-factly. "Would you like some tea?"

Deidre blinked. "Yes."

"Certainly," Freya replied, and went to the door. She summoned a maid, requested tea, and shut the door again, all without taking her eyes off Deidre. She came and sat back down and said, "Now tell us why the Hags were so eager for Elspeth's death."

The Nemain shrugged. "I don't really know. They seemed upset because Elspeth is looking around for a diary?"

"Maighread's diary," Elspeth leaned forward to say.

Deidre waved a hand. "Quite. But that doesn't really sound like a reason for execution."

"What if I found it?" Elspeth asked, ignoring Freya signing to be quiet.

"That would be interesting," the Nemain said. "Especially considering how much the Hags *don't* want it revealed."

Another knock came on the door, and they were silent as the maid brought in tea.

"Well," said Freya when the maid had gone away again, "I suppose we owe you thanks." She handed a teacup to Deidre.

"Hmm." Deidre sounded doubtful. "You're welcome, I'm sure, but I didn't kill Eve. Erm. Where exactly—?"

"The Thames," Freya said crisply. She waved the question of bodies and where they lay aside. "Will you be returning to the Wise Women?"

"No," the Nemain said. "I don't like how they've decided to live." She hesitated. "Though I could if it were for something important like delivering Maighread's diary."

Freya looked pleased. "Then perhaps you'll escort Elspeth?"

"I'd be honored to," Deidre replied. "I can leave tonight if you'd like."

It was settled, then, Elspeth supposed. There was no reason to delay any longer. She'd be off to Scotland by tonight.

She'd probably never see Julian again.

Elspeth set her teacup down, doing her best to hold in any wayward tears. Just until she got outside, anyway. "I'd better get my things from Whispers House, then."

"Take the carriage, dear," Freya said.

Elspeth could only nod.

The air was lovely and crisp when she stepped outside for the carriage to be brought around. She closed her eyes and lifted her face to the sky to cool her hot cheeks.

This should be the happiest day of her life. She'd found Maighread's diary, she had an escort to Scotland, and she was leaving tonight on her quest to save the Wise Women. It was more than she'd even dreamed of when she'd arrived in London.

She'd succeeded.

And Julian had told her flatly that he could not trust her.

Had her lies been worth it? Was making the Wise Women whole again worth the cost of Julian's trust?

She knew the right answer: Yes. Saving her family, her home, and everything she believed in, of course that was worth the loss of one man's regard.

Of course.

But that one man—Julian—weighed heavier than the world to her. Her heart told her she'd made a mistake.

Elspeth was so lost in her dreary thoughts that she

didn't even notice the carriage beside her before the door opened.

She turned and saw a woman, a familiar woman, and for a moment her brain scrambled to place her.

And then she realized. *Alice.* Alice from Adders Hall. The maid.

She opened her mouth to shout, but a large man wrapped his hand around her head, pulling the hood of her cloak over her face, suffocating her in the folds.

She fought, of course.

She elbowed a hard stomach. Clawed at the hands lifting her. Kicked at the body dragging her into the carriage. But the problem was she couldn't breathe. Black spots flooded her eyes, and soon she couldn't fight at all.

* * *

Julian glanced around the inn room, looking for any belonging he might've missed. He and Quinn had stayed here for over a month, but they had brought very few things with them to London. What there was fit into a trunk, sitting at his feet.

He nodded to the waiting porter. "Bring it down."

In the lower room, Quinn was meant to be settling the bill with the innkeeper, but Julian saw him at the bottom of the stairs, reading a letter.

His brother looked up as Julian approached him. "When did you last see Lady Elspeth?"

Julian scowled because Quinn had made no attempt to lower his voice, and the tavern was crowded. "Last night. Why?"

"Uncle has her."

Julian's heart stopped. Just stopped, and the world with it. Augustus couldn't—

Quinn turned to the door with his usual readiness to action, but Julian caught him by the arm. He had to think. "What does the letter say?"

His brother balled up the paper and shoved it in his pocket, his eyes concerned. "Better you don't read it. Augustus wants you at Windemere House."

Julian drew in his breath. It must be very bad if Quinn wouldn't let him read the letter.

He used all his control to ask with a steady voice, "Is she alive?"

To his credit, Quinn made no attempt to conceal his doubt. "The duke writes that she is."

Augustus lied. It was his defining trait. But if Elspeth was dead...the room started swirling.

No.

No. She was alive. She was beautiful, and unhurt, and her smile still held sunshine. Any other outcome could not be considered. He had to remain sane.

Quinn's arm flexed beneath Julian's fingers, but he made no move to pull away. "What do you want to do?"

And this was what Julian loved most about his brother: Quinn's willingness to follow Julian into battle without question or quarrel. "Go to Hawthorne. Tell him. Have him bring his men. All of them, and make sure they're armed."

Quinn nodded. "And you?"

Julian was already striding to the door. "I'm going to Windemere House. To bring back Elspeth."

Behind him, his brother grunted. "Don't die before I get there."

And then Julian was out the door.

CHAPTER NINETEEN

*"Who are you?" Lady Long-Nose
demanded of the fairy.
He gave her a long, unfriendly look. "I am the
Fairy King, of course."
Christina screamed and might have fainted had Lady
Long-Nose not pinched her arm.
The Fairy King settled in a throne made of human
bones, and as he did so, fairies appeared
from the surrounding woods....*
—From *Lady Long-Nose*

Julian had warned her over and over that the Duke of
Windemere was quite mad, and Elspeth had believed him.
But she hadn't truly understood how mad until now.

They were in Windemere's library, the place where
she'd met Julian all those weeks ago, which was ironic
and perhaps even funny, but Elspeth couldn't find it in
herself to be amused. She was chained to the fire grate at
the duke's feet. Literally chained with a padlock, which
forced her to crouch on the floor as Windemere aimed a
dueling pistol at her head from only inches away.

His Grace sat in an ornate chair facing the door and
paid her no mind at all. She might've been a cat on the
hearth. Or even less—the rug, perhaps. Which made his

words all the more chilling because he certainly wasn't speaking to her.

And there was no one else in the room.

"Bloody bastard," the duke said clearly. "Thinks he can win. Like his father. Like his bitch of a mother. He went to Swanson and Richfield. Who knows who else he talked to. All of them? No, he said he did, but it's not possible. Doesn't matter anyway. They wouldn't dare not do business with me." Windemere's eyes wandered to Elspeth, but he still didn't acknowledge her. "I'll make him watch. Have my men each take a turn at her, show him how his whore will share. No. I'll take her myself. Chain her to my bed. Chain him to the damned wall. Fuck her until she's big with my child, then kill them both."

He was insane, Elspeth told herself, slowly twisting, attempting to get to her pocket. She hadn't even been searched when Windemere's men had brought her here. The duke was insane, and he wouldn't ever touch her because Julian would come and—

But if Julian came, the duke would make him watch. Or kill Julian outright.

Her breath caught.

That couldn't happen. Elspeth had to get to her little pistol before Julian was lured into the house. He was smart. He wouldn't be fooled by anything the duke told him...except...

Except Julian was noble in the most maddening of ways, and if he truly thought her in danger, he might, he very well might, come walking in offering himself as an exchange, a sacrifice for a woman he couldn't even trust.

The fool. She nearly sobbed.

No. The pistol. That was all she needed to focus on.

But Windemere must've seen her move because there was a sudden loud *bang!* that nearly made her lose control of her bladder, and a hole appeared in the floor beside her knee.

She peered up and saw the duke staring at her as he set down the first pistol and brought out its twin. "I said, *stay still.*"

Elspeth froze, hardly breathing, because this man looked at her as if she were no more than a mouse he'd found in his bedroom. It wouldn't take but a twitch to shoot her.

There was a commotion in the hallway, coming closer, and it had to be Julian arriving to a trap, and she couldn't wait any longer, she couldn't.

The duke's eyes jerked to the door.

Elspeth rolled back on her bottom and kicked him as hard as she could in the knee.

The duke curled reflexively over his injury, but he pulled the trigger at the same time.

There was a bellow of rage, of desperate despair, and Elspeth struggled upright to see Julian fighting with what looked like dozens of men with more coming. His eyes were wild, he had a cut lip, and as she watched he brutally slammed one man's head into the wall, making his foe slump to the floor.

He was winning. She smiled. Julian was—

Something twinged in her arm, and she looked down.

Blood was pooling in her lap.

* * *

Elspeth was bleeding, lying against the hearth and bleeding, and still she smiled at him. Her beautiful smile, sunny and warm. And then her eyes closed, and everything went red.

Julian lost control.

Two men were holding him while a third hit him. He leaned to the side, into the man to his right, and saw his eyes widen just before Julian bit into his cheek. Hot liquid flooded his mouth, and there was screaming.

Elspeth wasn't moving.

He had a knife in his hand, and it was bloody, plunging in and out of another's stomach even as the man fell to the ground. Before him were others, but they were backing away now, trying to keep him and his knife from coming near but seemingly wary of touching him.

Julian had no such worries.

He charged the first, punching with the knife, stabbing as hard and as brutally as he could. Shoving, kicking, grinding knuckles into eyes, thumbs into throats. He didn't care. It didn't matter.

Elspeth wasn't moving.

He staggered to her, paying no attention at all to Augustus, his voice, or the other gun he was waving around. Julian's hands were on Elspeth, trying to lift her, but she was tied down somehow, his filthy uncle had chained her like a beast, and he tore at the padlock with his bare fingers because she wasn't moving and he couldn't lift her.

Somewhere behind him, he heard Quinn's voice. "Julian." And then more urgently, "*Julian*, you need to move. He's using you as cover."

Not even for Quinn. He couldn't look up, not even for his brother.

There was another shot, this one much closer, making his ears ring, the smell of gunpowder sharp in his nose.

"God's blood," someone said faintly.

Augustus was slumped in his chair, his head tilted to the side and half his face missing, and standing over him was the duchess, pale, blood-spattered, and strangely calm. "He tried to kill me."

CHAPTER TWENTY

Among the fairies was Sabinus, looking quite dazed.
At once, Christina started for the man.
The Fairy King clapped his hands, making her freeze.
"Give me a poem," he told her. "A fresh poem,
not the one in your pocket."
Christina opened her mouth and then
burst into tears.
Lady Long-Nose felt her heart seize with fear....
                                    —From *Lady Long-Nose*

When Elspeth awoke, the room was sunny, and Julian was staring at her. His gray eyes held tears.

"Don't move," he whispered. "You were shot. I thought I lost you."

She slapped him, which made her arm hurt very much. "Ow!" Belatedly, she noticed that her arm was bandaged.

His eyebrows snapped together. "What—?"

"You walked right into a trap," she said, her voice breaking. "He was going to shoot you. Make you watch and then...then sh-shoot you!"

And she started sobbing like a ninny, and he gathered her into his arms and gently scolded her. "I told you not to move. The bullet went in your arm."

"I wouldn't have been shot if you hadn't been so stupid," she said rather nonsensically. "I heard you in the hall, and so I had to kick your uncle. Couldn't you see it was a trap?"

He stroked a thumb over her cheek, his brows still drawn together. "You're very brave."

"Yes, I am," she said, swiping at the tears on her cheeks. Her eyes were never going to recover. "I won't ever have to do it again and be shot, if you simply use your intelligence and do *not* walk into traps trying to save me. Promise me."

He kissed her nose and murmured, "I would promise you nearly anything, but not that. If you were ever, God forbid, in such a circumstance again, I'd walk right into the trap. I couldn't not. You are my heart and I can hardly live without a heart."

She sniffled, her eyes welling up *again*, and said, "Oh Goddess, I've fallen in love with a fool."

"Have you?" he asked, almost shyly.

"Yes." She bit her lip, looking away and saying rather gruffly, "I know that you don't trust me, still—" He tried to say something, but she only talked louder over him. "But I've decided to trust you. I think trust is something that has to be free. You can't harness it, or confine it, in the hope that you'll be able to hold trust forever. You can only let it go and believe in your heart that it will stay." She inhaled shakily, turning back to him. "So I've decided to trust in you, Julian Greycourt."

"Elspeth," he whispered against her lips, kissing her softly, his breath leaving his body to enter hers, "I trust you as well, my love. I do. And I'm so sorry for my anger towards you. I think part of it was grief that I'd lost you."

"You haven't lost me," she murmured, closing her eyes and reveling in this moment between them, finally.

But she had to breathe after all, so she pulled back. "What will you do about the duke?"

"Nothing." His voice was odd. "Augustus is dead. Ann shot him in front of more than a dozen witnesses, including my brother-in-law and the Earl of Rookewoode. Apparently, he had been poisoning her."

"What?" she asked faintly, and then considered the matter. "Oh, good show, Ann."

He snorted. "I agree, but unfortunately there were witnesses."

"Oh, dear," Elspeth said, much more worried over Ann's fate than her late husband's. "What will become of Ann?"

"We can't hide who killed my uncle," he said, "and even as a duchess—perhaps especially as a duchess—the murder of one's husband is a grave crime in the eyes of England."

Elspeth frowned with concern. "She won't be sentenced to death, will she?"

He shook his head. "We called in a doctor, a friend of Rookewoode's, and the man made a statement to the court that Ann had a fit and is mentally and physically unwell. She wants to live with her older brother at his country estate. Of course, most of society will think she's imprisoned, but I won't make that stipulation with him."

"What if he doesn't treat her well?" Elspeth demanded.

"She seems certain that her brother loves her very much," Julian said. "It was their parents' idea to marry her to Augustus, not his."

She nodded. "Good." Elspeth suddenly thought of something. "The maid! Alice, from Adders Hall, she was one of the people in the carriage that took me."

But Julian was nodding already. "And she gave Augustus all the information about what I do in the bedroom. Don't worry, she's been arrested."

She sighed at the news and leaned back on her pillows to truly look at Julian for the first time since waking. There were dark patches under his eyes and a bruise turning a lovely shade of purple high on his cheek. "How long have you been sitting with me?"

He glanced away, and she rather thought he meant to prevaricate, but then he said, "Since you were shot. It's six of the clock now."

"Surely a new duke has better things to do," she said softly.

"Not this new duke." He took her hand firmly in his. "When I thought you dead, Elspeth...God, I think I lost my sanity for a time." He touched his forehead to hers. "I can never lose you."

"Oh, *Julian*."

Then his mouth was on hers, and she felt pure delight streak through her, like the parting of the clouds after a thunderstorm. The world was colorful again. She had hope.

She tugged gently at his bottom lip and then whispered against his mouth, "I suppose you'll be looking for a duchess now that you're a duke. An ordinary, proper lady."

His breath puffed against her lips. "If I wanted an ordinary duchess, I'd never have fallen in love with you."

EPILOGUE

"Come," said the Fairy King. "Simply give me a poem, and Sabinus shall be free. Don't you wish to save your love from our wickedness?"

"You can do this," Lady Long-Nose whispered to Christina. "Please try."

"I can't," Christina cried. "I simply can't because it was Lady Long-Nose who wrote those letters."

At this, Sabinus seemed to become more aware. He looked up in surprise, first at Christina and then at Lady Long-Nose. "What?"

The Fairy King slowly turned to him. "Did you know this?"

"I... I thought Christina had written those letters." The Fairy King raised one eyebrow dubiously and turned to Lady Long-Nose. "Tell us a poem."

And so she did, the words flowing from her lips like jewels tossed to the ground. Sabinus closed his eyes, smiling, as she recited, but when she finished, he opened them and winced when he saw her.

"You are a fool," the Fairy King said, and turned to Lady Long-Nose. "You love this man?"

Her heart was bleeding, but Lady Long-Nose tilted her chin up. "I do."

"Then I offer to you the same bargain that I would've offered Sabinus's true love: I will let this fool go now

*if you will take on his year's debt to my court
instead. Do you agree?"*
*"Yes," Lady Long-Nose said simply.
Christina sobbed, taking Sabinus's hand.
"Oh, please let me go with him!"
"If she goes with him," the Fairy King said, his gaze
never leaving Lady Long-Nose's own,
"then the debt is three years."
"Why an extra year?" Lady Long-Nose
couldn't help asking.
The king shrugged. "Because I wish it so. Normally
a mortal's debt would be ten years' time in the fairy
realm, or, if the mortal is especially intriguing, their
lifetime. But this man here"—he waved to Sabinus
without looking at him—"is nothing special.
He may be pretty, but otherwise he is a dullard.
I can do nothing with him other than add
his bones to my throne."
Christina screamed and fainted into Sabinus's arms.
Sabinus looked at Lady Long-Nose with pleading
eyes, but it hardly mattered, save for a pang in her
heart, for she'd already made up her mind. "Yes,
I will stay in the fairy kingdom for three years in
exchange for Your Majesty letting both
Christina and Sabinus go."
"Excellent," said the Fairy King, and
clapped his hands.
Instantly, the lovers were gone.
The Fairy King stepped down from his throne and
held out his hand to Lady Long-Nose.
"Come. I will show you my kingdom."
Now, the Fairylands are vast, encompassing forests
and fields, the oceans and rivers, mountains rocky*

and snowy, and caves so far underground that
the fish that live in the pools there have no eyes.
Wherever they went, there were fairies. Some had
gossamer wings; some covered themselves with
moleskin coats; some had scales on their bodies.
There were fairies of the sky who lived among
the clouds and delighted in sending rain down on
unfortunate travelers. There were fairies of swampy
lands, each with a small glowing light with which
they danced in the reeds on black nights. There
were fairies who disguised themselves with gray
lichen and lived in rocky hills.
And every fairy they met bowed to the Fairy King,
glancing at Lady Long-Nose with curious
but unhostile eyes.
After days, weeks, perhaps years, for there is no way
to tell time in the fairy world, they returned to the
Fairy King's own lands, stark and colorless.
Lady Long-Nose looked around the stark forest and
said, "All the other fairy lands are colorful and filled
with life. Why is your land so cold?"
"It is a curse," the Fairy King said. "Long ago, I
fought my cousin for the throne, a terrible battle in
which many, many fairies died, until at last,
I dealt him a killing blow. But as my cousin fell,
he cursed me."
Lady Long-Nose waited, but the Fairy King said
nothing more. So she asked, "What was the curse?"
"Ah," said the Fairy King with a careless wave,
"it hardly matters now."
That first year, Lady Long-Nose was called upon
each morning to recite a line or two of poetry, and as
the year progressed, more and more fairies attended

her recitals. The Fairy King never took
his eyes off her face.
She learned to eat honey and milk, tiny silver fishes,
berries and nuts picked fresh, and exquisite cakes,
beautiful and tasting of wine.
The second year, Lady Long-Nose learned to dance
as the fairies do, slow and stately, quick and leaping,
and wanton and wild. Soon she danced so well that
the fairies vied to be her partner, although the Fairy
King always took her hand for the last dance,
just before the dawn.
The third year, Lady Long-Nose learned to ride the
fierce fairy horses of the wild hunt. She gripped her
horse with thigh and heel, and when she shot her
arrows, she hit her target every time. The Fairy King
rode beside her, his eyes nearly warm.
But finally, the three years ended.
The Fairy King sat on his bone throne and summoned
Lady Long-Nose. "You have served your time in my
court," he said, his face blank and cold once more.
"A fairy of my court will escort you
to the world above."
Lady Long-Nose stared at him. "That is all? I've
lived and danced and hunted by your side for three
years, and you will dismiss me without
even a farewell?"
"If that is what you want," he returned.
"It isn't," Lady Long-Nose shouted. "I like it here.
No one seems to care about my nose at all."
At that, the Fairy King's brows drew together.
"Your... nose?"
She pointed to her own face. "It's huge."
He blinked. "And?"

*She waved her hands nearly hysterically. "Everyone
in the world above has always told me how ugly it is."
The Fairy King cocked his head slowly. "Sometimes I
do not understand humans at all."
"Why do you think they call me Lady Long-Nose?"
"I thought it merely descriptive," the Fairy King said.
"You dislike it?"
"Yes," Lady Long-Nose said. "It's not
even my real name."
"What is your real name, then?"
"Roxane," she whispered.
The Fairy King nodded briskly and held out his hand.
"Then, Roxane, will you remain with me in my realm,
reciting poetry for me, dancing with me, and riding
beside me as my queen forever?"
"Yes," Roxane said, "for I fell in love with you in my
first year here. And though you haven't said so,
I think you return my affection."
"I love you more than the stars above, more
than the sweetness of honey, and more than my
heartbeat," the Fairy King said with fervor.
"Please stay with me."
Roxane smiled as she took his hand.
And the forest bloomed with color.*
                                    —From *Lady Long-Nose*

ONE MONTH LATER
ADDERS HALL

Dear Ran,

*You would not believe the improvements that we've
made to Adders Hall. Already we have the broken*

*windows in the east wing replaced, and the portico
has been patched by a lovely local man who wears
the most awful wig. I thought I saw a beetle in it
the other day.*

*Have you finished reading that rather ghastly
anatomy book you told me about in your last
letter? Perhaps you ought to read something light
next time. I've heard many people are fond of* The
Compleat Angler, *although I don't really know
why. I've just finished the most marvelous book,*
The Other World: Comical History of the States
and Empires of the Moon, *by a man called Cyrano
de Bergerac, and it is quite interesting as...*

"There you are!" Messalina strolled into Elspeth's
study—actually one of the unused rooms on the first
floor, but if she wanted to call it a study, she could—and
plopped an armful of evergreen boughs on the table by
the window. "Do you think that's enough? Hawthorne has
declared a cessation to gathering evergreens and is sitting in the library with a glass of brandy. If we need to go
back out again, I should go get him before he becomes too
comfortable."

Elspeth set down her pen to eye her sister-in-law's
bounty. "Maybe? I don't really know. I've been surprised
by how much Julian is enjoying the Christmas festivities.
I suppose we ought to ask him."

"Whom are you asking what?" Quintus inquired as he
brought in a second heap of evergreens. "His Grace? Do
you want to ask His Grace a question? Because if so, I
think you should have to send a letter to his solicitors in
London and find out if His Grace has the time to—"

"For God's sake, Quinn," Julian called mildly by the

door, "are you ever going to stop gracing me?" Plum, who had been lazing by the fireplace, got up to greet him.

"No," Quintus replied, unperturbed at the interruption.

"Grace. Grace. Grace," Messalina chanted absently under her breath. "Do we need more evergreens? What do you think?"

Julian eyed the mound of branches. "I think that is enough to decorate the hall and dining room, and if you cut any more, my trees will be completely denuded."

"Oh, good," Messalina said. "Then I'm off to the library before Hawthorne falls asleep."

"Certainly," Julian said with a small smile as his sister passed him. He looked at Quintus. "May I borrow my wife?"

"You mean Your Grace would like to borrow Her Grace so that Your Graces might spend time all on your gracely..."

Elspeth giggled as she met her husband at the door. Plum had settled on the hearth again. "The more you object to Quintus's gracing the more he'll do it, you know."

Julian grumbled under his breath. "You'd think he might be more respectful now, and yet..."

Elspeth squeezed his arm. Her husband might complain, but she thought that he secretly enjoyed the gentle teasing from his family. Quintus and Julian had always been close, but the fragile accord with his sister—sisters, hopefully, if Lucretia could visit them for the Christmas season—was a new and beautiful thing.

"Where are you taking me?" she asked as they turned a corner of the hall. They were nearing their bedroom— Julian's old bedroom for now, until the master bedroom was done being renovated.

Julian leaned closer to her. "I have need of my lady."

She felt a lovely warmth between her thighs. "Do you, truly? Then I hope you have thought about the proper way to ask."

They were at their door now. Julian shoved it open, ushered Elspeth in, and shut the door firmly.

She turned and looked at him.

Julian dropped to his knees.

ABOUT THE AUTHOR

Elizabeth Hoyt is the *New York Times* bestselling author of over twenty historical romances featuring wounded, brooding heroes and the clever and caring heroines who love them. She lives in beautiful Minneapolis, Minnesota, with her family and spends much of her summers trying to outsmart the bunnies in her garden. In winter, she stays indoors and watches the snow fall.

Fall head over heels for charming dukes and sharp-witted ladies in these swoony historical romances from Forever!

BOOKSHOP CINDERELLA
by Laura Lee Guhrke

As an unmarried woman with no prospects, Evie Harlow is content with running her quaint bookshop. Until Maximillian Shaw, the devilishly attractive Duke of Westbourne, saunters in with a proposition: To win a bet, he'll turn her into the season's diamond. Slowly, Evie follows Max's lead and becomes the star of high society, even as their time together results in chemistry she's never felt before. But when Evie's reputation is threatened, will she trust that Max's feelings for her are more than just a bet?

MY ROGUE TO RUIN
by Erica Ridley

Lord Adrian Webb never meant to get caught up in a forgery scheme. But now a blackmailer is out to ruin him, and the most alluring woman he's ever met is trying to put him behind bars. Every time Marjorie Wynchester thinks she has Adrian figured out, her assumptions turn on their head. He's a heartless scoundrel. A loyal brother. A smooth liar. A good kisser. So is winning her affections just another attempt to avoid the law? Or maybe he's not such a rogue after all?

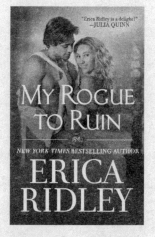

Connect with us at Facebook.com/ReadForeverPub

Discover bonus content and more on read-forever.com

NEVER MET A DUKE LIKE YOU
by Amalie Howard

She may have sworn off love, but Lady Vesper Lyndhurst is clever and popular, and she's afforded every luxury as a duke's daughter. Faced with an insolvent estate, the Duke of Greydon has no choice but to return to England in a final attempt to revive his family's fortunes. Not much about the ton has changed, including the beautiful and vexing heiress next door. But when an accident traps the enemies and total opposites in an attic together, the explosive attraction between them becomes impossible to ignore—and even harder to resist.

GOOD DUKE GONE WILD
by Bethany Bennett

Dorian Whitaker, Duke of Holland, needs an heir after his so-called "fairytale marriage" ended in disaster. But when the intriguing bookseller he's hired to liquidate his late wife's library finds love letters revealing an affair, he is drawn into a mystery alongside a lady whose dazzling intellect dares him to imagine adventures outside the ton—and whose own secrets threaten his heart.

Meet your next favorite book with @ReadForeverPub on TikTok

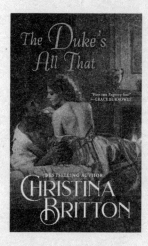

THE DUKE'S ALL THAT
by Christina Britton

Miss Seraphina Athwart never wanted to abandon her husband, but she did what was necessary to keep herself and her sisters safe. And while she misses Iain, she's made a happy life without him. But all that is put at risk when Iain arrives on the Isle of Synne, demanding a divorce. Despite their long separation, the affection and attraction between them still burn strong. But with so much hurt and betrayal simmering as well, can they possibly find their way back to each other?

A SPINSTER'S GUIDE TO DANGER AND DUKES
by Manda Collins

Miss Poppy Delamare left her family to escape an odious betrothal, but when her sister is accused of murder, she cannot stay away. Even if she must travel with the arrogant Duke of Langham. To her surprise, he offers a mutually beneficial arrangement: A fake betrothal will both protect Poppy and her sister and deter society misses from Langham. But as real feelings begin to grow, can they find truth and turn their engagement into reality—before Poppy becomes the next victim?

WAKE ME MOST WICKEDLY
by Felicia Grossman

To repay his half brother, Solomon Weiss gladly pursues money and influence—until outcast Hannah Moses saves his life. He's irresistibly drawn to her beauty and wit, but Hannah tells him she's no savior. To care for her sister, she heartlessly hunts criminals for London's underbelly. So Sol is far too respectable for her. Only neither can resist their desires—until Hannah discovers a betrayal that will break Sol's heart. Can she convince Sol to trust her? Or will fear and doubt poison their love?

THE PARIS APARTMENT
by Kelly Bowen

LONDON, 2017: When Aurelia Leclaire inherits an opulent Paris apartment, she is shocked to discover her grandmother's secrets—including a treasure trove of famous art and couture gowns.

PARIS, 1942: Glamorous Estelle Allard flourishes in a world separate from the hardships of war. But when the Nazis come for her friends, Estelle doesn't hesitate to help those she holds dear, no matter the cost. Both Estelle and Lia must summon hidden courage as they alter history—and the future of their families—forever.

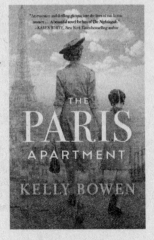